# STERILE JUSTICE

# BOOKS BY GENE RONTAL

*The Police Surgeon*

*A Lethal Dose*

*The Cruelest Cut*

*A Pre-existing Condition*

# STERILE JUSTICE

## A Detective Ben Dailey, M.D. Mystery

# GENE RONTAL

CAVEL
PRESS
Kenmore, WA

A Camel Press book published by Epicenter Press

Epicenter Press
6524 NE 181st St.
Suite 2
Kenmore, WA 98028

For more information go to:
www.Camelpress.com
www.Coffeetownpress.com
www.Epicenterpress.com
www.generontalbooks.com

This is a work of fiction. Names, characters, places, brands, media, and incidents are either the product of the author's imagination or are used fictitiously.

Design by Scott Book and Melissa Vail Coffman

Sterile Justice
Copyright © 2021 by Gene Rontal

Previously published by Sterling House

ISBN: 978-1-60381-787-5 (Trade Paper)
ISBN: 978-1-60381-788-2 (eBook)

Printed in the United States of America

*To Ellie, Sara and David*

"Chance favors the prepared mind."

—*Louis Pasteur*

# PROLOGUE – 1972

I SNAKED MY '66 CHEVELLE THROUGH THE GRAY MUSH of the prison parking lot, shut the ignition off, and waited impatiently through the inevitable engine run-on. A few more jiggles of the key and it finally stopped coughing. My eyes drifted up to the rearview mirror and focused on the reflection of my furrowed brow. It wasn't the car that was ticking me off. What was it my college football coach used to say after I missed a block? Something about steeping my senses in forgetfulness? He must have studied nights to find those quotes to push my button. Unfortunately, he was usually right. Like now. *Dailey, you were the fool who left your research papers behind here. You're late already. Go get them!*

Sliding out of the car, I put my feet right into a puddle. It was shaping up for one lousy day.

By the time I had stopped feeling sorry for myself, I had made it to the vine-shrouded, red brick building overlooking the iced-over St. Croix River. Rural Minnesota. A little farther up or downriver the scene would have looked picturesque. But the sign announcing "Stanfield State Penitentiary" turned Norman Rockwell into Norman Mailer: rough, raw, and on the edge, the hardest time in Minnesota.

Every time I had gone there, the same eerie feeling of foreboding consumed me, my persona changing from that of medical resident to prison guard. An unmistakable transition left my muscles tense, my teeth clenched, my eyes furtively dancing from side to side. I was incarcerated, just like the inmates—except my prison was my imagination.

By the time I'd made my way to the front desk, I had myself under control. Leon was there: bulging neck, close-cropped mullet mohawk, gnarly hands that could snap you in two if he wanted. I think he enjoyed knowing I was always unnerved walking in there.

Right now, I was too irritated at myself to bother about what he thought. I flashed my Minnesota State Prison ID: Ben Dailey, age twenty-eight, surgical consultant. It sounded a lot more impressive than the dismal reality: fourth year resident surgeon, North Central University Medical School.

Leon popped his fingers, listened to the cracking sound echo down the bare cement hallway, and looked down at his list.

"Ain't you ever goin' to finish that university program, Doc?" he asked. Leon might not have been a grammarian, but he knew how to get to the nub of the problem.

"Fourteen more months, Leon, but who's counting?" At least I'd never have to see this place again after today. My term here was up. But accident seemed determined to keep me here. Leon interrupted my musings.

"Marge Fredrickson in the infirmary told me if one of you guys showed up, to hustle your ass back to the hospital ward as soon as you got here. Some kind of trouble."

Damn. Just what I didn't need. "Any idea what the problem is?"

"I just guard 'em. You guys save 'em." He turned for a second to the trustee at the revolving metal pass gate. "Joey, escort the doc here down to the infirmary. Chop-chop."

Joey was Joseph Dunbar, a three-time loser who just couldn't make it on the outside. Inside he'd found a home, exchanging his freedom for the security of prison life. He was the only exception to my strict rule about avoiding unnecessary conversation with inmates. I'd gotten to know him well over the past couple of years. Especially in the few touch football games between staff and inmates the warden had cooked up.

'Hey, Doc, you ain't limping no more. Guess you'll be fine just in time for the spring game."

"Forget it, Joey. I want to make it into private practice alive." By this time, we had entered the outer courtyard, a circular area fifty feet in diameter with gun turrets pointing down from the four compass points. Near the gate a couple of Native Americans stood, arms folded, looking a little too grim for my liking.

"What's with the welcoming committee?"

Joey shrugged. "They just showed up today, some kind of Indian ceremony thing. The guards let them stay as long as they behave." Looking up at the .50 caliber machine guns, I reflected that the administration could afford to be ecumenical.

"They kind of give a fella warm feeling inside."

"How do you think I feel living here? Them Indians are a big group, and they never let no one inside." As we walked toward the gates, I saw an inmate through the slatted bars, running down the corridor.

"Joey, what's going on in the infirmary?"

"The Big Chief is sick."

"Who?"

"Johnnie Willson. Meanest sombitch in the yard," Joey grimaced, extracting his keys to unlock the first of four metal doors. "Scuttle is he ain't doin' too well." There wasn't much regret in his voice. "He got a fever after surgery and nobody seems to know what to do." By this time, I had heard the repetitive slamming locks of one-inch solid high tensile chrome-moly steel gates. The only person who could bend them would be Superman, or someone with about three tons of explosives.

"Just what I need," I groaned, as the last nuke-proof tumbler locked behind me.

We had rounded past the laundry and entered the infirmary. By modern standards it had advanced only to the Middle Ages. Old rusted iron beds, porcelain bedpans, and thermometers that looked like relics from the Boer Wars. In the twenty-bed ward, I saw Marge and three or four inmates standing next to a patient. Her look of relief at the sight of me told me we had no ordinary problem on our hands.

Marge wasn't easy to miss. Close to six feet, short blond hair swept back in a D.A., starched nurse's outfit, and those white high-heeled shoes fit to kick your balls through the goal posts. Beneath the image, she was warmhearted; but nobody ever messed with Marge. Not even the toughest in the house.

It was one of the few times I had ever seen her acknowledge the worth of any resident. She didn't seem to approve of having us embryo physicians practice on her inmates. It was a moral issue for her. I liked her.

"Thank God you're here," she exclaimed. "I've got a patient with septic shock. Fever 105, 22,000 white count, and an IV running with ampicillin. I started an aramine drip." One look at the enormous man with a swollen, but distinctively Native American face, lying in the bed with tubes emerging from every one of his orifices reinforced everything Marge's facts and figures had recounted.

"How long has he been like this?" I looked up at the four inmates surrounding his bed, reading the stenciled names on their prison garb: Featherstone, Strong, Graywolf, and Martinez. I had interviewed them for my research on voice identification, but otherwise had never talked to any of them. I glanced at their faces, hardened, grim, and angry. It was hard to believe they were only around my age, except for Featherstone, who was at least fifty, though hard and lean. For a moment my stare met the eyes of the inmate at the foot of the bed: Martinez. His gaze bored into my head with a burning hatred that made me feel not only uncomfortable but oddly exposed in its glare. Marge's voice jolted me back to the emergency.

"He had an acute abdomen yesterday. A routine appendectomy, the residents on duty said. About four hours ago, he started spiking a fever. At first, I thought it was a fluke, but he's been going steadily downhill. His pulse has been going up and the pressure's been dropping steadily. A few minutes ago he lost consciousness."

Cross of death. When the blood pressure dropped and the pulse rose, the point where they met on a graph usually coincided with the patient's death. Which, looking at Willson's corpulent, pale face, looked imminent. Just then a beeping went off on the EKG overhead, confirming my fears. I looked up at the wildly erratic line.

"V-tach, Marge. Give me some IV lidocaine now!" I commanded. Marge was good in a crisis. She handed me the syringe within seconds.

I pumped in forty milligrams and waited. Nothing.

"Christ, Marge, I'm a head and neck surgeon, not a cardiologist. I haven't handled a code since I was an intern."

"You're all the Big Chief has until the internal medicine guys arrive," she said sternly. Nice sentiment, like the hockey coach telling the rookie that he was filling in on the ice for Gordie Howe. Then there were those hard, blank stares from the inmates. I figured if I didn't save Johnnie Willson, I'd be going out more or less the same way.

"Give him a vial of sodium bicarb, now!"

Marge reached over and quickly pushed it into the IV. I looked back at the monitor. The V-tach was back to bigeminy. That's when I remembered the ABC's of resuscitation: airway, breathing, circulation. *Get a tube in him, dummy.*

"Marge, give me a six tube with a stylet and an intubating laryngoscope."

The equipment was in my hand almost as soon as I finished speaking. I was in the flow now. Finding an airway was my thing. I pried open his mouth, put in the scope, and peered down the blade of the battery-powered instrument. The airway appeared, a dark hole deep inside the throat. One fluid motion and the tube was in.

"Nice job, Ben!" Marge shouted. My face flushed as a feeling of relief came over me. The expression of the inmates at the end of the bed didn't change. You couldn't please everyone.

I stood there looking at the huge man prostrate on the bed. What to do next? The latest antibiotic therapy for septic shock wasn't in my armamentarium. Just then I heard the squeak of rubber-soled shoes trailing down the linoleum hallway. I turned and saw two internal medicine residents I knew.

A few moments later, the case off my hands, I was headed down the hallway. About halfway there, I remembered I had come back in the first place for my research papers. I turned around and went back to the office. The voice spectrograms were where I had left them.

As I started walking out of Stanfield for the last time, I heard voices from the infirmary. "He's going out. Put on the paddles!"

Looked as if Johnnie Willson and I were leaving Stanfield at the same time. *It's funny the way lives touch each other,* I remember thinking.

# CHAPTER 1

FOR SOME REASON THE BELL ON THE PHONE seemed louder than usual. Maybe it was because it had torn me away from the excitement coursing through me from the long legs and taut body undulating on top of me. Being a doctor had inured me to most intrusions from the telephone, but somehow I had never gotten used to being rung up in mid-stroke.

"Hello," I croaked. Jordan already had a petulant look on her face and that cut me almost as much as my suddenly limp male hood.

"Ben, what the hell's the matter? You sound like you're half dead." I quickly recognized the voice of Bruce Sanderson, Coastal Life Insurance Company's main man in Detroit. I'd formerly done medical investigations for him, in the days when I'd been down on my professional luck. Before my "rehabilitation" —and before Jordan.

I looked down. "Only part of me is half-dead, Bruce."

"Well, listen, wake up all over, 'cause I need something done in a hurry." The urgency in his voice suggested that Coastal was on the hook for some big bucks in a malpractice case.

I looked at Jordan lying next to me, her legs scissored over mine, her nipples rubbing against my chest. "I don't do that anymore, Bruce."

"This is important, Ben. I need you. Come down to the office as early as you can. Please."

I looked at Jordan again. She was already slipping to other side of the bed to put on her robe. So much for the sex life of a middle-aged man.

"What could be so important at seven in the morning?" I asked Bruce testily.

"I haven't been able to sleep all night worrying about this case."

"It's too early in the morning to be beating around the bush, Bruce. What case is it?"

"How about the trial of the century?" Sanderson wheedled.

"I thought that was finished with O. J.?"

"I'm talking about Dr. Larry Burkinette," Sanderson retorted.

That did it. I'd lost an intimate moment with the most beautiful, auburn-haired, green-eyed Federal district attorney in the greater Detroit area over that bastard Burkinette? To hell with him *and* Bruce Sanderson.

"Forget the explanation, Bruce. Trouble follows Larry Burkinette like a bad rash follows a wet diaper. Which is a good description of him."

"You know him?"

"You're the only person I'd ever admit that to, Bruce. And that's because I don't give a damn what you think."

"Come on, Ben," Sanderson pleaded. "He's in real trouble. And so am I. Don't you remember who gave you work when you needed it?"

"For chump change," I reminded him sourly. But I was weakening.

He must have sensed it, because he pursued eagerly. "Don't all you medical guys have a code of helping each other out or something? Brothers, ain't that right?"

"That's cops," I corrected. But for some reason I didn't understand, I felt a willingness to hear him out rise within me. I interrupted Bruce's renewed pleas. "No promises, Bruce, but I'll listen. Get your files together and I'll be down in a while."

I cut off his expressions of gratitude by hanging up, then sat on the edge of Jordan's bed for a minute, trying to gather my senses, and mourning our stillborn orgasm.

By the time I got to the breakfast room Jordan was reading the newspaper and sipping her coffee from one of those Villeroy & Boch cups I had given to her as a thank-you-for-being-with-me present.

"What was that all about?" she asked, looking up from the front page.

"It's Bruce Sanderson. He wants me to look at some case of his," I answered with an assumption of carelessness, shoving aside some of my spectrography papers on the table and reaching for the sports section.

"At seven in the morning?"

"It's a malpractice case. You know Bruce, he's real nervous."

"I'll say." There was a definite edge to her voice. I couldn't say I blamed her, considering the past. Sanderson was a seedy part of a seedy past Jordan Dalkind, who'd helped me regain my respectability and also my self-respect, considered a closed chapter in my life.

How could I explain being interested in investigating Larry Burkinette? I picked the paper up again and started reading, trying to avoid answering any more questions. But Jordan wouldn't let me get away with it.

"I don't know about Bruce. He's got a certain . . . unpleasantness about him."

"You mean sleazy, don't you?"

"I didn't want to come out and say it."

"After my last experience with him, I can't dispute it." Almost being electrocuted by a psychopath had a way of making one lose confidence.

"Then why have anything more to do with him? You're director of research at the hospital now. Isn't that enough?"

Funny how two people can see the same thing so differently. She saw the job as something to be proud of, worthy of admiration. On the other hand, I looked at it primarily as a public-conscience salve for the board of trustees of St. Vincent's for their earlier injustice to me over the Scotten case. The only reason I'd taken the position was because it gave me a chance to do my beloved voice research. I knew full well that the hospital didn't give a rat's ass about voice spectrography, voice identification, or any of my other work. And it would take me a long time to get over the bitterness of being disavowed by the very institution I had helped build.

These were strong feelings, but also very personal and not worth mentioning. I didn't want anyone to know I was still hurting. Especially not Jordan—she had helped negotiate the deal.

"Sure, it's a good job," I said unenthusiastically.

"I'm worried that Sanderson might get you into something you can't get out of."

"Like what?"

"Like trouble involved with the law. You seem to have a peculiar determination for finding the truth."

"Are you saying the law and the truth don't match up?"

"I'm saying that finding the truth and getting into trouble usually go hand in hand. You're not a kid anymore." As usual, I was finding it hard to argue with my beautiful lawyer.

"I might be old, but I'm not ready for the undertaker yet."

"Is that it? Is working with Sanderson a response to some kind of midlife crisis?" Now I had done it. I was going to have to try and extract my size four-teens from between my jaws. Why couldn't I learn to keep my mouth shut?

"You know," I counterattacked, "I've spent a lifetime studying people's voices, doing research, and all that."

"So?"

"Your voice speaks to me of disparagement, maybe even a touch of anger."

"Try worry. What can I say? You're over twenty-one and in full control of your faculties. You're also one of the brightest men I have ever met. Look at those papers. I'll bet there's more information crammed into that work than a lot of people amass in a lifetime."

I looked at the pages of spectrographs and voice research.

"This stuff is just a hobby. Kind of like stamp collecting."

"What is it?"

"Just some voice identification stuff I've been looking over. See, look at the patterns on this spectrograph, you can see the similarities between the voices of these two people, and the differences." I pointed out the horizontal black lines and then the irregularities of the thin vertical lines on the strip of paper. Maybe I *was* successfully redirecting the conversation.

"You should see how your eyes light up when you talk about it," she said encouragingly.

"It's just the sunshine through the window. Most people wouldn't give this stuff a second thought."

"Whatever it is, it's safe. Remember how you almost got killed the last time you worked with Sanderson?"

"I'm not lyin', I'm denyin'," I said in my best Wolfman Jack voice.

"I hate it when you laugh off situations this way. Remember, for every ten jokes, there are a hundred enemies." She got up from the table. When she reached the doorway, she stopped.

"I forgot to tell you last night. I'm going to Miami tonight for few days. My drug case is still going on. Maybe we'll continue this when I get back." Then, as if to make clear she wasn't holding a grudge, she came back to kiss me goodbye.

I sat there, staring at Steve Yzerman sprawled across the sports page, as if he could give me an answer to why I was risking Jordan over Larry Burkinette. Ten jokes and a hundred enemies. I had a sinking feeling that maybe Jordan was right.

BRUCE WAS AT HIS USUAL POSITION at his desk behind a mountain of documents, coat off, suspenders stretched across his gut like bowstrings ready to release. When he saw me, he smiled.

"Sorry to call so early this morning."

"Too early to hear Burkinette's name," I agreed.

"We can't pick our clients, can we?"

"What's the deal?"

"The deal is that it seems Dr. Burkinette has gotten himself in big trouble. A sixteen-year-old kid died after a tonsillectomy. Widespread infection from a bacteria nobody had ever heard of."

"Pack it in, Bruce," I advised, sliding into the imitation leather chair next to his desk.

"Why?"

"Burkinette's a scumbag. All they'll have to do is drag up his past history and go to the cashier's office. They've got him by the *cojones*."

Bruce looked at me quizzically. "Co-what?"

"It's what us medical types call balls."

"Shit. I told the Chicago office we shouldn't have taken on this guy. He's had ten lawsuits in twenty-five years of practice. But his premium was three times what everyone else was paying, so they accepted him. Shit!"

"They should have talked to me. He was a resident a year ahead of me at North Central University Medical School in Minneapolis. He had all the makings back then. Smart, but ruthless."

"You've known him that long?"

"One of the slickest surgeons I've ever seen."

"This is a big problem for me. The boys in Chicago have a short memory. They don't seem to recall it was their decision to take him on. Suddenly, it's all my fault."

"Relax, Bruce. It's simple physics."

"What do you mean?" he replied, totally dumbfounded.

"Shit rolls downhill. Now what do you want me for?"

"You're my last hope. There's got to be a loophole here somewhere. The guy's bad news, no doubt, but it was a tonsillectomy, for Christ's sake. By his own account he's done over two thousand of them the same way. Never a problem."

"Try over three thousand. When I was head of the county peer review committee, we did a Q.A. review on him."

"English, please," Sanderson begged, wiping his forehead with his handkerchief.

"Quality assurance, making sure that the indications were proper. When you do that many cases of one kind or another, it raises suspicions. The insurance company asked for the review."

"What did you find?"

"Most of them didn't need to be done. We tried to sanction him at the State Board of Medicine."

"Did it work?"

"Too smart. His lawyer threatened the board members with personal suits. They all caved."

"Where were you when we issued him a policy?" Sanderson grumbled.

"You wouldn't have found out that information anyway. The lawyers put a gag order on it. If you say I told you, I'll deny it."

"This whole business is making me gag."

"What do you want me to do?" I repeated impatiently. "Not that I've said yes."

"I want you to go over everything, lab results, x-rays, depositions. Then call John Franklin. He's our attorney. Top defense man in the city."

"I thought that was Nick Lidstrom of the Detroit Red Wings," I quipped. I'm what you might call hockey obsessed. I'd driven Jordan crazy once by exhorting her to memorize the roster of the entire NHL, including, of course, the Red Wings. The price of my love.

Sanderson didn't smile. Instead he shoved the mountain of paper over toward me, along with Franklin's number, and looked up at me plaintively. "Ben, find me an answer. We're six months into the case, the depositions are starting, and the attorneys are worried. If I don't do something soon, there's going to be hell to pay. You have to find something positive for me, like no one has ever seen something like this before in the medical literature." He reached into the top drawer of his desk, extracted a bottle of Mylanta, took a swig, and slowly put the cap back on.

"Does Burkinette know you've talked to me?"

"Not yet. I'm going to tell him today."

"He might not like it, when he finds out."

"Goddammit, Ben, I don't give a shit what Burkinette wants. It's my ass on the line, and I'll put the best person I can get on the job. That's you."

I looked at him for a moment. "Relax, Bruce. You're going to work yourself up into a B.E."

"B.E.?"

"Yeah. A brain evisceration."

"What the hell is that?" he asked fearfully, as if the Ebola virus was about to consume him.

"It's when you worry so much your brain pops out of your skull. But don't get scared. It's nothing a couple of stiff martinis wouldn't help." I picked up the papers. "Relax. I'll do this one. And this one only. For old time's sake."

I admitted two things to myself as I walked to my car. First, that Jordan had been right. The detecting bug had bitten me good when I'd solved the Scotten murder and cleared myself. And second, my predilection for uncovering the truth from beneath layers of deceit and corruption would bring me trouble as the day brings on the night.

What I didn't admit to myself was my own personal stake in bringing to light the truth about Dr. Larry Burkinette.

# CHAPTER 2

I STOOD OUTSIDE COASTAL'S OFFICE in the slanted rays of the mid-November sunshine. Where was I going to begin? A stiff breeze from the southwest washed over my face. It made me wish I was broad reaching in the North Channel. There it was. I was going to begin at my "office."

My "office" was really a sailboat moored at a marina on Lake St. Clair. My second boat. The last one had been sunk during the Scotten affair. Fortunately, my restored fortunes—a timely investment with Herb Albright, my stockbroker, in Friendship Labs stock, and an ample settlement for a wrongful dismissal suit at St. Vincent's—had given me enough cash to replace it with the boat I wanted. At St. Vincent's I now directed my voice research—I had a small lab to do my own studies on voice disorders—and held a tenured professorship at the medical school. I was recovering financially, but somehow I never really felt totally secure.

I blamed most of that on my ex. She always seemed to find some way to get a piece of whatever I had. Ergo, I was never too cocksure of my financial state, still always looking for a bargain.

I found it in a ten-year-old CS 40. Sloop-rigged, winged keeled, and set up for single handling. I jumped at it when I first saw it resting on the cradle. It was what we sailors call a good fit. I called it my office, but it was something more. Deep inside, where the bare truths lie, I knew it was the last battle flag of my waning intransigence—my independence. That's why I called it the *Second Chance*.

When I got down to the docks in the early afternoon of a November Indian summer day, the breeze had chilled slightly; cold enough to play hockey, but warm enough to sit inside my boat without turning on the heater. I swung on board, opened the hatch, and lowered myself into the cabin. Not as lived in as my other boat, but who cared? Living with Jordan made up for a lot of my past losses.

Once inside, I switched on the cabin lights and went over to the answering machine to play back the messages: two solicitations for the Policemen's Benevolent Association and some unintelligible guy doing a survey on my preference for TV programs. They were working on bad material. The morning news, Red Wing hockey, and the Stanley Cup were about all I could tolerate by way of television.

I spread Coastal's armful of papers onto the dinette. Larry Burkinette. Would I help him, if the evidence inclined his way—or was I hoping it would indict him, so I could help nail him with a clear conscience? I brushed the thought aside and resolutely concentrated on the file.

It was all as Sanderson had said. Sixteen-year-old boy comes in for a tonsillectomy and dies of septic shock. I had never heard of the bacteria before—*Acinetobacter calcocetious*. I'd have to look that one up. The file contained mounds of lab tests and nurses' notes. When I'd waded through them, I was no nearer a conclusion. I picked up the complaint again. According to the particulars, Burkinette had violated every medical standard left on the face of the earth.

I looked at the plaintiff's attorney's name: Tony Bidora. I'd never heard of him, and, after being crucified in the Scotten case, I knew the names of all the big ones in Detroit. How had a no-name like Bidora gotten this cash cow case?

By the time I had finished it was close to four o'clock. Just enough time to head over to the hospital and check out the medical library. I knew all the answers were there, buried in the thousands of bound journals.

Midweek in a hospital library in early November isn't exactly prime time, especially on a beautiful day. I guess most of St. Vincent's doctors subscribed to the "gray days make gray matter" theory. The sun passed through a tinted window, illuminating the dust in the air, emphasizing the library's deserted state. I saw the tight-lipped, bespectacled librarian behind her desk. Fortunately, I remembered to use my library voice.

"I'm looking for a book on microbiology. Anything on your bestseller list?"

A smile creased her face for a moment. I don't think jocularity made its way into her domain too often.

"Long version or capsule?"

I did a quick mental status exam and realized ruefully I was a long way from medical school state-of-the-art currency on micro-b.

"Short version."

"Over on the 'J' shelf. *Review of Medical Microbiology* by Jawetz."

She seemed disappointed in me. I didn't take it personally. A lot of people thought I was smarter than I was. I found the book and started fumbling through it until *Acinetobacter* came up in the index.

*Acinetobacter calcocetious*—an opportunistic organism, something that normally grows on the skin or in the throat. Not infective unless the patient is debilitated or taking some type of medicine that reduces their immunity; then the organism can take over like Attila the Hun. It was commonly seen in AIDS and diabetes patients, and in patients receiving chemotherapy. Definitely not to be expected in an otherwise healthy sixteen-year-old boy coming in for a tonsillectomy. The discussion went on to say that *Acinetobacter* occasionally responds to certain new antimicrobial drugs such as Cefzil.

I put the volume back on the shelf and walked over to the library computer. I punched in postoperative infection and *Acinetobacter*. A couple of papers on immune deficiency and opportunistic infection came up. The same information I had just read. There was nothing about these bacteria being seen as a complication of tonsillectomy.

JOHN FRANKLIN, TOP LEGAL DEFENSEMAN in Detroit. His office was downtown near the river, in one of those remodeled warehouses, fashionably understated. But looking at the plush carpeting, marble entranceway, and well-dressed receptionist, it was plain Franklin was in the high rent district.

But right now I wasn't interested in his rent structure. I was irritated and hungry. A bad combination when you're about to speak to an attorney, especially for me.

I was startled by the unimposing figure behind the mahogany Sligh desk. The placid-looking forty-five-year-old, with wire rims and Brylcreemed, thinning blond hair parted precisely on the side, hardly fit my image of the "top defenseman in the city." He stood up and extended his hand. The clamminess of his handshake struck me. If I was hanging off the side of a cliff, this wasn't the hand I would want to depend on to drag me up.

"I've heard a lot about you, Ben. Please sit down."

As I sat down, the door opened and a tall, well-dressed man of Franklin's age walked in.

"Sorry I'm late, John."

Franklin smiled. "You and I both know you're never late, Al. Al Heath, Ben Dailey. Al is from Honnicutt, Garrity and Meyers." They represent Metropolitan Hospital."

Heath fit my image, all right. Elegantly tailored suit, white monogrammed cuffs and a crisply starched collar offsetting his regimental tie. A high-class guy, the kind who was an expert at billing every five-minute call at a quarter of an hour. The kind only hospitals could afford. Which is how I recognized him. He was with the firm that had ousted me from St. Vincent's.

Heath eased himself into the leather chair opposite mine and unbuttoned his gray pin-striped suit coat. His gold cuff links sparkled.

"Al and I have both read over the complaint from Mr. Bidora," Franklin began. "Basically, we're depending on you to shed some medical light on this case."

"Right now, I don't have much light to shed," I replied. "I see the death of Paul Versanti as a tragedy, but so far I don't see it as negligence."

"Unless Bidora is shooting blind, he must have something. Aside from the usual fluff, according to the complaint, he says Burkinette violated the standard of care in allowing the infection to incubate. What do you make of that, Ben?"

"The only way to prove that would be to show that either the young man was infected prior to the surgery, or that in some way Burkinette introduced the bacteria into him."

"Is that possible?" Heath queried in a slightly nasal voice reminiscent of his native Boston.

"Anything is possible in medicine. I've just never heard of it. Neither has the MEDLAR search." I went over everything I had learned from the chart and the library.

When I finished, Heath said, "We need a strategy." I guess for his price he did.

"I think before we get a strategy, we'd better get some facts," Franklin interjected. "Only the depositions will tell us that. We have a couple coming up, including the scrub nurse's tomorrow. I'd like you to meet us at Bidora's office tomorrow, Ben."

"That's why I'm getting paid the big bucks." I looked at Heath as I said it.

Heath bit.

"I want you to know, Ben, that I didn't represent the hospital in the Scotten matter. If you want the truth, I admire the hell out of what you did."

As he spoke, I got up to leave. I might be living with an attorney but working with two of them was making me claustrophobic.

"I've found that it's nicer to be admired while you're still alive. Forget about the past. I'll see you for the deposition tomorrow."

As I left, I reflected on how aggravating it was to have my profession probed by laymen. Had they ever had to deal with losing a child, or had to take the everyday risks that a physician did? Of course not. It almost made me sympathetic towards Larry Burkinette. Almost.

All of this thinking was putting my jaw into spasm. I knew I needed to spend some time at the Pipeline.

The Pipeline was the jazz place where I did stand-in on the piano while the real musicians took a break. Tonight, after I grabbed something to eat, Sid Blanton, the owner, gave me a little extra time, allowing me to try out my

Thelonius Monk version of "My Melancholy Baby." It actually turned out decent. At least the audience was polite. The bouncer, Charley, my gauge of success, gave me a big bright grin from the door as I got up from the piano.

I went over to a small table near the bar and sat down next to Sid.

"Not bad, young man," he growled with the voice I had rescued from cancer of the larynx years before.

"I had a little more impetus tonight," I said, bringing two Diet Cokes over to the table.

"Why's that?"

"I spent the whole day working to save the neck of one of the worst assholes in the city. At least I think I was. I'm not sure whether I want to save his neck or break it."

"I know what you mean, my man. Got my share of assholes here, too."

"How bad can the people be here, Sid? A little music, a few drinks."

"That's just it. Something about jazz and booze, it brings out the best and the worst in people sometimes. Take tonight, for instance. A guy comes in, real greaseball type; slicked back hair, twelve-hundred-dollar cashmere coat, and a hoochie-coochie in a low-cut dress. He has a few drinks and starts getting real loud, annoying the customers."

"What did you do?"

"I didn't have to do anything. It was Charley. He kind of quieted him down if you know what I mean."

"I'd think you'd be used to stuff like that."

"I am. I just didn't like his attitude."

"Didn't you just say something about booze and jazz bringing out the worst in people?"

"My point exactly. He could have just left. He didn't have to insult my music." That was the worst thing you could do around Sid. He didn't care if you didn't like his skin color or the price of his drinks or the decor of his joint. Just never make fun of his music.

"What happened?"

"Charley got a little carried away. Kind of messed up his suit." Sid grinned. "Oh, yeah, and he must have known you." Here it was. Sid never mentioned anything without a purpose.

"Why?" I said cautiously.

"He shouted something about knowing you worked here. Charley heard him call you a meddler in other people's affairs. I think those were the words."

"Is he still around?"

I didn't have to wait for an answer. I looked up to see Dr. Larry Burkinette in all his disheveled splendor hovering over the table.

"You know, Dailey, a simple ass like you can't seem to get out of the way of your own shadow." Even without his breath, his incoherence was sufficient testimony to his drunkenness. I looked up into his perfectly capped teeth and neatly styled hair.

"What's the matter, Larry, can't find enough places uptown to screw up?"

"I don't know what the insurance company had in mind when they hired you. I'd think they'd want someone with a little better reputation than you to look over my case."

I shrugged my shoulders. "I guess they thought differently. Anyway, it's not my call. From my standpoint I'd just as soon see you get what's coming to you."

"Everyone knows you've been out to get me, Dailey. Well, I'm too smart for them. I eat attorneys for breakfast."

"I always knew you had a strong stomach, Larry."

"Always the wise guy, aren't you? But in this case, you're dead wrong."

"That's not what I hear."

"This suit is a pile of shit. I tried to tell Sanderson that. Instead, what does he do? He hires you."

"Hens roost in a hen house and roosters just have minds of their own." I think I was talking over Burkinette's head. But Sid guffawed.

"You're probably the happiest guy in town now. You finally got what you wanted, a chance to really get me."

"Not me, Larry. You've been out to get yourself. And you know what, you might eventually succeed."

Larry took a step toward me and swung. Before I could duck my head in anticipation, I saw his arm come down as if struck by lightning. The next thing I knew Charley had him by the elbow. This time Dr. Burkinette was out the door for good. Sid looked at me for a moment, trying to find an answer in my eyes to one or two uncomfortably shrewd questions.

"What was that all about?"

"Business, Sid, just business."

"Take some advice from a guy that knows. Maybe you should stick to your regular line of employment. Y'ain't no gumshoe, my good friend. You're only a doctor and that means you need to keep your hands clean. Know what I mean, my man?"

Jordan and now Sid. Two of my favorite people in the world. Two people with the same message in one day. Both of them telling me to keep my hands clean, like a good doctor.

Maybe I should have learned to be a better listener.

# CHAPTER 3

IN HIS YOUTH LARRY BURKINETTE COULD CHARM the rattles off a witch doctor. I'd always thought that was how he'd never gotten in trouble in the residency. That thought still made me angry. Why did no one else see what I saw?

I remembered the quality assurance interview the peer review board had had with him. He had been cool, suave, unflappable. Red tie perfectly knotted, blue double-breasted suit, polished cap-toes flashing, a look of benevolence cast over all of us. He had an answer for every question. On the surface his response to our inquiry seemed reasonable, quoting studies on surgical incidence and indications. When we got done, the look on the other board members' faces stuck with me. It was a look that said: *What are we doing here? This guy is too smooth.* But that was Larry, always smooth. So far it had worked for him.

These thoughts flashed through my mind as I sat the next morning in the outer waiting room of Anthony Bidora's office with John Franklin and Al Heath. Larry was someone I couldn't shake. He kept popping up in my life. Never pleasantly.

I looked around the waiting room. Quite a difference from Franklin's upscale place. It was one of those low rent single story buildings on Woodward Avenue flashing "personal injury" on the marquee. A touch of understated elegance.

Inside were bright fluorescent lights, prefab paneling, and uncomfortable plastic waiting room chairs, the kind that stack one on top of another. Fancy offices don't make the man, but this was a bigtime case.

My level of surprise heightened when I met Anthony Bidora. His black hair was what I called a "four-strander," each strand about a foot long and circled four times back on itself to cover his bald head. He had let the fringe of hair in back grow in long Rastafarian curls, with thick muttonchop sideburns sticking out on his cheeks like steel wool. He had pale, jowly cheeks, and puffy eyelids encircling the two beady slits of his eyes. A poorly fitting charcoal gray suit coat barely covered his protruding midsection. The final impression was of a grandmother in male drag.

He shook hands with Franklin and Heath.

"This is Dr. Benjamin Dailey, he's working for us and will sit in on the deposition," Franklin introduced me.

Bidora stuck out his flabby paw. Furtively, I wiped my palm after a reluctant shake.

"Follow me, gentlemen, into the conference room." The conference room turned out to be a converted lunchroom with a big Formica table. At one end sat a demure African American woman. Brenda Palmer, witness for the plaintiff, the best scrub nurse I had ever worked with.

Brenda looked a little embarrassed to be there under the circumstances. "Hello, Dr. Dailey. It's been so long."

I didn't wait for her to get up. Instead I went over and gave her a big hug.

"Brenda, you get better looking as you get older."

"Now quit that, Doctor. You know me too well to embarrass me in front of all these people."

I raised my arms in surrender. "Okay, I'll put on my deposition face."

She was right about one thing. I did know her well. You don't work twenty years in an operating room with someone without finding out who they are. Brenda lived in the world of personal dignity and possessed a wariness of anyone she didn't know.

The dignity was earned, the wariness justified. Brenda had been raised in an austere Southern home, imbued with a Christian ethic and a strong sense of duty to her country. But the death of her son, Lucius, from a Vietcong land mine ended any trust she had ever had in her government. She viewed his demise as the direct result of laws written by slick, uptown, white attorneys, whose own children never got drafted. In her mind such lawyers as those I had just walked in with were never to be trusted. Knowing her as I did, I was sure she was sitting here today only because she had to.

By this time the court reporter had set up her dictation stand, the tape recorder was rolling, and Bidora began to speak.

"Mrs. Palmer, I'm Anthony Bidora. I represent the plaintiffs, Mr. and Mrs. Versanti. I'm going to ask you some questions. If you don't understand any of them, please ask me to repeat the question. How long have you worked at Metropolitan Hospital?"

"Six years."

"And before that?"

"I worked at St. Vincent's for twenty years."

"Any reason for leaving St. Vincent's?"

Brenda looked directly at me. "I didn't like the way they were treating some of the staff." I smiled affectionately at her.

"What capacity do you now work in at the hospital?"

"I started out as a nurse's aide and worked my way up to scrub nurse in the operating room." I knew that she had been the sole support for her family ever since her alcoholic husband had left her shortly after Lucius was born.

"A scrub nurse. That would be someone who helps the doctor during surgery, is that right?" Bidora's voice was irritating, high-pitched, and whiny.

"Yes."

"As a scrub nurse, you would have ample opportunity to work in close contact with the surgeon, right?"

"Yes."

"I take it you have worked with Dr. Lawrence Burkinette during your time at Metropolitan?"

"Yes."

"Would you say you have worked with him more than any other surgeon at Metropolitan during your time there?"

"He did an awful lot of cases, so I guess that could be true."

"What kind of cases have you worked on with him?"

"Well, we do mostly tonsils, ear tubes, and deviated septums."

"Would you say you do more tonsillectomies than any other procedure?"

"I would think so." Brenda agreed tersely. I could tell she was starting to get a little irritated with this patronizing man questioning her.

"Do you remember a patient named Paul Versanti?"

"Yes."

"How do you remember him?"

"I heard from the people in the hospital that he died after surgery."

"Well, aside from what you heard, do you remember anything specifically about Paul's case?"

I could see myself suffering in my own misery. Same forum, except I had been on the receiving end of the inquisition. A young boy had died, supposedly from my negligence, a sponge left in the wound. It had taken five years and two deaths to prove my innocence. A cold sweat started running under my arms. Brenda's voice brought me back to reality.

"What do you mean?"

"Well, let's start with conversation in the operating room. Do you remember anything about what was said that day?"

Brenda, as I knew well, possessed a photographic memory. She would have total recall of the events from the day in question.

"I remember Dr. Burkinette talkin' 'bout music. They were playing "I Heard

It Through the Grapevine," and he was saying something about a group that he thought sang it better than Marvin Gaye. I didn't believe him, though. It's pretty hard for a white person to tell someone black how a black person should sing."

Bidora smiled ingratiatingly.

"Was there any breakdown in sterile technique at any time during the procedure?"

"Now, look here, Mr. Bidora, I've been scrubbing for twenty years and any-one at the hospital will tell you that I'm the most careful scrub tech around, so don't you be accusing me of no breakdown in sterile technique."

"No, I didn't mean to imply that, Mrs. Palmer. I was referring to Dr. Burkinette."

Brenda looked at him resolutely. "Well, we did have to change Dr. Burkinette's gloves during the procedure."

"Why was that?"

"Well, I saw that he had a hole in his glove. It's standard procedure under such circumstances."

"What did Dr. Burkinette do then, go back outside and rescrub?"

"Oh, Dr. Burkinette never scrubs before a tonsillectomy."

Bidora looked at her with astonishment, feigned or otherwise I wasn't sure.

"Are you telling me that before the tonsillectomy, he never washed his hands?"

"Look, Mr. Bidora, I remember what happened. I put my hand on the Bible before I testified. What I told you is the truth. I gave my word on that."

"Thank you. I have no further questions," Bidora said triumphantly.

I looked at Franklin. He appeared disturbed as he heard the testimony. Bidora was evidently confident that he had come away with testimony useful to his case.

"Mrs. Palmer, I'm John Franklin, and I represent Dr. Burkinette. I'm going to ask you a few questions. How many cases would you say you scrub on each year?"

Brenda thought for a minute. "Maybe a thousand."

"Out of those cases, how many are tonsillectomies?"

"Probably a couple hundred."

"Can you remember any of the other two hundred tonsillectomies?"

"Maybe one or two."

"What makes those cases stand out in your mind?"

"What was said during the case."

"Why?"

"I've always remembered things. Useless things most of the time, like what someone was wearing at a wedding, or where someone was when something happened. In this case it just stuck in my mind what Dr. Burkinette said about my music."

Franklin knew when to stop. "Thank you. I have no further questions." He turned to Heath. But Heath no more desired to ask a question he didn't know the answer to than Franklin.

I didn't make the effort to tell them it was usual not to scrub for a tonsillectomy. Why not? Because it would help Burkinette? Because I was lazy? What was I doing here at all? I thought suddenly of Jordan in Miami. I missed her.

Bidora redirected a few more questions, but it was clear Brenda's deposition was over. As we walked out of the room, I noticed a couple seated in the waiting room. A tall good-looking man in a blue sport coat and creased gray flannel trousers. Definitely not the client I would have expected to meet in Bidora's office. Next to him was a woman, slouched in her chair, looking at the wall. Her face was hidden behind large dark sunglasses.

Outside on the street the cool wind was swirling leaves around the sidewalk. I hugged Brenda goodbye and turned to Heath and Franklin.

"Those were the Versantis, weren't they, John?"

Franklin nodded. "Judging from the look on the missus's face, she seemed a bit under the weather."

"'Battered' would be a better word," I retorted as I got into my car.

Something about the deposition's revelation bothered me. It had been a little too pat. A torn glove turning up so conveniently with an infected patient. Nobody was that unlucky, not even Larry Burkinette. Damn it. I was going to go over to Metropolitan Hospital and try to find out how Anthony Bidora had gotten on this case.

HOSPITALS HAVE ALWAYS HAD THE POOREST SECURITY. Even the rankest of amateur impersonators could don a white coat and a phony name tag and enter the hospital milieu. It follows without saying that hospitals leak confidential information like gigantic sieves.

A ward clerk telling her friend about so and so, a nurse leaving a diagnostic test lying on a countertop, or a doctor talking about a patient with another physician. But attorneys operate on a whole other level.

The impetus to find information is much stronger, especially when thousands, maybe even millions of dollars are involved. The legal profession found ways to permeate the hospital system. For the unscrupulous among the legal profession, it was like taking candy from a baby.

Not that lawyers skulk around the corridors late at night with crowbars and explosives. It's much easier than that. They can hire the people who work there to get them the information they desire.

These "runners" can be a nurse on the floor, a ward clerk, or maybe even an orderly. My experience had taught me that the best informers were found in the emergency room. That's where most of the tragedies took place, where most of the money could be made. I headed for the E.R. after I pulled into the parking lot of Metropolitan Hospital.

I extracted my white coat from the back seat of my Jeep, put it on, and turned my name tag backwards. I doubted anyone would ask me any questions.

Metropolitan was located on the northern border of Detroit, a middle class, racially diverse neighborhood with a solid school system and a good police department. The hospital stayed alive by being just outside the city limits so that potentially frightened clients could retain the psychological satisfaction of being in the 'burbs.

It had the layout of most city hospitals: side lot, emergency room, and patient information. I walked in the main entrance, clutching my coat around me to keep out the chill.

The security guard nodded at me as I resolutely walked toward the emergency room. About fifty feet ahead I saw the entrance sign. Coming out of the E.R. was a young man dressed in scrubs, probably around eighteen, pushing a gurney. I shucked my coat on some carts to the side and walked up to him.

"Hi," I said casually. He looked up for a moment and nodded. Open face, disappearing acne, and a certain dullness to his look told me he would like to be doing anything but pushing that cart around.

"Busy today?" I asked.

"The usual, a couple of auto accidents and some guy with chest pain."

"Pretty boring stuff, huh?"

"Yeah, well, it's a job. I'm starting college next year and I need the money."

"Oh, yeah? Where you going?"

"State. I want to be a veterinarian."

"This is as good a place as any to start. Say, speaking of money, I'm looking for some information."

"What kind?" He looked at me quizzically.

"Oh, you know, auto accidents, slip and fall. Anything I could use to help my practice."

"You're a lawyer, huh?"

"Yeah, a struggling one at that. Hard to compete with those guys who advertise on TV."

The youth looked around the hallway in both directions. "I can't tell you anything about that. But I know someone who can."

"What do you mean?"

"One of the guys that works here. Anybody that wants information, I send to him. If I don't, well . . ."

I got the picture. "Who is this guy?"

"Freddie Robinson. He's around the corner. Black guy, medium build. You can't miss him, lots of gold. Listen, make sure to tell him that Jim sent you. Sometimes he gives us a cut."

"Thanks." Capitalism at work. The insurance company pays, and everybody gets a piece.

Freddie Robinson was just where I'd been told he'd be, standing in the corner, holding onto a mop, and talking into a pay phone.

"Yeah, baby, I mean it. You and me tonight." With that he hung up the receiver, his dark eyes flashing, the corner of his mouth curving in anticipation.

He paused for a moment and then turned back to his work. Yes, it was my man. Medium build, tight cropped hair, small mustache, two gold earrings, a large gold pinky ring, and three chains.

When he saw me, he put his mop in the pail and stood nonchalantly with his hands on the hips of his white pants.

"You looking for someone, boss?"

"Yeah. Freddie Robinson."

"You found him," he said, eyeing me cautiously. "What do you need?"

"Maybe some information."

"What kind of information?"

"A little P.I. work. I hear you're the man to talk to."

He flashed a smile, exposing a single gold tooth with a diamond in it. "Depends on what we have to talk about."

I took a twenty out of my pants and held it in my hand. "How's this for a start?"

He smiled again and palmed the bill. "It's a start. But you don't look like a lot of the Brooks Brothers boys that come down here."

"I don't like attention."

"Well, boss, let me tell you. Anything you get from me is going to cost a lot more than this." He held up Andrew Jackson and scoffed at it. I thought it was very unpatriotic of him.

"Depends on what you get me. I want something like Paul Versanti."

"Who?" His hesitation told me what I wanted to know.

"You know, the kid that died after a tonsillectomy. Now that's a real score."

"Not that I know anything, but how'd you find out about that?"

"Bidora told me. He's a friend of mine."

When I mentioned Bidora, Freddie seemed to relax. "Big Tone sent you. Now there's a piece of work. Man's gonna make himself a pile." He dragged the last word out to give it emphasis. "And when Big Tone makes, I make."

"Kind of like the gold rush, isn't it?"

"Yeah, that's right, like the gold rush," he chuckled.

"You do many cases with him?"

"I don't keep a record, man. You know what I mean?"

"How'd you two get together? This sounds like a case for one of the TV attorneys."

Freddie looked a little wary. "He found me. He started asking some questions, man, and I gave him some answers. Now what you need is some cash to get started, like Big Tone. First case up front. After we establish ourselves, I'll work on credit. But don't you never fuck with me, man." I knew from the way he said it that he meant every word.

That was it. Robinson to Bidora to Versanti. A regular Cooperstown keystone combination. The only loser was the young boy.

"Okay, Freddie. I just wanted to make the contact. I didn't bring my card with me, so I'll write my number down on this piece of paper. Call me if you find anything and we'll get started."

He picked up the paper for a second and looked at it. "I've seen this number before. You sure you're not on TV?"

"You're probably mistaking it for something else." As I said it, I started walking away. I wasn't surprised the number was familiar to him. It was the main number of the Detroit Police Department. Lieutenant Sennett, my friend from the Scotten case, had made me memorize it.

# CHAPTER 4

I GOT UP EARLY THE NEXT MORNING and cleaned Jordan's house. I guess I was feeling a little guilty about Jordan. I was increasingly sure she was right. Today I was flying to Chicago to interview some medical hired gun who would tell me that Larry Burkinette was a bad doctor. I already knew that much. Soon the rest of the world would know it too—without any help from me.

Actually, it seemed ironic that I was going to Chicago today to interview Bidora's medical expert. Medical testimony was one of Larry's fortes. I had heard through the grapevine that when the tonsil business got slow, he could always count on a substantial income from testifying against his peers. Money had always meant a lot to Larry. No one else in the residency ever seemed to have the things Larry had. Sleek car, nice clothes, a fancy apartment. As struggling young doctors, integrity gave little solace to the rest of us living in shitholes and eating at McDonald's. Maybe I *had* been a little jealous. It was hard not to be.

My thoughts were jangled by the sound of the TV in the background. A special report, Len Wendel, investigative reporter. "How bad is medicine in this country?" I looked at the screen. Wendell was standing outside Metropolitan Hospital.

"Six months ago in Detroit Circuit Court, one of the most bizarre cases of this decade was filed, defining the issue of whether the basic standards of medical care can survive the carelessness of one doctor, Larry Burkinette. The suit alleges that through a breakdown in sterile technique, a teenage boy lost his life.

"This may turn out to be another example of the deterioration of health care in our country. We spend enormous sums on medical care, but have only the seventh lowest mortality rate in the world. Yet our physicians are among the richest professionals in society. Perhaps the reason for this is the rush by our doctors to perform more and more cases. Maybe they don't have time for such elementary procedures as the age-old tradition of scrubbing before surgery.

"If, in fact, what has been alleged is true, it's time that the public take a stand against such slipshod quackery. It's time doctors become accountable for their mistakes. It's time for justice to stop being sterile. I for one am going to watch this trial closely, for in it lies the seeds of a rich harvest of negligence that must never be planted again."

Wendell's diatribe made me pause. Burkinette's wasn't the first faulty case to be filed for malpractice. But most of them didn't get this kind of publicity.

Even so, I didn't experience my usual outrage at this kind of scare journalism. Maybe I even felt satisfaction that Larry Burkinette was going to get his at last.

I looked at my watch and realized I had better get my ass on that plane.

I MADE IT TO THE GATE with ten minutes to spare. Franklin looked nervous, but then he didn't know me. I always ran it a little close.

Not that my absence would have mattered much to Dr. Curtis Armbruster. He got paid whether I was there or not.

Armbruster was the hired gun Bidora had engaged to dispense his opinion, truthful or not, on Burkinette's case. Like a lot of plaintiff attorneys, Bidora had found it difficult to find anyone in the Detroit medical community to testify against another physician, even Burkinette. That's why we were flying to Chicago for the deposition.

The plane made it to Midway in forty-five minutes. I figure in fifty years the Detroit-Chicago area will be the Midwestern megalopolis.

Hardly futuristic, Curtis Armbruster's second floor Michigan Avenue office was a dump. Peeling wallpaper in the waiting room, papers scattered on the receptionist's desk, lime green indoor-outdoor carpeting in the hallways that still bore a ground-in dark mixture of blood, dirt, and coffee stains.

The inner office was separated from the waiting room by a clouded sliding glass window announcing that the doctor required payment at time of service. In the waiting area the orange plastic chairs formed a haphazard circle around the perimeter, separated from one another by simulated-wood Formica tables strewn with old magazines. Before each chair, a dark stain on the carpeting where patients had sat with muddy shoes. On the walls hung prints: Lester Johnson, Georgia O'Keefe's "Santa Fe Opera," a Carnival Line cruise ship.

When we walked in, Bidora was already there, and so was the court reporter. He registered little surprise at seeing me. I was about to sit down when Armbruster made his entrance, sidling into the room with an odd air of diffidence. I studied him for a moment. Stained lab coat, greasy black hair, a pale, waxy face that looked as if he hadn't seen the outside in months. I bet if I'd looked closely, I would have found dirt beneath his fingernails. He and Bidora, The Malpractice Twins.

Armbruster sat down next to Bidora as the court reporter adjusted the paper in her shorthand machine. She nodded to Armbruster as if they had seen each other before. From what Franklin had told me on the ride over, he made most of his living chewing on the carcasses of other doctors.

Franklin began the deposition in his low-key voice. "Dr. Armbruster, I'm John Franklin. I represent Dr. Burkinette. Did you bring a curriculum vitae with you?"

"I did."

The CV held no surprises. Graduation from a small southern Illinois high school. Undergraduate education at the University of Illinois, and then Chicago Medical School. What the rehash of his career didn't show was the probable years of being picked on in grade school and high school. I could see him then: always the brain, always hoping to be accepted by his classmates. Years of feeling superior because he was so much smarter than his tormentors. Then, when he became a doctor, the awful realization he was no smarter than any of his more successful peers, who practiced the kind of medicine he wished he could. I had seen that movie before.

"I take it you've had a chance to review the file of *Versanti versus Burkinette*?" Franklin began.

"Yes," Armbruster answered.

"Have you come to any conclusions about it?"

"Yes. I think that Dr. Burkinette practiced outside of the standard of care for other throat surgeons practicing in the same specialty." He spoke in a derisive, flat monotone.

"Why do you say that?"

"Because he did not scrub before surgery and tore his gloves during the procedure. All that's needed is to culture the bacteria off his hands, and you'll have him. *Ergo post propter hoc.*"

Franklin's head jerked. "Wait a minute. Do you have some information I haven't?"

"Mr. Bidora showed me a culture report," Armbruster smirked.

"I object to this slyness, Mr. Bidora. Why wasn't I notified before the deposition?"

Bidora smiled. "I just got it today. Affidavit from Miss Janie Denso, circulating nurse, Metropolitan Hospital. She obtained the culture from Burkinette's gloves. You can accept its veracity or not. I'm sure Dr. Burkinette will give us a culture to contradict this one at any time. If you wish, we can end the deposition right now, or reschedule."

"I'd like a moment to talk to Dr. Dailey."

We walked out into the outside hallway.

"What do you make of this, Ben?"

"If it's true, they'll satisfy Koch's postulates."

"What's that?"

"The scientific method: make a hypothesis, set up a controlled experiment, get a culture from Burkinette, and match it up with the culture taken from Paul Versanti. Of course, if you don't let Burkinette give a culture, the chain breaks, but then he looks guilty as sin. With Brenda Palmer's deposition they've got a lock on the deal."

"Are there any possible outs?"

"I need to check with the pathologist who did the autopsy and examined the tonsil specimen. But it doesn't look good for the home team."

Franklin paused for a moment. "Let's go on with it. He can't hurt us any more than he has, and I think I'll find a chink in his armor."

As we sat down, Franklin said, "Okay. Before we start again, I warn you that I am going to object to the court on the nature of these proceedings and the withholding of evidence. That may require us to do this over again. Notwithstanding, we elect to continue. Now, Doctor, what do you know about *Acinetobacter*?"

"It's a common skin contaminant that can become pathogenic under certain circumstances."

"Isn't it true, Doctor, that it only affects patients when they have been weakened by an underlying disease?"

"It's called an opportunistic organism," corrected Armbruster patronizingly.

"Yes. Thank you. Since Paul Versanti didn't appear to have any underlying disease, why do you conclude that the organism alleged to be growing on Dr. Burkinette caused the boy's infection?"

"Obviously there was a sufficient number of bacterial colonies on his hands to inoculate the patient."

"Have you ever heard of this happening before?"

"No."

"Then what makes you think it could happen here?"

"It's the only plausible source. The tonsils were clean of this organism, as was ascertained from previous cultures. The doctor had a tear in his glove. Someone cultured the organism off his hands, and he didn't scrub his hands before the surgery. What else do you need?" Armbruster concluded.

"Doctor, I'm here to ask the questions, and you're here to answer them. Now, what is your standard of practice regarding scrubbing before a tonsillectomy?"

"I always wash my hands." I was certain that was a lie. Many doctors didn't bother to scrub before a tonsillectomy. The throat is such a breeding ground of bacteria that the bacteria on the doctor's hands can only cause trouble under very extraordinary circumstances. But I was also sure that Franklin could never prove him wrong.

To my surprise, Franklin had anticipated Armbruster's response. "I just want to read an affidavit we obtained from a Mrs. Sonja Paulson. Do you know who she is?"

Bidora jumped from his chair. "Just a minute, Mr. Franklin. I'm entitled to see your evidence before you show it to the witness."

"Be my guest." Bidora read it over. He handed Franklin the paper back, saying nothing.

Franklin continued. "Now, Dr. Armbruster, do you know Mrs. Paulson?"

Armbruster answered reluctantly. "She was a nurse at Methodist Hospital. They got rid of her because they said she wasn't doing a good job."

After a moment he added, "Besides, she'd had something against me ever since I'd joined the staff."

"What kind of a thing?"

The pitch of Armbruster's whine increased. "There was another group that did their cases there. She just liked them better than me. She always gave me a hard time."

"Does that happen often?" Franklin asked politely.

"That's none of your business," Armbruster snarled. "I'm just as good as any of those guys. Just because I don't do as much work . . . . I deserve the same respect. Besides, I'm sure they were paying her on the side." He slumped in his chair, glancing evasively at the yellowed posters on his wall.

"What does the content of the affidavit say?" Franklin pursued.

"It says that she had been present on a number of tonsillectomies I had performed where I didn't scrub before the case."

"Now, referring back to your previous testimony, didn't you say you always scrub before a tonsillectomy?"

As Armbruster squirmed in his chair, his upper lip began to perspire. "She may have seen me do that one time, but I'm sure she's just telling you that because . . ."

"Thank you, Doctor. I've got only a couple more questions. Do you know of or recognize Dr. Benjamin Dailey?"

"I've heard of him before."

"How have you heard of him?"

"I've read some articles he has written, and I've heard him speak at the national meetings."

"Would you consider him an expert in his field?"

"Probably, but what's that got to do with this case?"

Franklin ignored him. "One last question. Do you often testify in malpractice cases for the plaintiff?"

"Occasionally."

"What does 'occasionally' mean? Ten, twenty, over fifty times?"

"I would say over fifty times." Armbruster looked around the room, avoiding Franklin's eyes.

"Have you ever testified for the defense in a malpractice case?"

"I think once or twice."

"Isn't it true that you have testified for the plaintiff in over fifty malpractice cases in the Detroit area alone?"

"I would have no way of knowing for sure."

"If I told you that I had scanned the cases in the Wayne and Oakland County courts over the past five years, and found your name as an expert for fifty-one of those, what would you say?"

"I wouldn't dispute it."

"How many times have you testified for Mr. Bidora?"

"Probably about twenty times."

Armbruster seemed to feel almost proud of this accomplishment; he wore a self-righteous expression as he confirmed his efforts on the plaintiff's behalf.

Franklin had a different view of it. "I see. So, you are something of a regular with Mr. Bidora. Is it true that you are what some people might call a 'professional witness'?"

"What do you mean?"

"You know, as they say in the vernacular, a 'plaintiff's whore.'"

Armbruster's face flushed. "What do you mean by that?"

Franklin looked at Armbruster with his best deadpan, adjusting his wire-rimmed glasses. "*Res ipsa loquitur*. Let the fact speak for itself."

Bidora had little to add, but he did get Armbruster's qualifications as an expert. But nothing changed the fact that, unless I was able to find a break in the chain of medical evidence—the autopsy report or Burkinette's glove culture —Bidora had more than enough to bring the case to a jury if he wanted to.

By the time we were done it was three-thirty in the afternoon. The plane to Detroit left at four. We finally got a cab in front of the Trib building and made it to Midway with ten minutes to spare. It wasn't until we finally sat down on the plane that we had a moment to talk about the deposition.

I cut to the heart of the matter. "Have you changed your opinion about the case?"

"My approach will be that this was an isolated incident and Burkinette was a victim of fate," Franklin evaded thoughtfully. "The question is, will a jury buy it? What did you think?"

"It seemed to me that Armbruster was awfully smug. I think he really believes that what he has is invincible."

"What do you think?" Franklin repeated inexorably.

I hesitated. Finally, I said, "I think no one is that unlucky. Not even Larry Burkinette." It cost me something to admit that, but after the words were out of my mouth, I was glad. Glad that, in spite of everything, I was still better than Larry Burkinette.

"Maybe," he mused. "How common is it not to scrub before a tonsillectomy?"

"It happens all the time. Hell, dentists work in your mouth without scrubbing."

"Even so, it's going to be tough to defend this case in front of a jury."

"Why don't you settle the case?"

"Bidora appears to want to take it all the way. We're scheduled to take Mrs. Versanti's deposition tomorrow, and there's a mediation scheduled for the beginning of next week. How soon can you get to the pathologist?"

"The pathologist shouldn't be a problem, he's a friend of mine."

I stared out the window as the plane circled Detroit. It seemed that the city was always cloudy when I landed. As we circled in from the east, the sun suddenly broke through the clouds, illuminating the magnificent inland waterway where Lake Huron emptied its waters into the St. Clair River, past the great inland yacht basin of Lake St. Clair, through the Detroit River's great industrial complex, and into Lake Erie. It was a kaleidoscopic marvel of man and nature. Iridescent red reflected off the General Motors Building, contrasting with the blue water.

The jolt of the wheels touching down shook me out of my reverie. I looked over at Franklin putting his briefcase on his lap.

"John," I said suddenly.

He looked up inquiringly.

"Do you think Burkinette is guilty?" I didn't know why I was asking the question.

He shook his head, fussing with the Mark Cross catches.

"It's my job to have no opinion on that point," he answered calmly.

If I hadn't known Jordan Dalkind, I'd have thought there were a lot of lawyers as bad as Anthony Bidora. Then I stopped for a moment. Maybe anyone who'd encountered Larry Burkinette might feel the same way about doctors.

# CHAPTER 5

B Y THE TIME OF THE VERSANTI DEPOSITION the next day, I was getting sick of the deposition routine, and especially sick of Bidora's office. I showed up only a few minutes before the start.

Actually, this time my tardiness was all my fault. I shouldn't have let Gus Katsopopoulos bend my ear for so long. Gus owned Mr. K's Coney Island, the chief source of my calories and personal confidant to my problems. However, today it was my turn to listen to his. It was his house. He had just built it in the suburbs, and he wanted to show me plans for his in-ground swimming pool. An in-ground pool?

"How much do you think it would take to open up my own shop, Gus?"

"C'mon, Doc. You can't be serious. You're a doctor, not a hashslinger."

"You never know, Gus. There could be a future in it. Look at you."

"Yeah, look at me. Down here early, get home late. Talking to people all day. Listening to their complaints. You know what I mean?"

"Know what you mean? Yeah, I know. I spent twenty some years doing that practicing medicine." I didn't make the usual pleasantries when I walked into the conference room. Instead I nodded and took my place next to Franklin. No Heath. It looked as if the hospital was bailing on Burkinette. Just as they had with me six years before. But I had been innocent. Was Larry Burkinette?

Across the table, I saw the couple from the waiting room the other day. The wife still had on sunglasses, and a scarf around her neck. Her well-dressed blonde husband sat sullenly next to her. Quite a pair, Mr. and Mrs. Robert Versanti.

Karen Versanti's appearance presented an incongruous mixture of dishevelment and style. The ring on her finger must have been three carats, her Prada handbag went for four hundred a pop, but the scarf around her neck looked like a K-Mart special. She fidgeted with a pencil.

Robert Versanti fixed Franklin and me with a steel-hard glare. He looked like a man used to getting what he wanted.

Franklin began. "Now, Mrs. Versanti, how long have you known Dr. Burkinette?"

"We met about three weeks before the surgery."

"Was there anything about that visit that you recall as unusual?"

"Objection," Bidora interrupted. "That is a matter of conjecture on Mrs. Versanti's part." The objection was frivolous, but Franklin, somewhat disdainfully, acquiesced.

"Let me rephrase. Until this episode with your son, had you experienced any misdealings on the part of Dr. Burkinette?"

"No. Everything was very businesslike. I thought he was a little brusque and quick in recommending the surgery, but then our pediatrician agreed it was a good idea."

"I see. Did he explain the surgery to you?"

"He said there wouldn't be much to it. We were to come in for a fifteen minute surgery and go home the same day."

"And during that three-week time period before the surgery, I assume that if you had thought Dr. Burkinette a man of less than good moral and ethical character, you would have found another physician?"

"Objection. You're leading the witness."

"Objection noted. Please answer the question." Franklin didn't bother to conceal his contempt for Bidora this time. I had to admire his strategy on these upscale clients. Mrs. Versanti appeared even more rattled than before.

"Yes, but that wasn't the case. Everything seemed in order."

"How did you hear of Dr. Burkinette?"

"My pediatrician said that Paul had too many episodes of tonsillitis, and that we should see someone about taking them out."

"So it was your pediatrician who encouraged you to see Dr. Burkinette?"

"Yes, I heard from some other people who had taken their children to him that he was very good." Bidora started sinking deeper into his chair.

"When you saw Dr. Burkinette, what did he do?"

"He talked with me about Paul's infections, and then examined him."

"How did Dr. Burkinette examine your son?"

"He put a tongue depressor in Paul's mouth and asked him to say 'ah.' That was about it."

"Did he explain any risks of the surgery to you?"

"He said the recommendation was that if a child had more than four or five episodes of strep throat or tonsillitis in one year, the tonsils should come out.

He said they didn't have to come out, and that Paul could keep taking antibiotics, but Paul was missing a lot of school and was sick all the time. Dr. Burkinette also gave me a sheet explaining the surgery and the risks that went with it."

Of course, we already had Burkinette's standard disclaimer. Franklin made a pretense of reading through it. About halfway down was a paragraph on the possibility of post-operative infections.

"Did you read this?"

"Yes."

"Infection is mentioned here."

"I know, but I never dreamed of anything like what happened to Paul."

"Let's talk about that. How long after the surgery did Paul show signs of not doing well?"

I could see her jaw stiffen as she began to describe the events after the surgery.

"It happened so fast. It was a blur. He just started to get warm, and then I called Dr. Burkinette." She began to cry as she spoke of her son's last hours.

"I'm sure this is very difficult for you, Mrs. Versanti, and I will try to be as quick as possible, but you know there are certain questions I must ask."

Karen Versanti nodded.

"When you called Dr. Burkinette, did he respond right away?"

"Yes."

"What did he tell you to do?"

"He told me to take Paul to the emergency room at Metropolitan."

"Did he meet you there?"

"It took him a while, but, yes, he did."

"What did he do then?"

"At first he acted as if it were all routine, but after an hour or so, he began to look worried. That's when he called another doctor named Fazio."

"Did Dr. Burkinette go home or did he stay with Paul?"

"He stayed with us the whole night." I was surprised to hear that, knowing Burkinette. At least he didn't forget everything from the residency.

"How would you characterize his concern and professional manner during this time period?"

Bidora must have seen enough to know Mrs. Versanti was being dismantled as a witness.

"Mr. Franklin, you know this isn't admissible under the court rules. You're leading the witness shamelessly."

"Mr. Bidora, whether the question is correct or not is for the judge to decide. Personally, I think he will have no objection to the question. Now, Mrs. Versanti, would you please answer the question?"

Karen Versanti looked at me. I didn't suffice as a source of help. She turned back to Franklin, as if in defeat.

"I felt that Dr. Burkinette had done everything possible for Paul."

Franklin looked puzzled at this point. "I'm curious, Mrs. Versanti. If you thought everything had been handled properly, what prompted you and your husband to start the suit?"

Mrs. Versanti glanced from Bidora to her husband. Glares from each of them told her she had gone too far. I could see she was at a loss, not knowing which way to turn. After a moment she looked disconsolately at Franklin and shrugged her shoulders.

"I don't know. We just changed our minds."

"I have nothing further to ask at this point," Franklin said smoothly.

Bidora began his damage control.

"Mrs. Versanti, has there been any change to your personal life since the death of your son?"

She looked at him curiously, obviously not understanding what he wanted.

"What do you mean?" she asked.

"I mean, is there a difference in the way you and your husband interact?"

Mrs. Versanti glanced furtively between her attorney and her husband.

"Why, no. We're the same as we've always been. That is, except that we don't have Paul, and sometimes we . . . ." She stopped. Her hands started to shake. Unable to speak, she stared at the table in front of her.

Mr. Versanti erupted.

"Why don't you tell them it was all your fault? How could you have insisted on taking Paul to see Burkinette? I was never in favor of the goddamned surgery. Now you see what's happened!"

"How can you accuse me of that?" Mrs. Versanti cried. "I saw his pediatrician and he agreed."

"Fucking doctors are all in collusion. Burkinette probably had him on the payroll."

"But doctors are careful. They wouldn't have operated on Paul unless he needed it."

"Bullshit. It's a business just like everything else. You heard about Burkinette's fancy cars. I see him at the club playing golf two, three, four times a week. Who the fuck do you think pays for that?"

Mr. Country Club got angrier by the moment. "But no," he continued, "you badgered me to have it done because you couldn't stand being inconvenienced.

"He was standing over her, his face reddened and his eyes bulging with fury.

Terror rose in her eyes. I was about to get out of my seat. Then Mrs. Versanti flung off her glasses.

"Here, big shot, show them how tough you are." She pointed to her face. Two enormous blue-black lids hid the reddened and swollen eyes behind. She tore off the scarf that covered the dark purple fingerprints on her throat.

Mr. Versanti swept back the blond hair from his forehead and walked slowly to the door. As he did he looked back pitilessly at his wife, her head buried
in her hands.

"Just remember your son's face every time you start to feel sorry for yourself," he snarled. He slammed the door behind him.

That slam ended the deposition. A few minutes later Franklin and I walked
out the door and into the chill fall air without saying a word. When we got to
the corner, Franklin stopped and set down his briefcase.

"What was your sense of all that, Ben?"

I frowned. "I think," I finally said slowly, "That in this case, anyway, Larry
Burkinette's best friend is Karen Versanti. And his worst enemy is Robert
Versanti."

I had conflicting emotions about the latter fact, but overall, I was relieved
that someone had taken my place in my own mind as Larry Burkinette's
archenemy.

# CHAPTER 6

AFTER SEEING KAREN VERSANTI, I wanted to talk to Jordan and tell her I loved her, but she was still out of town. I'd call her at her hotel that night. In the meantime, I caught a sandwich at the deli, then went to one of those Steven Seagal movies. Fifty-two people got blown away, garroted, or eliminated by every type of anti-personnel weapon known to man, and Steven didn't muss a hair on his ponytailed head. If I was going to be exposed to violence, I was going to do it right.

I got ahold of Jordan later that evening. We had a good, lighthearted chat, both of us studiously avoiding any mention of the Burkinette case. I knew better than to believe she'd changed her mind; she was merely too practical to argue long-distance. Before we hung up, she said she thought she'd be back in a couple of days.

"I can't wait," I growled in a fair rendering of lust.

"Well, if you can't be good, be careful," Jordan suggested sweetly.

"You're too broadminded for me. I like jealous women."

"All right. I'll start staking out your boat, where you meet all your bimbos."

"What do you mean 'start'?"

She laughed. "Good night, Dr. Dailey."

"Good night, Jordan Dalkind, Esquire."

THE NEXT MORNING AT NINE I started making calls on the Burkinette case. My first one was to the pathology department at Metropolitan. My old friend from medical school, Tim Fenninger, worked there. After graduating Tim and I had crossed paths several times when I was doing my original research on voice analysis. In pathology he was an expert on the head and neck, especially diseases of the voice box. Nowadays we didn't see much of each other, but back in medical school playing golf with him for points had been one of my main sources of ready cash.

"Still playing with the same handicap, Tim?" I asked.

"Would you believe I'm down to a two?"

"You always were persistent. I'm glad I put your money in the bank."

"All I want is another shot at you, old boy."

"Emphasis on the 'old.' That's why I wouldn't take you on anymore." There was a brief pause.

"You didn't call to talk golf, Ben. What's up?"

"Paul Versanti. Does that ring a bell?"

"The case with *Acinetobacter* sepsis, wasn't it?"

"Yeah, that's him. A sixteen-year-old who died following a tonsillectomy. Anything interesting you can tell me that wasn't on the pathology report?"

"Just interested or working?" he asked.

"A little of both. A lot of things are never mentioned in reports."

"In this case it's all there."

"Have you ever seen this before?"

"Not in twenty-plus years of practice. *Acinetobacter* is such a common organism, it would be hard to eliminate. When we find it it's usually a nosocomial infection."

"You mean an opportunistic organism."

"Right. Of course, with AIDS and chemotherapy, I suppose we're going to see more. Usually it's seen with pneumonia, or even sepsis, as with this patient."

"How do you figure this happened?"

"Your guess is as good as mine. Preexistent infection or it was introduced to his body somehow."

"That's how the plaintiff's attorney views it. He claims that somehow the bacteria on Burkinette's hands inoculated the child."

"I suppose it could happen, but it would have to be a pretty massive inoculation."

"What if I told you he didn't scrub before surgery?"

"Uh-uh. It just doesn't ring true."

"Maybe it doesn't ring true to you or me, but from what the lawyers tell me it would play pretty well in front of a jury. Doctor doesn't scrub, and the patient dies."

"Hey, I just section, stain, and diagnose. I leave that other stuff to the lawyers."

"Tim. Any suggestion where to go from here?"

"Try the CDC. They probably have a record of something like this in their files."

Of course, the Center for Disease Control in Atlanta. I paused before I went on. "What do you know about Burkinette?"

Tim hesitated. "You mean regarding this case?"

"No, in general, in the hospital."

"He's the worst. To him money is everything. But we're working on it."

"What do you mean?"

"The hospital has an ethics committee: Medicaid business, that kind of thing. Beyond that I can't say anything else." I knew it was useless to press him right now. When I was chief of staff at St. Vincent's I had had the same problems. Still, he'd told me something useful. Burkinette was being investigated by the hospital for ethics violations.

Tim changed the subject. "Anything new in the voice business?"

"I haven't done much lately, but I read some reports out of Sweden on voice analysis using voice spectrography. They even quoted that crazy article I published back when I was a resident."

"From what I remember it wasn't so crazy, being able to identify a specific voice, almost like a fingerprint."

"If it was so great, how come I'm not the one being asked to lecture all over the world?"

"Dumb luck," he said.

"You know, Tim, I might have beaten you up on the golf course, but you were always smarter than me."

"Funny, that's what I used to try and convince myself when we were in medical school. It never worked. I'd rather have beaten you."

"Next summer. I'll give you your chance."

"Promise?"

"Promise."

I quickly picked the phone back up and called information in Atlanta. A couple of minutes later I was talking to the operator at the Center for Disease Control, the main repository for every weird infection reported in the world, and certainly the largest source of information regarding infections as unusual as *Acinetobacter calcocetious.*

After three connections I finally got Mrs. Jeanette Wilkins, Senior Technologist, Section for Hospital Infections. I quickly recognized that I was talking to someone interested in what she was doing. I didn't try to pretend I knew more than I did.

"Mrs. Wilkins, I've got a child here in Detroit who died from an overwhelming sepsis secondary to *Acinetobacter calcocetious.*"

"*Acinetobacter*, the scourge of the hospital. Silent and ubiquitous, yet deadly. Was this child immune-depressed?"

"No. It followed a tonsillectomy. As far as we know he was otherwise healthy."

"Then where did the bacteria come from?"

"Some people have speculated that it came from the surgeon's hands through a tear in his gloves."

"Not *Acinetobacter*. It's too slow growing. You need massive numbers for that effect in a healthy person."

"Where would you look for the source?"

"That's a tough one. Somewhere in the operating room, probably. I'd have to do some thinking on that, but offhand I'd look at the anesthesia equipment."

"Have you ever heard of a result like this before?"

"Never. And I hear them all. *Acinetobacter* is my specialty. Fascinating bacteria. It has an unusual cell structure, with an ability to survive under adverse conditions. It's an amazing bacteria. Gram negative rod found in food, water, and on the body, in the hands and throat. In a way I kind of admire the damn bug."

"Funny, I never looked at bacteria that way. All I ever wanted to do was kill them."

"That's the difference between a researcher and a clinician. When you see the survivability of these bacteria, you begin to respect their ways."

"That's where you and I differ. As long as I can control it, I can admire it. This one got out of hand. Aside from the anesthesia equipment, where would you look?"

"Just be methodical. Follow the course of the patient through the hospital and check the various spots along the way where he could have received the infection. And remember the three C's."

"The three C's?"

"Culture, culture, culture."

"I'll try and remember that. I'll start with the anesthesia equipment. I might give you another call."

"That's what we're here for. If you want, I can do a computer search of similar infections and see if anything comes up. I'll mail you the results."

"Thank you. That'd be great," I replied, and gave her my address at the boat.

After I hung up, I thought a moment, then dialed John Franklin. He came on the phone immediately.

"I've got some information, John. Whether it's going to be helpful is another story."

"Before you begin, I think you and I had better have a heart-to-heart." The sternness in his voice put me on alert.

"What's up?"

"I got a call from my client, Larry Burkinette. He says he thinks there is a direct link between the incriminating bacterial cultures and certain material you have in your office at St. Vincent's. He's demanded the police be called."

"The police? What's the deal?"

"Larry Burkinette is filing charges against you. He claims you've set him up."

At least I didn't have to feel guilty anymore for hating Burkinette for what had happened in the past.

# Chapter 7

B Y THE TIME I ARRIVED AT MY OFFICE at St. Vincent's, there was already a crowd. A couple of suits, John Franklin, and a stocky African American man standing in the corner. When he turned around, I realized with some relief that there was at least one friendly face in the room.

"You know, Doc, for a friendly guy, you sure get yourself in a hell of a lot of trouble." He stuck a paw out at me, and I quickly shook the hand of Lieutenant George Sennett. It was a hand that had saved my life, the hand of a man I respected.

"What the hell's going on here, Lieutenant?"

"Maybe you'd better ask Mr. Franklin."

I turned and faced Franklin squarely in the middle of the room. Franklin's previous cordiality had vanished as if it had never been.

"So what did you find, Counselor?" I asked.

Franklin nodded to Sennett. The policeman offered, "I don't know what to make of all this, but there was a bunch of dishes and some literature on bacteriology." I looked over at a stack of red agar plates, culture swabs, and pamphlets on bacteriology that I had never seen before.

"I have no idea how those things got here. But even if I knew, what difference does it make? Doctors have all kinds of things in their medical offices. Cut me some slack, Lieutenant."

"Relax, Ben, no one's accusing you of anything. Yet."

"Oh, yeah? From the look on Mr. Franklin's face, and the presence of those two guys with their collecting bags, I'd say there *is* something of damaging importance in this office."

"I called Burkinette. He indicated that you and he had an altercation at the Pipeline the other night. You still playing there? I haven't been in lately."

"We had words, a little pushing and shoving, that was it."

"He quoted you as saying that he would get his someday."

"No. What I said was that most roosters come to roost in the henhouse because that's where the action is." Franklin looked unimpressed. What did he know about blues lingo anyway?

"Whatever you said, he figured you were out to get him."

"Ridiculous. Kid stuff. I'm beyond that now." I hoped it was true.

"Not according to Larry. He said only a few years ago you filed charges on him, through the county medical society, for Medicaid fraud."

"The guy was abusing the system, for Christ's sake. I just did what I had to. He hired some fancy downtown lawyer, paid him a king's ransom, and beat the rap. What's he crabbing about?"

"He figures you're still out to get him. He says he told the insurance company he didn't want you on the case, but they prevailed."

I turned to face Franklin squarely. "Listen, John, I wasn't running around looking for this business. Bruce Sanderson begged me to get involved. Ask him."

"I will. I'll be in touch." Without another word Franklin nodded to Sennett and left my ransacked office.

I turned to George Sennett.

"Looks like more of the same for you, Doc," he shook his head grimly. "This Burkinette says you set him up good."

"Do you think I purposely infected that boy and murdered him to get back at Burkinette over some ancient history?" I asked angrily. I had suddenly gone from the hunter to the hunted. Again. Goddamn it. I wanted to talk to Jordan for being so right.

"Don't matter what I think," Sennett said stolidly. "That's what he thinks."

"It'll never stand up. He needs witnesses. He needs proof that I would do such a thing. It's crazy."

"Burkinette says you've had a vendetta against him for years, dating back to your residency. He claims this is just another attempt by a sick and demented person to somehow get even."

"This is crazy, George. I would never do anything like that."

"I know that, man. Can you prove your whereabouts on the day of surgery?"

"I'd have to think. I don't even remember where I was that day."

"Better think hard. My advice is to get an attorney. Luckily, you have one in the house." He grinned at me.

He wasn't joking, though. I suddenly desperately wished Jordan would get back from Miami.

"I'm going to get this cleaned up before Jordan even needs to hear about it," I declared.

Sennett eyed me shrewdly. "Doc, I was there with you last time, remember?"

"I remember."

"Well, then, listen to me. Don't be an asshole twice." He shook my hand, collected his men, and left me alone in my office.

If he knew me so well, why didn't he recall that I had never learned to take good advice?

I WALKED OUT OF MY VIOLATED OFFICE with my mind in a turmoil, looking for a friend. I felt robotic as I got back into my car. I sat for a moment behind the wheel and then swung out of the parking lot, headed nowhere in particular and wanting to be somewhere that I knew. Instinctively, I made my way over to Gus's diner. Some of my best thinking was done over one of his red hots.

It was cold out, yesterday's Indian summer gone. The wind swirled the leaves in front of the diner into a mini dust devil. Up and down the deserted street, I seemed to be the only person in the world looking for food or comfort.

"Did my coming down here chase all the customers away?" I said to Gus, leaning on the counter.

"Only the paying ones. I got plenty of mice, squirrels, and dogs to eat whatever I got left over."

"That's a good appetite stimulant. At least we're all omnivores."

"Omni what?" he asked.

"Just a word, Gus. I'll take the special with extra onions."

"You don't look so good, Doc. You coming down with the flu or something?"

"I didn't know it showed."

I told him the whole story, start to finish.

"It sounds to me like someone's setting you up."

"Not 'sounds,' someone is setting me up. This guy Burkinette is such a slimeball, he would do anything to anyone to get himself off the hot seat."

"You know, Doc, back in the old country we had this game of cards I used to play with my friends. Kinda like poker. Except we never had much money, so anything we lost meant a lot. That's why we played it straight, no bluffing."

"Bluffing's part of card playing. How'd you restrain yourselves?"

"Real simple. We had this fire of charcoal, and when it got real hot we spread it out on the ground. Then we'd bet. If a guy bluffed and got called, he had to walk the coals."

"You ever get caught, Gus?" I asked, biting into my sandwich.

"I'm still walking, ain't I?" he winked.

"How am I going to see if Burkinette's bluffing?"

"There's always a line of coals in life, Doc. Make him walk it."

I finished the sandwich, washed it down with a Coke, and went over to the phone to call Sennett. Time to hear what the police lab had made of the strange cultures found in my office. As if I didn't know.

It took a moment for the lieutenant to get on the line.

"What did they find, George?"

"I'll spell it. A-C-I-N-E —"

"*Acinetobacter*," I said coldly.

"Yeah."

I hung the phone up slowly. Somebody was trying to make me walk the coals.

# CHAPTER 8

Not only had they found the lethal bacteria in Paul Versanti's death in my office, they found sheets on how to incubate the damn bug, and documents on *Acinetobacter* infections and how they spread. There was also an operative schedule with Paul Versanti's name on it and the number of the operating room. It was a setup. Somebody was after me, and the obvious person was Larry Burkinette.

Well, if the trail led to Burkinette, I'd follow the trail and see if I could trace the steps of the setup. With luck, I could clear myself before Jordan got home.

I waited until late in the afternoon, during the shift change at Metropolitan Hospital, when there was the most confusion. Dressed in scrubs, I headed down to the operating room in the basement of the five-story hospital.

The three C's. Armed with a bag full of culture plates and my copy of the surgical chart, I was determined to culture my way through the entire route that Paul Versanti had taken from the moment he entered the hospital the day of surgery to the time he left to go home. Some of the cultures would be useless, but I was determined to leave no stone unturned.

My first stop was the admitting office. The admitting record said that Florence Birdwell had been the admitting clerk. As luck would have it, she was at her desk. A pleasant lady, with gray hair brought back in a bun and a white satin blouse with a neat bow tied at the neck.

It took about five minutes of explaining that I was working for an insurance company on a malpractice case before she would let me take the cultures from her. A throat and hand specimen was all I needed. I carefully took the swab, crushed the container, labeled it, and put it back in the bag.

Before I left, I asked her to tell me the various places that Paul Versanti would have passed through on his way to and from the operating room. My charm must have worked again—she gave me names and instructions as to how to follow his path through the hospital. I stopped at the transportation services office and found the transporter who had wheeled Paul Versanti down to the preoperative holding area. From there I went to the preoperative area, then to the cleanup area. As soon as I said I was working for the defense, I got immediate cooperation. Everyone was pulling for the home team.

Fortunately, I didn't run into Larry Burkinette. I cultured everything I could think of from the cleanup room, from the sterilization room. By the time I was finished I had fifty or sixty plates in my bag.

My last stop was in the post-anesthetic care unit. I sat down at a table and started sorting my specimens, making sure everything was in order.

About halfway through my labeling I saw a familiar face. The orderly I had met in the emergency room on my first gumshoe prowl a few days before.

"Hey, didn't I see you upstairs the other day, looking for Freddie Robinson?" he asked.

"One and the same," I admitted. "How come you're down here tonight?"

"Freddie got mad at me for telling you to see him. Got me transferred."

"Sorry, I didn't mean to get you in trouble."

"Hey, I'm glad. He gave me the creeps." Then he looked down at my plates. "What's this all about? I thought you were a lawyer."

"Nope. Doctor. Just some cultures from the operating room. All I'm missing is Dr. Burkinette's culture. I don't know how I'm going to get that."

"Just take his glove from the bag over there." He retrieved a wastebasket from an adjoining examining room. "He was here about an hour ago, doing something to a patient. I watched him for a while. He was the only one there. When he was done, he threw his gloves in the corner."

In excitement I put on a pair of sterile gloves and extracted Burkinette's gloves. I took out a culture stick and quickly made the transfer from the glove to the culture plate. I thanked the kid and wished him well in veterinary school.

That was it. I had everything I had come after. If *Acinetobacter calcocetious* was growing somewhere along the chain of surgery, I was going to find it. I took my bag and started walking toward the elevator. As the door opened my luck ran out. Larry Burkinette stepped out.

No swollen eyes and puffy face this time. Instead I saw the sharp cunning eyes of a schemer who had pulled himself together, and then some.

"Dailey, what the hell are you doing here?"

"Just checking up on you, Larry."

"Maybe you should be checking up on yourself, old man." His drawl and smirk didn't quite cover up his uneasiness at finding me there.

"Just trying to grow old. Now if you'll excuse me, I'm on my way out."

"What have you got in the bag?"

"Nothing that would interest you."

"Let me take a look." He reached over to pull at the plastic sack.

"Not now, Larry." I pulled it back with my left hand, but he was too quick. Before I could respond he had spilled the contents of the sack onto the floor.

"What do we have here, an amateur microbiologist? Or maybe a detective? Which is it, Dailey?"

I reached down to pick the cultures up, but he kicked them aside. In doing so he struck the heel of his shoe into the side of my leg. A bolt of pain shot down my leg, and for a split second I felt dizzy with rage, staggering backward. Then my head started to clear. I needed the cultures back.

"That was for the other night, Dailey, and there's more where that came from."

I bent my head down, hoping he would back off. He did, bending down to pick up the cultures to read them. That's when I leg whipped him. Nothing pretty, just a trick I learned playing football. I spun my leg around, wrapping my heel behind his knee. With a sudden move I jerked backward. A scream of pain, then I saw him holding his knee.

"That was for a moment ago, Larry." As I said it, I picked up my culture sticks, put them back in the bag, and headed out the door.

"I'll get you, Dailey!" he yelled, holding his leg with one hand and shaking his fist at me with the other. I wondered if he finally would, this time.

I left Metropolitan and hustled back to St. Vincent's. I knew a woman in the bacteriology lab whose son I had treated years ago. When I explained what I needed, she was only too glad to help.

WITH EVERYTHING ELSE ON MY PLATE, informing Bruce Sanderson at Coastal Insurance of my new conflict of interest *vis-à-vis* the Burkinette case seemed to me an item that could wait. Unfortunately, he duly called me early the next morning. I knew he must have been doing somersaults when he realized I might have become his company's main escape from the lawsuit.

"What do you make of all this, Ben?"

"Bruce, as much as I dislike Larry Burkinette, there's no way I'd do such a thing."

"I know it, Ben," he said sympathetically. "But from what I read, you've got a tough road ahead of you."

"What do you mean?"

"Didn't you see the paper this morning?"

"No."

"Go get one and then call me."

I picked it up off Jordan's doorstep. Front page news.

*"Dr. Benjamin Dailey, noted head and neck surgeon, has been implicated in an investigation of the death of a young man following routine surgery at Metropolitan Hospital. Although sources would not confirm, the* Times *has learned that Dailey will be named next week in an indictment for conspiracy.*

*"Dr. Dailey was the subject of a sensational investigation last year in which he uncovered a plot to market an electronically flawed implantable device, a plot that nearly cost him his life. Now he is back in the spotlight.*

*"Sources report that this conspiracy may have been an attempt to discredit a former colleague of his, Dr. Lawrence Burkinette. Attempts were made, but Dr. Dailey was not available for comment."* Attempts made. Uh-huh. And so much for Jordan not finding out 'til things had blown over. Shit.

I dialed Sanderson back. "Who leaked the information, Bruce?" I demanded.

"Not me, Ben. My company wants to be as far away from this case as it can." How unexpected.

"Any guesses?"

"Robert Versanti."

"The plaintiff?"

"Best guess."

"Why?" As I asked the question, I conjured the image of his battered wife sitting in Bidora's office. I'd answered my own question.

"Because he's crazy, he's rich, he wants revenge, and he has connections to the media all over town . . . ."

"Okay, okay. I get the picture. What exactly does Versanti do?"

"He owns the largest PR firm in the city. Deals with people on the highest level—media executives, advertising people, even the entire automotive world knows Bob Versanti."

"And now he knows me."

"Now he knows you. This guy doesn't want to win this lawsuit for the money, Ben. He has more money than he'll ever need. He wants to get even with whoever killed his kid. Now he thinks it's you, not Burkinette." Bruce could no longer hide the relief in his voice.

"Burkinette knows what he's doing, all right. I should have been on my guard."

"You know, Ben, we're going to have to sever our relationship on this case." "Friends to the end and this is the end, right?"

"It's just business, Ben. What are you going to do now?"

"Follow Koch's postulates."

"Huh?"

"It's a bug thing, Bruce." I hung up.

A few minutes to clean up and I was out the door. I decided to stop by the boat and pick up my messages, then head over to St. Vincent's. The cultures I needed should be done. It took about thirty minutes to get across town on the

Reuther Expressway. Detroit had a thing about naming freeways after autoexecs: Ford, Chrysler, Lodge, Jeffries. I suppose they'd named the Reuther as a concession to the working people of the city. Walter Reuther was a straight-up guy who formed the UAW, improving the lives of millions of people in the process. He deserved the recognition.

I drove down to the dock where my boat lay gently rocking against the pilings, white, sleek, and ready to move. In front of the parking spot were a couple of cars. Probably a few workmen battening down the place for the winter.

I pulled up my Jeep. I was about to walk up the wooden ramp of my boat when the door from a blue sedan opened and a nondescript man dressed in a wool mackinaw stepped out.

"Dr. Dailey?" he called out.

"Yeah, that's me," I said warily. He approached rapidly.

"I'm here to deliver this to you." With that he handed me an envelope and walked back to his car before I had a chance to reply.

I stood in front of the dock and slowly pulled out the six-page document. The first words were *Subpoena ducas tecum.* I scanned the rest of the page and saw the words "*Versanti versus Dailey*, obstruction of justice, conspiracy." *Shit, it was starting all over. Not again.*

I could feel the anger rise with the bile in my throat. How was I allowing this to happen to me again? Out of the corner of my eye I saw a door open to another car. Out of it stepped a well-dressed man in his mid-forties. Robert Versanti.

He strode up to me. A fixed grin crooked the corner of his mouth, giving his face a lopsided appearance. Everything else in his affect was PR perfect.

"I got Burkinette and now I got you. But unlike Burkinette, you're going to prison. I'll see to that." He hissed the words out like a cobra toying with an animal. As he spoke, my heart almost stopped. I knew it was a possibility. It could happen.

"You're making a big mistake, Mr. Versanti. I had nothing to do with your son's death, or with Dr. Burkinette."

"Sure. The prisons are full of people who never did anything. I'm going to send you there to exchange stories with them." That was enough to flip my switch.

"Are you going to treat me the way you did your wife? The media loves that stuff. I can see it now: big-time PR man batters wife, then takes on an innocent doctor." His face reddened as I spoke. Nothing like getting to the base of emotion.

"You go near the press and I'll tear you from limb to limb."

"First Amendment, Mr. Versanti. A document called the Constitution, which also guarantees the right to a fair trial. See you in court." I walked back to my car, forgetting my messages, my boat, and everything else. It's hard to think straight when you're shaking with fury.

I drove out of the marina, trying to clear my head. Nothing like a little *ducas tecum* to jangle the nerves. One thing was clear from my discussion: I might have fronted a good speech, but that was about all. He had all the legal cards, all the media connections, and all the money. Apart from Jordan, I had nothing except my mouth. Still, as I drove around, I felt better for telling him off. There was something about a good verbal body shot that really made the blood flow.

MY SEEMINGLY AIMLESS DRIVING did eventually find a purpose, ending at the front entrance to St. Vincent's. I parked in the staff lot and walked through the side entrance. Funny how a difference in your legal status makes you look at things differently. The same door I had freely gone through a day before now became a source of anxiety. Would someone confront me? Was I still free to come and go as I pleased?

That question was answered as soon as I passed through: no one cared. I walked past the guard and down the hallway to the bacteriology lab, straight for the office of Mary Henderson.

I had known Mary for years. We first became acquainted when she brought her son to see me for an ear infection. A routine visit that I ordinarily wouldn't have remembered, except that about five minutes after I had seen them, Mary rushed back into the office with her child in her arms, his lips turning blue.

"What happened?" I'd exclaimed.

"Joey swallowed a Lifesaver. It's gone down the wrong way and he's choking on it. Please help me!"

With the whole office staff watching, along with four or five startled patients, I spun the young man around, clasped my arms around his abdomen, and squeezed forcefully. Out shot the Lifesaver, eight feet down the hallway, accompanied by a chorus of applause from his mother and everyone else. A couple of years later the boy came in for another infection and brought me his own handwritten note thanking me, along with a box of Lifesavers. I still had the note on the wall of my office. The Lifesavers were long gone.

Mary reminded me of the episode every time I saw her. Today was no exception.

"How is my boy's lifesaver?" she asked. "I read the newspaper. I don't believe a word. Neither does anyone else around here."

"Thanks, Mary. I'm trying to save my own life today. Did you find anything on any of those cultures?"

"I was just running through them now. Twenty-four of them grew out nothing, all I have left is this last one. I'm checking it out under the scope now."

She looked intently through the oculars of her Zeiss microscope. "Gram negative rods in chains." She flipped the high power on. "Cell wall structure puts it in the contaminant category." She looked up from the scope.

"I'd say this was *Acinetobacter*. Probably the *calcocetious* variety. I see it all the time."

My heart was pounding. "Mary, where did the culture come from?"

"Let's see." She thumbed through her list. "Says here, Burkinette, L."

How unexpected.

# CHAPTER 9

I WANTED TO MEET WITH BURKINETTE, but I knew he wouldn't do it. My only option was to wait for him at his home.

Burkinette lived in the swank northern suburb of Lakeland Hills. I got the address from the hospital and then did a drive-by while it was still light out. The house was on a lonely cul-de-sac off a quiet gravel road. A few random cars occasionally moved through the neighborhood, an old man was out with his dog. Pretty benign place.

Benign and also ritzy. Burkinette might have alimony payments and a few mistresses here and there, but it hadn't affected his lifestyle. I saw his house, a massive stone and brick Tudor affair set back from the road, through a column of huge Colorado blue spruce that faced a small lake. The trees distanced it from the road, the lake from its neighbors. People with seven-figure incomes lived in houses like this one. I knew what the average head and neck surgeon earned; it was certainly not enough to afford this kind of establishment.

Once I had the layout memorized, I decided just after dark to park away from the house. Around five thirty I pulled onto the gravel road and stopped on a grassy shoulder about a hundred yards off the main drag. I shut the lights off, put the engine in park with the motor on, and took a pair of binoculars and a Maglite from behind the seat. With my equipment in hand I returned under the cover of the large trees next to the road that shielded me from the emerging beams of the rising three-quarter moon.

When I was near the entranceway to Burkinette's house, I moved onto the grass, keeping the trees between me and the driveway. The only thing I heard was the annoying crunch of leaves under my shoes, until I came within twenty feet of the gate. I halted at a new sound. I looked up. Two huge Dobermans growling from behind the gate. In the beam of my flashlight their eyes seemed deep red, flashing up from their snarl-bared canines. The only thing keeping them from tearing me into dog food was the underground electric fence. Above the gate I saw the red light of an alarm. The place was an armed fortress.

I backed away slowly and returned to my car. I got in, shut off the engine, and settled down to wait. No sense in alarming those mutts anymore. If I was lucky, Larry's established nocturnal habits would bring him out to me.

Waiting in the car with the engine off, the time passed agonizingly slowly as I shivered inside my jacket. The more prolonged the wait, the more apprehensive I grew over my resolve to confront him.

At about eight o'clock the front door opened and Burkinette came out. From the way he was dressed, he was ready for something fancier than the Pipeline. If he had been concerned about his dogs barking, he didn't show it. He got in his car, started it up, and moved down the driveway and into the street. By this time I had started the Jeep.

When he was twenty feet from me, I turned on the lights, pulled out from the curb, and braked in front of his car. His brakes screeched. Angrily, he burst out of his Mercedes—not like an arrogant patrician, but a man driven to recklessness by the extreme of nervous tension.

"What the hell is going on?" he yelled, his voice trembling. Rage? Or fear? I had gotten out of my car and was walking slowly toward him, my head down.

"Sorry," I called out, "I got a flat and had just fixed it when you pulled out." I was almost upon him.

"Well, get out of here. This is a private road."

Typical Burkinette. Too late. I was already within reach. I rushed him, pinning him against his Mercedes before he had a chance to react. With one hand I spun him around and put him in a chokehold.

"It's time to shut up and listen," I barked.

Even if he could have shouted, in this far-flung neighborhood no one would have heard. I took his coat and pulled it down his shoulders. The more he struggled, the more the straitjacket constricted him.

When he saw my face, his showed astonishment, followed by what looked like scornful relief.

"Back on the town again I see, Dailey," he said, leaning against the side of his Mercedes.

"Just working," I answered grimly.

"C'mon, Ben. Isn't this a little melodramatic? I mean, we're both doctors, for Christ's sake." The conciliatory tone of his voice almost made me feel guilty. Almost, except that I'm usually not at my arbitrative best when someone is trying to frame me.

"Every time I hear the word 'doctor' in front of your name, I hear sham and deception. Now quit the bullshit, Larry." I stared at him for a few seconds. "All this time. Even when we were residents it seemed inevitable that I'd have this Hallmark moment with you."

"Well, here we are. What do you want?"

"You're setting me up, aren't you?"

"I don't know what you're talking about," he said insolently.

"I'm talking about planting that *Acinetobacter* culture in my office, and those papers."

"I didn't put anything there," he denied. He actually sounded halfway convincing.

"Do you also believe you didn't kill the Versanti kid?"

"It was a fluke occurrence. You know medicine: always expect the unexpected." His body relaxed and his voice cooled, no sign of lying or guilt. But then he'd always been a cool liar.

"If that's the case, why are you worried?"

"Who's worried?"

"You are. I know you. You'd never confront me in a public place the way you did the other night at the Pipeline unless you were scared."

"Worried about you? Not in this life."

"Bullshit. You're really scared you did it."

"They need proof, old man."

"They've cultured your hands; they know the bacteria is there."

"It's too common a contaminant. It could come from anywhere." Doctors were becoming more like lawyers every day.

"Including your hands. That's why you framed me. You knew the plaintiff's attorney had cultured your gloves. Franklin told you. You had to try to make them think someone else did it. Given our past, and my work for Coastal on your case, I was a perfect setup. There was only one problem."

"Oh?"

"I cultured *Acinetobacter* from your gloves, too."

He started laughing uncontrollably, as if it were the greatest joke he had ever heard.

"So that was the culture you were taking. Who's going to verify it? Do you think they're going to take *your* word?"

"We'll see, after I show the results to Lieutenant Sennett at the police department."

"Do whatever you want. I'll never let them do a confirmatory culture on my hands. Fifth Amendment, old boy. Without one it's all speculation and hearsay."

"We'll see," I said. But suddenly I realized my mission had been foolish. What was I going to do, beat him to a pulp? I'd had my chance to confront him. He hadn't broken. In fact, he seemed more confident.

"Not feeling so good anymore, are you, Ben?" I'd had enough of this. I reached inside his pocket and pulled out his keys.

"Get in the car, Larry." I pushed him inside, still straitjacketed. "When you get yourself loose, your keys will be at the end of your driveway. See you in court."

Misgiving came over me as I looked back at him in the car. He was pushing frantically against the dashboard trying to get out. I figured I'd wait around for five or ten minutes and then let him out. Yeah, I was one tough gumshoe. My worst enemy and I couldn't even inflict a little claustrophobia on him. Sid at the Pipeline had me pegged, all right.

About the time my conscience had made the decision, I heard a slapping noise on the blacktop. I looked around and saw Larry's two hounds in pursuit, thirty feet off and gaining. This time there was no electric fence to protect me, and they were a hell of a lot faster than I was.

I ran to my Jeep, fumbling with the latch. Just before they were on me, I yanked the door open, threw myself across the seat, and dragged my legs inside, slamming the door behind me. Ten seconds more and I would have been ground chuck.

Breathing heavily, I cursed myself a fool. Naturally, he could open his gate by pushing a button on his dashboard. No wonder he'd been thrashing around. *First rule*, I castigated myself. *Never feel sorry for a snake, Adam._*

I started up my car. As I drove past his Mercedes, he was almost out of his straitjacket. His dogs were there, growling at me. All I could see of his face from the lights of my car was a nasty smile. Would he always win? Thirty years. Had I lost for good this time?

But the more I drove, the better I felt. It would take some doing, but I knew Sennett would believe me. When I walked into Jordan's front hallway I saw the answering machine light on. It was Jordan.

I didn't call her back. I couldn't. Not until I'd gotten myself out of the mess she'd warned me I was stepping into. She'd already helped save my ass once. I'd be damned if she had to do it again.

AFTER YEARS OF BEING ON CALL I knew how to sleep on demand. When the phone woke me, I felt as if I had been in a coma.

"Ben, this is George Sennett."

I looked over at the clock. "Jesus, George, it's five in the morning. Couldn't it wait?"

"I don't think so, Ben. We just found Larry Burkinette outside his gate in the front seat of his Mercedes, a single shot through his forehead." He paused. "I think you better get your damn fool butt down here."

# CHAPTER 10

"WHAT THE HELL HAPPENED?" I asked innocently, sitting across from Sennett at the station.

"It looked like someone had used his coat to disable him up in the front seat. He had a single bullet hole through the left eye. Our guys are telling us he died instantly. Both his dogs were found dead next to the car."

I was surprised to find that I was sorry for Larry's violent end. Maybe I could afford to be. After all, I was still alive. But that didn't mean I had won. If I didn't clear myself now, I'd spend the rest of my life in prison hearing Larry Burkinette's mocking laughter.

"Any suspects?"

"Well, right now you could be top on my list."

"C'mon, George, you know I'm incapable of murder."

"I know, Ben. But those who don't include my captain, a grand jury, and a judge. From what I hear you had plenty of motive. You'd be the first person they'd look at."

"What about Robert Versanti?"

"We're going to check him out."

"But not too hard." I thought about my fingerprints all over the car. A shiver ran down my back.

"Had you seen him recently?" I felt a great temptation to lie, but Sennett would forgive me anything but that.

"I stopped by to see him. Tried to talk things out."

"Anything else?"

"Nothing. I left him alive." I paused for a moment. "You must really believe I had something to do with the murder, don't you?"

"No. I told you no. That's why I'm going to stick my neck out and let you do your thing. Only one restriction."

"What's that?"

"Stick around town for a while. I've got some digging to do. It'll take another four or five days. In the meantime, I might have someone nearby."

"You mean following me?"

"I have to, Ben. I'm already stretching my coat to cover you. Don't make me sorry."

I had to do some thinking. The best place was my boat. But my fears were unfounded. The marina was empty when I arrived. It was the beginning of the winter season, and most of the boats were in their cradles now, enshrouded in blue transparent shrink wrapping like cold, drowned ghosts.

I stepped on board, took the mail out of the box, and headed down below. I'd anticipated that someone might have broken in, but everything was in its place. I threw the letters down on the dinette. A Center for Disease Control return address caught my eye. The information Jeanette Wilkins had sent me.

I opened the envelope and two pieces of paper fell out. The first was a letter addressed to me:

*Dear Dr. Dailey,*

Thank you for your recent inquiry. Acinetobacter calcocetious is a common contaminant in food, water, the skin, and oral cavities. It is a gram negative, rod type bacillus with very little in the way of infective potential, except in debilitated individuals, causing the so-called nosocomial or opportunistic infections. These are usually found in the form of pneumonia or blood infections. The current therapy is with third-generation cephalosporin antibiotics. Enclosed please find a computer printout from the last five years of Acinetobacter infections in surgical patients. Obviously, we can't list every infection with this organism, only the unusual or cases associated with surgery.

I hope my information is useful.

*Sincerely yours,*
*Jeanette Wilkins*

Nothing I didn't already know. I scanned the list of cases, about fifteen of them, with doctors' names and hospitals. Culture, culture, culture, look, look, look.

The cases were from all over the country. Fortunately, Jeanette had included the addresses and phone numbers of each of the treating physicians. I started making the calls. Usually doctors were more willing to talk to a colleague than a hospital bureaucrat.

Most of the doctors were in when I called, and when I told them I was doing a study on *Acinetobacter*, they were helpful. But these were sad stories with no answers. All were debilitated patients on chemotherapy or suffered from AIDS.

There were three I couldn't get hold of. I'd wait until tomorrow and call back. Exhausted, I put the list back in my pocket, closed up the boat, and went down to the local deli for a sandwich.

When I got there, I found a newspaper on the table next to me. I reached over for it and pulled out the sports section. I judge my anxiety level by how long it takes me to read the sports page before I feel relaxed. If I was still uptight by the time I finished the box scores, I was in trouble. It was close tonight, but by the time I read Steve Yzerman's name, I was all right.

All right enough that the thought crossed my mind to go to the Pipeline and play a few sets, but instead, I decided to call it a night and head back to Jordan's.

On Jordan's street my sense of anxiety returned. There were more cars than I was used to and a few more people on the street. My instincts told me to stop, so I pulled into a driveway a block away. I saw the local news station camera crew and the lights shining on a reporter in front of the house. Versanti at work again.

I realized there was no way I'd be able to go back to Jordan's. Not unless I wanted to do the headless monster walk under my jacket. I swung my Jeep in the opposite direction, driving toward the Reuther Freeway. There was a Holiday Inn I'd often passed on the outskirts of town.

As I drove, I realized afresh that I was on a free fall into criminal space. I had gone from investigator to murder suspect with a flick of a TV set clicker. I had to find out who had murdered Larry Burkinette. The best place to start would be his office.

Surprisingly, when I called next morning, the office of Lawrence Burkinette, M.D., Head and Neck Surgery, was still open. Even though he had died, the practice still had to sort out the mess his sudden death had created.

When I said I was working for an insurance company on a claim and wanted to pick up some papers, the secretary made no objection to my visit.

I drove to a high-rise office building just off the expressway. Burkinette's suite was on the fifteenth floor. Pretty much what I had expected: fancy paneled waiting room, repro Georgian furniture, subdued lighting, copies of *Vanity Fair* and *Town and Country*.

"I'm Dr. Dailey. I'm the one that called earlier."

"Oh yeah, come on in."

The oak door to the inner office opened, and I stepped through. I was surprised. Instead of the computerized, mechanized office of the nineties, I found cardboard boxes on the floor filled with charts, a pegboard, and billing slips in disarray on the desk.

"Sorry about the mess, but everything is torn up."

"No problem. It looks like my office."

"It's been such a hassle trying to keep up with things."

"Didn't you computerize?"

"I talked to the doctor about it, but he never wanted to spend the money. He said he was a solo practitioner, and the expense was unnecessary."

"I suppose you're right, but with a practice the size of his it would have been a good business investment."

"Oh, we weren't that busy. At least while I worked here." I was surprised. I had always figured Larry had been the master of the eighty-patients-a-day routine.

"How long did you work for Dr. Burkinette?"

"About a year. Would you like a cup of coffee?"

"Thanks," I said, following her to the small lunchroom. "Was the turnover high in the office?" She looked at me with a questioning expression on her face.

"Say, you sound like the police that were here yesterday. Cream?" I nodded, and she heaped in two teaspoons of that powdered stuff that ruined whatever coffee flavor had survived the drip-maker.

"No, just an insurance representative. How was it working for Dr. Burkinette?" I pressed my luck.

"He didn't talk much except on business. Patients seemed to like him all right. The only complaint I ever got was that he was too quick."

"You said he wasn't busy. Was that since you had been here?"

"The other girls said things had been slow for a while before I started."

"It must be hard working here now, knowing it's not going to last."

"Oh, his lawyer called and told me to take as much time as I needed."

"I take it Larry was never late with a paycheck."

"Never. It always came from his accountant's office." I looked around for a moment, then took the plunge.

"Listen, the reason I came over is that Dr. Burkinette told the insurance company he was working on a paper about the effects of antibiotics on tonsillectomies. He had the draft here in the office. I came to pick it up." She seemed surprised.

"That's a switch. Dr. Burkinette doing medical research. He seemed so uninterested in medicine. It makes me feel better to know he had that kind of curiosity. You know, everyone likes to be proud of who they're working for."

"Sure."

"Just go back in his office. If it's there, it'll be in his desk or in the file cabinet next to the wall. But don't be too surprised if everything's a mess. The police went through his things with a fine-tooth comb, especially after the murder."

I walked back through the office. Four small exam rooms and a tiny lab. Pretty spartan equipment for a big-time practitioner: no strobes, no flexible laryngoscope, and no x-ray machine. Hardly a new-wave office. No match for the expensive waiting room. That was Larry: all show, no substance.

In Larry's private office I picked up the operating room schedules from his littered desk and started reading them. There were about thirty of them, each a week apart, each with Burkinette's name highlighted in yellow.

I looked at the caseload. Every week he performed two to three tonsillectomies and a tube insertion. I had always assumed from my previous experience on the peer review committee that Larry was doing six times that many cases. I put the papers down and took one more look around his office. Avarice, ambition, and lust, the species of madness that had consumed him. Now this was all that was left of him, a dingy cubicle filled with emptiness. I got up slowly from the desk and walked back to the receptionist's office.

"Did you find what you were looking for?"

I shook my head. "I guess they're somewhere else," I said to the secretary. She looked disappointed.

"If I find them, I'll let you know. It would be a shame to let his last work go unrecognized. I think he would have wanted that recognition."

"What makes you think that?"

"Oh, just the lawsuit. I think he felt he'd been disgraced."

"You knew about the suit?"

"Oh, everyone did. He never talked much about it, but Dr. Burkinette got upset if there was a mention of it. I'd never seen him act like that before."

"In what way?"

"He was real jumpy, never liked taking phone calls, and was always changing his office hours."

"A suit like that would make any one jumpy," I agreed. She glanced up at the clock on the wall. "Maybe you're right. Say, I've got to get going. I want to go to the funeral."

"Where is it going to be held?" I was instantly thinking of going myself. You never know what might turn up.

"It's at Oakdale Cemetery, over on Coventry and Waddington Road."

"I know the place. What time?"

"In about an hour. I'd better get going if I'm going to make it." As I turned to leave, she stopped me.

"Thank you for telling me about Dr. Burkinette's research. I feel so much prouder having worked for him." I smiled and nodded. At least my lie had done someone some good.

MARK TWAIN SAID WE REJOICE AT a birth and grieve at a funeral because we're grateful we're not the person involved. In the case of Larry Burkinette, there wasn't much grieving. The assemblage at the Oakdale Cemetery was underwhelming. In attendance were his secretary, of course, a couple of men in business suits, the pastor, and a blonde woman in a black coat near the edge of the burial site.

I stood toward the back of the burial site and watched. No matter how much I'd disliked Larry Burkinette, what did it matter now? A waste of a mind, somehow lost in the empty search for the material goods that the practice of medicine can bring. What had happened to the young man who'd stood up at Saturday morning conferences and effortlessly quoted the latest journals? What had happened to the surgeon with such promise, once described by one of his professors as the "boy with the golden hands?"

The pastor gave a eulogy, but it was clear he had never known Larry. No one else came forward to say anything. So after Lawrence Burkinette had passed through the valley of the shadow of death, the workers shoveled clods of dirt on top of the shiny walnut casket and that was that.

I started walking. I was almost to my Jeep when a voice stopped me.

"Did you know Larry well?" I turned around to see the tall, blonde woman, devoid of makeup, her hair pulled back in a ponytail.

"I'm just an old acquaintance from his residency days."

"Oh, really? Larry never talked much about his past. What's your name?" she asked. I noticed her blue eyes were dry.

"Ben Dailey," I said, extending my hand. "What's yours?"

"Samantha Burkinette. I'm—er—was, Larry's wife." I was surprised, both that she was here and that she still considered herself married. My face must have shown my surprise, because she elaborated, "Larry and I had separated, but the divorce wasn't final. I still cared for him."

"Did Larry ever mention my name to you?"

"Not that I remember. But that's not unusual, there were a lot of things we never talked about."

"I wonder if he ever told you anything about a patient named Paul Versanti."

"Well, I knew about the lawsuit, of course. But I think he had more on his mind than that."

"What do you mean?" She looked at her watch.

"You know, I'd like to talk to you more, but I've got to go. Maybe you could see me later?"

"Sure." I took the address she had written down, looked at it for a moment, then pocketed it. Somewhere across the river in Canada.

IT WAS AFTER EIGHT O'CLOCK by the time I had made my way across the Ambassador Bridge and into the Canadian city of Windsor. The Motor City's twin sister across the Detroit River was a sharp contrast to the teeming cauldron that hid itself behind the skyscrapers of the automotive capitol of the world. Most of Windsor's downtown was ringed with grassy waterfront parks and low, unobtrusive buildings. It was an intentional statement that Canadians did not fully share in the raucous American culture across the river. Except for the casinos. In ten years, Windsor's casinos had become the largest tourist attraction in Ontario, and consequently one of its greatest moneymakers.

I followed the address that Samantha Burkinette had given me down to the casino area. Over the years, my occasional trips to Windsor had never taken me to the waterfront. Throwing away money was never part of my ethic, and more importantly, luck was not my strong suit.

Finally I stopped my Jeep. I checked the address again. No doubt, the Pink Ostrich was the place. The doorman came to the side of my car.

"You want valet parking, mister?" He must have seen my hesitancy. He added, "Cost you twice as much at the casino and it's a four-block walk to boot."

Sold. I handed him the keys.

"Pretty busy tonight, isn't it?"

"It's the auto show, eh. These guys come from across the river. They're wild, eh. The place is jammed." Great. I had heard of the strip joints across the river, but I'd never had the urge to go. And now, with Jordan, I got every thrill a man could desire *and* brain-friendly pillow talk.

I walked past the six-foot-six, three-hundred pound bouncer with a ponytail and goatee and made my way to the back of the crowded bar. In the center stage a spotlight focused on a well-built woman in a G-string, circling the stage in a catlike prance, breasts bouncing from side to side, arm outstretched with a fistful of bills signaling the end of her act. The shouting of the men along with the bump-and-grind music was making my head pound already.

As the dancer exited stage left, the music suddenly changed. The spotlight moved to another girl, dressed in leopard-skin tights, suspended in a bird cage above the floor. The cage lowered slowly to the ground as the seated blonde with extravagant makeup extended her legs and slithered out onto the stage, bringing a roar from the crowd.

The girl stalked the stage, eyeing the customers lasciviously. She slowly began to disrobe, taking off her long gloves first and then slowly, painstakingly removing her skintight top. Her firm, protruding breasts produced another roar. Her eyes focused on the crowd through her heavy mascara and fluorescent blue eyeliner. Her tight buttocks and muscular thighs were adorned only by the glittering piece of string between her white, flawless legs.

The crowd of men, mostly in business suits, showered the floor with dollar bills. Each time she bent to pick them up she undulated her smooth rear in the face of one of the customers. A red-faced fifty-year-old man in a business suit waved a twenty-dollar bill in front of her. It must have been what she was waiting for because she lowered herself to her knees and moved sinuously across the floor to him.

She came off the stage and walked sensually around his chair. As she circled him, she brought her body next to his head and rubbed her breasts against his face. Taking the bill from his hand, she held it up to the crowd, then slipped it inside her string. In unison the crowd began yelling, "Lap, lap, lap!"

The girl laughed as she straddled his knees, her pelvis touching his stomach. The band struck up "Honky Tonk Woman" as the girl pressed her nipple against the man's lips, lowering her hips and grinding her pelvis against his evident erection. The man had obviously had too much to drink, and couldn't control himself, because his body began shaking. As he released in his pants, the girl shouted derisively in French, "*Il m'a baisse!*" The crowd went wild with applause as the embarrassed and deflated man sat foolishly, trying to figure out a way to exit the bar without being noticed.

The act finished with a roar of laughter as the girl climbed back on the stage and strutted off. There was no doubt who she was. It was Samantha Burkinette.

I followed her backstage until I came to the door leading into the dressing area. I ran into the first bouncer's identical twin.

"You can't go back there, man," he growled.

"I'm here to see Samantha Burkinette. Tell her Dr. Dailey is outside. She'll let me in," I shouted above the din from the bar.

I guess I must have impressed him with my polite manners, because he headed back into the dressing area. Within a couple of minutes, I was ushered into the one place every other guy in the joint would have liked to have been.

There were women in various states of dishabille everywhere. Somehow, close-up, they didn't look quite the same. Breasts a little slouchy, faces painted to hide the crow's feet around their eyes, blank, expressionless faces that bespoke a boredom disguised on the stage.

Samantha Burkinette's dressing room was at the end of the corridor. The bouncer knocked and showed me in. I was a little surprised when I saw her. Dressed in sweatpants and a Florida State t-shirt, she certainly didn't look like the woman who had just lap danced the businessman into an ejaculatory orbit. I pushed a couple of her costumes aside and sat down on a chair next to her cluttered dressing table. She must have seen my surprised gaze before.

"Everybody looks that way when they see me dressed like this offstage. It makes me feel good, like I don't really belong here."

"Do you?" I asked.

"It's the only job I know. I grew up in New Orleans and spent a couple of years at Florida State. My old boyfriend got me into exotic dancing, and here I am."

"Is this where you met Larry?"

She nodded. "He used to be a regular. He never yelled like the other guys, and something about him caught my eye."

"Do you usually go out with customers?"

"No. But he was persistent. He used to send me flowers and sometimes a note with a present. Like this necklace." She held up a gold heart with a small diamond in it. "It's a pretty nice gift from someone who doesn't even know your name, don't you think?"

"That sounds like Larry, all right."

"Did you know him for a long time?" she asked.

"We were residents together back at North Central University Medical School in Minneapolis." I looked around the room at the bras hanging from hooks, the G-strings scattered on the dressing table, and bottles of makeup on the table. Then I looked at her. Hers was an innocent face, simple, uncomplicated. No wonder Larry fell for her.

"What happened between you and Larry?"

She seemed eager to talk. "When we first started dating, he was all over me. Calling me, telling me he couldn't live without me. He proposed on his boat on a moonlight cruise. It was all so romantic. He made me feel like a princess."

"Then what?"

"We were married for about a year. He told me it was the first time he really felt happy in his life. Then he started getting the calls I was telling you about. Someone named Buzz, that's all I know. Every time Buzz called, he became a little more distant, a little more angry." As she spoke she started playing with a makeup brush on the table in front of her.

"He never told you what was bothering him?"

She shook her head. "He would lash out at me. The things he said, they were so unlike him. At first I thought it was just something that went wrong at the office. I didn't understand medicine that well, and he never told me much. Then that boy died and that was the end."

"What do you mean?"

"He told me he had talked to his attorney, and he was filing for divorce. He said he'd take care of everything. He wanted to put me up in an apartment. I told him to forget it. I was out the next day." Tears were starting to brim in her eyes, welling onto her cheeks.

"So that's when you went back to dancing?"

She nodded weakly. "When I married Larry, I thought I had finally gotten my life together. Respectability and a husband who cared. I didn't want his money, only his love."

"Was money ever a problem?"

"For Larry? He always had plenty of money. Maybe he had too much."

"Anything else you know of?"

"The only times I ever saw him really get upset were when he lost that boy and when he got the letter."

"What letter?"

"Just a plain envelope, no return address and a piece of paper inside."

"What did it say?"

"I didn't see the whole thing, but it looked like three red lines on a piece of paper."

"Do you have any idea what it might have meant?"

She shook her head.

"Did he ever tell you about his difficulties at the hospital, insurance things or patient problems?"

She shook her head again sadly. "I wanted him to. Every now and then I'd ask him how his day was. But I think he thought I wouldn't understand. Honestly, I tried as hard as I could." Her body shuddered slightly as she spoke.

I wanted to go over and put my arm around this little girl grown, but I knew better. One woman was enough for me. Instead I got up to leave. But a couple more questions.

"By the way, who were those other two guys at the funeral?" I asked.

"Larry's attorney and accountant."

"You know them well?"

"Not really. I think I'm just a pain in the neck to them. Jack Rembertson, he's the attorney, asked me to stop by his office in the next week or so. He said Larry had provided for me. I think he's worried I'll want more."

"Should he be?" I still couldn't figure out why Larry would have wanted to provide for her at all, if he was discarding her.

"Let me tell you one thing," she said angrily. "Happiness is Detroit in my rearview mirror. Larry can take his money and shove it. As soon as I make enough from this job, I'm out of here."

"I'm sorry if I upset you. Maybe I should leave."

"You don't have to," she said, wiping the tears away. "Actually, in some strange way you remind me of Larry. Maybe it's because you're a doctor, too.

Maybe that's why I talked to you without asking why you're so interested in Larry's problems."

Good shot. I couldn't think of an answer right off the bat. Come to think of it, why *had* she been so willing to talk to me without even knowing what I wanted?

"Or maybe I just liked the company." There was an innocent allure to her voice that stirred me. Damn, she was good. Larry'd never had a chance. Lucky for me I had Jordan to keep me straight. Larry and I had been with the same girl once before. The idea of repeating that catastrophe held no appeal for me.

"Goodbye, Mrs. Burkinette. Thanks," I mumbled. She seemed disappointed. As I left, I caught a last glimpse of her sitting in front of the mirror, the yellowish light from the table lamp tinting her pale skin. That single look told me her whole life. Often adored, rarely loved. Too bad the one she'd chosen to belie her fate had been Larry Burkinette.

I walked out the door of the Pink Ostrich and into my Jeep. Thank God for Jordan.

# CHAPTER 11

A CANDIDLY OUTSPOKEN LITTLE MAN roots around in all of our brains. Given his temperamental disposition, he usually makes his appearance at the most unpredictable times. When he does, he speaks only for a moment, then disappears as fast as he came. Most of the time his voice is loud and clear: *You don't need that cake*, or, *Keep your hands off the secretary with the cute ass.* Unfortunately, sometimes his voice comes from a distance, making it hard to perceive, easy to ignore. From experience, I found those are the moments that what he has to say is usually significant, and almost always associated with something painful.

I'm not always the best at heeding the little man, but the morning after I met with Samantha Burkinette, I was all ears. The death of Larry Burkinette had put me at the edge of a cesspool filled with quicksand, and I was slowly being sucked into it. If I waited for someone to help me, I would drown, another victim of life's bad luck. The little man evidently thought I needed reinforcement in this realization. I heard his message loud and clear: *Don't believe in luck, and don't ever be a victim.*

Larry's killing and the setup of me as a suspect were not random events. The key to both lay somewhere in Larry's sullied past. Something even worse than I already knew. I had a feeling that when I was finished it was going to take me a long time to feel clean.

But right now, I needed to get dirty. I had to start digging. And not just for some sexual gossip told in the surgeon's lounge at the hospital, or the legal testimony in peer review sessions. Whoever had killed Larry in that gruesome way had done it for something even less forgivable than screwing someone's wife or bungling surgery.

All I had wanted, as far as Larry Burkinette was concerned, was to keep my life as far away from his as possible. Well, "as far as possible" had turned out to mean right in the thick of his murder.

So, I needed to find out even more about him.

I was at the offices of Jack Rembertson the next afternoon. I had only a couple more days until George Sennett was going to have to put the hook on me. I wasn't going to be stopped by a little thing like giving a false name to Burkinette's tax lawyer.

Rembertson had agreed to see me when I'd told him I'd replaced Ben Dailey for Coastal Life on Burkinette's case. I drove over there after a fruitless morning trying to reach the last three doctors on my CDC *Acinetobacter* list, a gloomy meal of chili dogs with Gus, and a quick drink with Sid and Charley in the quiet golden light of the Pipeline. All three of them together were the next best thing to Jordan, lost to me in Miami.

"You were at the funeral yesterday, weren't you, Dr. Griffin?" Rembertson asked as we shook hands.

"Larry and I went way back to residency days."

"Were you good friends?"

"'Friends' wouldn't be the word people would have used to describe our relationship. We always seemed to be on the opposite end of arguments."

"I can understand that, knowing Larry."

"Had you been Larry's lawyer for long?"

"About eighteen months."

"That was before the Versanti malpractice case was instituted, is that right?"

He nodded. "That case was really sad. From what Dr. Burkinette told me it was going to be a tough case to defend because of the sterility aspect."

"Did Larry talk to you much about the case?"

"We talked about nothing except estate planning. That's my forte. He had me setting up trusts to prevent any attachment of his assets."

"I didn't know Larry had anyone to leave anything to."

"Larry's family members were all dead. Everything is going to three beneficiaries."

"Any names?"

"Well, the will hasn't been read yet, so technically I can't divulge the names. But I suppose the insurance company would want to know, especially if any award goes over policy limits."

"Why's that?"

"Well, these trusts were formed after the death of the Versanti boy, but before the serving of the papers."

No surprises here. Larry had been trying to beat the justice system, just as he'd exploited every system he'd ever worked in. Except as a presumption of his awareness of his guilt in Paul Versanti's death, that predictable fact gave me nothing I needed. In fact, this whole visit seemed like a waste of time. I excused myself, thanking Burkinette's tax scammer for his time.

Down in the lobby, I looked around. All I could see was a janitor and a guard at the desk. On the way out I noticed a large Lichtenstein intaglio on the wall. I looked up at the accusing eye of the Roman head staring back at me as if it was Sennett's cop trailing me. It gave me the chills. *C'mon, Dailey, forget it. You're just getting jumpy.*

I decided to go back to the boat to see if I had any messages. I could have phoned in for them, but I needed the solace of my water-bound office. It was getting late, and the traffic near Rembertson's suburban office seemed to be increasing. I made a quick decision to avoid the ditches and take the less traveled road along the lake. Dusk was falling as I swung down Jefferson, through the low-income district that separated Detroit from Grosse Pointe.

To a stranger, entering Grosse Pointe was startling. First came Detroit, with blocks and blocks of boarded-up shops, abandoned cars, and the faces of the dispossessed on every street corner. Then, suddenly, the city limit sign for Grosse Pointe: like magic, ornamental streetlamps, large stately trees, houses that reeked of auto money.

At the Grosse Pointe line Jefferson Avenue turned from a six-lane thoroughfare into a four-lane parkway with a new name, Lakeshore Drive. I often wondered why Grosse Pointers had changed the name. Jefferson represented everything they stood for, I thought—independence, wealth, the pursuit of happiness.

Tonight, the traffic on Lakeshore Drive was light, a surprising occurrence for a midweek rush hour. Then I remembered it was November, the season of the mass exodus from the city for hunting. It was surprising, the effect on a large metropolitan city like Detroit, though less so on a wealthy neighborhood like Grosse Pointe. Shops closed early, and for a couple of weeks the expressway madness that usually consumed the area at five o'clock seemed like a bad dream.

The few car lights I saw swung past me quickly. All except one, whose bright headlights kept piercing my rear view. Maybe a cop tracking my speed, or maybe Sennett's promised man tailing me. I checked my speedometer and slowed down. So did Sennett's man.

I still looked on Sennett as my friend, but I guess the pressure was getting to me. A light at the corner had just turned red. I wheeled out of the left lane and made a turn into a side street. There was no one coming. I'd lost my tail as successfully as the missing link. I was gloating at my driving ability for about twenty seconds. Just enough time for me to realize that the revolving blue flashing light coming down one of the small exclusive side streets that bordered Lake St. Clair was coming at me. Damn, not only was I going to get twenty to life for Larry's death, but I'd nabbed a reckless driving ticket to boot.

I was slowing down to pull over when another flasher pulled in front of me. I was boxed in like a captured felon. I waited while the first policeman sauntered out of the car. The second joined him. Both were young John Waynes. I guess Grosse Pointe got first crack at the photogenic graduates of the police academy.

The first officer tapped my closed window with his night stick. I guess I didn't roll the window down fast enough, or maybe he didn't like the way I was dressed, because the next thing I knew there was a crash on the seat behind me. My side door window was all over the back seat of my car.

"Out and assume the position!" he shouted.

I wasn't taking any chances now. I had heard stories about the Grosse Pointe cops—you either lived in the Pointe or you were the rankest criminal. I opened the door slowly and slid my feet out onto the pavement. I no sooner got them on the ground than Officer One spun me around and pinned me against the car, his left foot inside my right leg. Two black-and-whites, frisking me on a quiet side street for a moving violation? No wonder the crime rate was so low in Grosse Pointe.

When he was convinced I wasn't carrying a concealed weapon, he turned me around again.

"Driver's license." He even sounded like John Wayne.

"My wallet is in my left rear pocket, officer." I pulled it out, and he looked at it.

"Illegal turn on a red light and driving with an expired license," he growled. *Shit, the guy could read after all.*

"I suppose that's justification for breaking my window." He thumbed through my wallet.

"You're a doctor, huh?"

"Yeah, I'm a neuropsychiatrist. I take care of all the paranoid schizophrenics who break innocent motorists' windows." Even in the cruiser's blue glare I could see his face redden.

"Cool it, Rich. You want us on *Hard Copy*? The camera's taking pictures from the squad car. Give the guy back his license. I doubt we'll see him back this way again for a long time." Boy, was he right about that.

"Okay, mister. It's a standoff. I don't get your license revoked and you get your ass out of our city, now." They were gone as quickly as they'd appeared.

At least now I understood why Grosse Pointers had changed the name of Jefferson Avenue. They didn't want to remind themselves of how far from the values of the author of the Declaration they had strayed.

I sat there, trying to calm down. After a few minutes a car pulled up next to me. Nice guy, business suit, on his way home from the office.

"Is everything all right?" he asked through his window.

"Yeah, fine, just fine," I said shakily.

I was angry, and not just at local disregard for the rights of the individual. I was even more pissed at George Sennett for having me tailed. Who the hell did he think he was, a one-man vigilante squad? What kind of friend was he, anyway? As far as I was concerned, he was the kind of friend I didn't need. I had just had a lesson in the foolishness of trusting the police to behave well. To the police, there was no innocent man.

And I was a suspect in a murder George Sennett had to solve.

In the meantime, a light rain was falling, and if I didn't get my car sealed up it was going to resemble a leaking Noah's Ark.

I drove to a shopping center near the marina with a hardware store. I came out with some plastic sheeting, duct tape, and a small dust broom. With the rain misting under the glare of the lights of the shopping center parking lot, I swept out the car and then closed up the side door window. Just like those other unfortunates I'd seen on television, I had fought the law and the law had won.

I decided to pass on the boat. The less I frequented my usual haunts the better. I took a circuitous route back to the Holiday Inn. Every car light that got close to my Jeep gave me a stab of anxiety. It was eight o'clock by the time I got back to the motel. No visible tail. My "friend" Sennett must have called off his dogs for the night.

I called Jordan's hotel in Miami. She was out again. I told the operator to tell her I had called, but didn't leave a number.

Ben Dailey, fugitive.

# CHAPTER 12

THE NEXT MORNING I FACED THE same question: Why would someone want to kill Larry Burkinette?

I remembered how impressed I had been the first time I had worked with him when he was chief resident. I was convinced he was destined to be the new king of head and neck surgery. Had he kept to the medical ideals of the program, I don't think I would have been too far off the mark.

He'd been brash, but I'd shrugged that off. All residents were, to some extent. It was all part of the machismo of being a surgeon—the ones I knew had strong egos. But the ego's best master is humility, and when it came to that, Larry was lacking. That's why it hadn't taken much for him to fall victim to his own superiority. When he fell, his greed made for a ready accomplice.

During the first few cases we did together as residents, I was a ready student, eager to learn what he had to teach. But then, of course, the cases had gone smoothly. It wasn't until we had a problem that I realized what he was really like. I shouldn't have been surprised. Dealing with crises always brings out a surgeon's real personality.

I relived the case when I had first realized how peremptory he could be. We were doing a radical maxillectomy to remove a cancer from a patient's facial sinus. I had just cut through the posterior wall of the maxillary antrum when suddenly there was a gush of blood. As the junior resident, I panicked, reaching for the suction, shouting orders, trying to find the bleeder, all at once. Larry stood by and let me do my thing as I put pressure on the vessel.

"Larry," I said finally, "both my hands are in place. If I move them, we're going to lose exposure, and this artery is going to retract. We can't afford to lose this one. I think it's the internal maxillary."

"What do you want me to do?" he asked calmly as he took the suction from me to remove the bright red blood from the wound.

"I'm not sure," I said, sweat pouring down my face.

"Just relax. With one hand hold this suction, and I'll clamp the vessel."

The steadiness of his hands impressed me most as he picked up the hemostat, isolated the pumping vessel, and calmly stopped the flow.

When he finished tying the vessel, he turned to the anesthetist. "That was good, wasn't it? No, it was better than good, it was great! No one is better than the Big Kahuna." He thumped his chest as he stood beside the patient. It had been good, but nobody had needed to be told. It was a small thing, but I think that was the moment I began to dislike him. I had grown up in a working-class neighborhood, played years of football when I was a kid, and seen hotshots like Larry come and go. They were usually the people who came up short in life. I'd learned the hard way that if you've got it, you don't need to talk about it.

But not everyone felt as I did. Larry was a smooth salesman, and some people bought what he was selling. Especially Norman Larson, the chief of the department, until they had a falling out over some problem no one ever identified. It was a surprise to everyone, because the rumor had been that Larson wanted Larry Burkinette to take his place when he retired.

I decided to call my former chief, Dr. Norman Larson.

It took me a while to find him. He had retired to Arizona, it turned out. When I finally reached him, his voice was as vigorous as it had been twenty years before.

"How are you doing, Dr. Larson?" I asked.

"Is that Ben Dailey's voice I hear?"

"How did you know it was me?"

"The voice is my business, or have you forgotten the work you and I did during your residency?"

"No, I haven't, Dr. Larson. In fact, I'm going to come out with some new material in a few months on voice spectrography in the analysis of vocal cord dysfunction."

"You know, Ben, I always thought it was a shame you didn't go into academics full time. You could have taken over the department."

"I thought you had reserved that spot for Larry."

"Who? Burkinette?" he harrumphed. "He was the biggest damn disappointment of my academic life. In all my years of teaching I never saw a man with that much potential, both surgical and academic."

"So I would have been a second choice," I laughed.

"I said 'potential.' You had the goods, and you were willing to work. Larry always sought the fast way."

"Actually, Larry is the reason I'm calling."

"Oh, what about?"

"Larry died a couple of days ago," I said solemnly. There was a moment of silence at the other end.

"How?"

"He was found dead in his car, shot through the head." More silence.

"I almost can't say I'm surprised," he said quietly.

Here I was. I plunged in without giving myself time to think.

"Dr. Larson, they think I'm responsible for Larry's death." I was ashamed to have to tell him.

"You? Nonsense. I knew the two of you didn't get along, but never to the point of violence. Actually, when it all washed out, I realized there was merit in how you felt."

"What do you mean?"

"I mean that I had problems with Larry in the residency."

"What kind of problems?"

"I suppose that now that he is dead, and if it will help you, I can talk about it. For all these years I've kept my mouth closed about certain things he did during his time as a resident."

"Like what?"

"Like being a runner for some shyster lawyer in Minneapolis. I found out about it toward the end of his residency."

"I never heard about that. What did you do?"

"I had one hell of a session with him. At first, I didn't believe he had done it. I told him I had planned a career for him in the department. I wanted him to tell me he hadn't done it. Do you know what his answer was?"

"What?"

"He said he had a lawyer and this fella had told him I couldn't do anything to him. Further, if I persisted, he would sue *me* for slander. Slander, can you believe it?"

Larry Burkinette, lowlife. "What happened?"

"I went to the university lawyers. They told me he was right."

"What do you think changed Larry?" I asked. There was a long pause.

"I'm going to give you my opinion, but that's all it is. Take it for what it's worth, from an old man who has an indomitable faith in human good. Larry was an orphan. No family to speak of when he came to apply for the residency. I liked that. He entered as a single guy, committed to learning, without outside responsibilities. Then came his marriage, and that friend of his, Belender."

"Belender?"

"Yeah, some general surgery resident he teamed up with. Looked real sharp, the kind of kid who would play all the angles. I met him a couple of times when we had joint cases with general surgery."

"Did Larry ever give you any more problems after you confronted him?"

"Not that I know of. He was the model of decorum. But I knew now it was all a show. Naturally, I never trusted him after that. That's why I would never have offered him a job in my department, and why I would have made you chief. Personal integrity, that's what it's all about."

"That's what you taught me, Dr. Larson. Unfortunately, not everyone believes in that." In the midst of all my trouble, I felt humbly proud that such a fine man believed in me.

"I see it more and more nowadays. Too much concern about the economics of medicine and not enough for the patients. It's happening even at the medical school level. I talk to some of my friends who're still in academia. They're muttering things about collection rates, profit margins, and participation rates. Nothing about research, teaching, development of new ideas."

"Some of us are still trying to do it right, Dr. Larson." I paused, thinking back on my own problems again. "By the way, whatever happened to Larry's friend Belender?"

"To tell you the truth, Ben, I never asked."

"Who do you think I could talk to, to find out?"

"If you want to find out anything more about what happened, try talking to Doris, Larry's first wife."

"Any idea where I could find the former Mrs. Burkinette?"

"Right there in Detroit. She divorced Larry and married some guy who works in the auto industry. Name's Spencer, I think."

"Retirement hasn't touched that your memory, Dr. Larson. Now that you mention it, I remember Doris. She was a nurse at the hospital."

"To tell you the truth, I never got over Larry. I guess that's the reason I kept tabs on what happened to him."

"With as many residents as you taught, there was bound to be a Larry Burkinette somewhere in the mix," I tried to console the conscientious old doctor.

"Maybe. Still, I think the whole business shook my confidence in my judgment of people."

"I'm sorry I had to be the one to tell you about Larry. And thank you for your help."

"You let me know when you are cleared of this ridiculous charge, won't you? If it gets that far, I'll gladly testify as a character witness."

I couldn't help the lump in my throat at his kindness. "Thanks again, Dr. Larson. But I'm sure I won't need to bother you. I'll get this cleared up."

"I hope Doris Spencer can help," Dr. Larson said, concerned. "Goodbye and good luck."

"Goodbye, sir. Thanks." I hung the phone up and stared at the floor for a moment. I had never known the chief would have asked me to work for him.

# CHAPTER 13

AFTER TALKING TO DR. LARSON, I checked out of the Holiday Inn and moved myself to a Motel 6 near the airport. On the drive over, I kept looking for someone tailing me. I even cut through a couple of side streets and doubled back at an intersection near the motel. I felt a little stupid playing cops and robbers, but my anger at Lieutenant Sennett was still simmering as hot as it had last night.

At the motel I registered under the name of S. Federov and paid cash. The clerk gave me a strange look. I guess I didn't look like his idea of a Red Wings hockey player.

My next job was to get the Jeep fixed. On my fourth try I finally found a dealership sympathetic enough to fix it for me while I waited.

I stopped down at Gus's to find a friendly face and someone to talk with.

Unfortunately, when I walked in Gus wasn't there. The waitress told me he'd gone home early, because his kid wasn't feeling well. But he wanted me to call if I came in. She gave me his number and I dialed. He answered in a panic.

"Doc, I'm so glad you called. My son, Tony, he's so sick. He's got pain in his ear, a high fever, and the right side of his face is numb."

"Slow down, Gus. Did you call the pediatrician?"

"Yeah, he gave him some antibiotics, but it don't seem to be doing any good."

"How old is Joey?"

"He's sixteen. Great kid, Doc. You should see him, captain of the basketball team, all-A student, and . . ."

"Listen, Gus. It sounds like a routine ear infection. I'll grab something to eat here and then meet you at St. Vincent's emergency room. I'll see you in an hour." While I waited for my fast food, I called Doris Spencer.

I had found her unlisted number by shrewd gumshoe work. Auto executives play golf, and most of them play at Fairwood Country Club. I told the receptionist I was the florist for a party she was giving and had only the club's number for a contact. After couple of minutes of pleading she relinquished the home number.

Strangely, Doris didn't seem too surprised to hear from me.

"When I heard about Larry's death, I thought maybe I'd hear from one of his colleagues. Especially with the way he died."

"Did anyone else call?" I asked.

"No, you're the only one. It makes me sad."

"Why?"

"I was married to Larry for four years and went with him for two years before that. That makes me a part of his life, doesn't it?"

"I suppose. I'd like to talk to you about Larry. Do you think you could meet me later this afternoon at Sisters' Deli over on Potomac in Clarkston?"

"I think I'd like that."

"I'll see you at four-thirty." I put the phone on the hook and looked at my watch. I could leave now, meet Gus and his boy at the hospital, and be there on time.

Gus's sick boy turned out to be a more urgent case than I'd thought. Entering the emergency room, I saw Gus standing next to a young man on a gurney. He looked like a younger, taller version of his father: curly black hair, the beginnings of a five o'clock shadow, dark, thick eyebrows over two piercing brown eyes. The boy was sitting up, holding his right ear, in obvious pain.

"How long has he been like this, Gus?"

"It started a couple of days ago, Doc. I thought it was just a cold, you know, a little sore throat and fever."

I turned to the boy. "Okay, Tony, where does your ear hurt, front, back, or inside?"

"Deep inside, Doc," he replied, slurring his words.

"Wait a minute, smile for me." As he tried to curl his lips, I could see the right side of his mouth wasn't working.

"I thought you told me his face was 'numb,' Gus."

"It is, isn't it?"

"No, it's partially paralyzed."

He looked devastated. "It's my language, Doc. Sometimes I can't find the right word."

I wasn't listening. I had already picked up the otoscope and was looking into Tony's ear. Inside I could see the eardrum, bright red and bulging.

"He's got an acute otitis media."

"Is that serious?" Gus paled at the unfamiliar words.

"Only if I can't drain it." I called over a nurse to help me.

"Tony," I explained, "I'm going to have to look at your ear a little better. That means freezing it up with a needle." I could see his eyes widen.

"Is it going to hurt?"

"Who, me?"

He laughed softly. "No, me." The joke seemed to ease his anxiety.

"Only for a moment after I stick the needle in. After that you should be fine." Gus was right, he was a good kid.

"Do what you have to," he replied. "Just give me something to squeeze."

"How about your dad's hand?"

"Fine." Gus held his son's hand as he lay his head back on the pillow.

"Give me some one percent Xylocaine with epinephrine in a tuberculin syringe with a twenty-seven gauge needle," I said to the nurse. "Then get me a myringotomy knife from the cabinet."

The nurse scurried around for a moment and then handed me the syringe.

I took off the sheath and slid the needle down the speculum of the otoscope.

"Little stick now, Tony." I inserted the needle and injected the local anesthetic. The boy's head was motionless as the medicine went in. The skin blanched. I touched the eardrum with the tip of the needle.

"Do you feel that?"

"No."

"Okay, give me the knife."

She handed me the angled blade, and I slipped it through the speculum, pointing the tip at the front part of the eardrum. As it penetrated the thin membrane, there was a sudden gush of fluid rolling into the external ear canal. I suctioned it out.

"How's that feel, Tony?"

"Like a ton of bricks have been lifted off my ear."

"Can you hear better?"

"Yep."

"Great. Now lie on your back and let's look at your face." Almost miraculously, the muscles of his lower lip began twitching as motion started to return.

"My God, Doc. It's coming back. What did you do?" Gus almost shouted.

"The nerve to the face runs right through the ear. In a small percentage of people, the bony covering to the nerve is absent. If the patient gets an ear infection, like Tony, it can directly affect the nerve, causing a paralysis. It's a medical emergency. The eardrum had to be punctured and the infection let out."

"What happens now?" Gus asked fearfully.

"Tony's lucky. The nerve will probably return to normal function. He just needs some different antibiotics and some cortisone."

"How can we ever thank you, Doc?"

"Just be my friend. You got a terrific kid here, Gus. Not every sixteen year old would sit so still."

"Yeah, well, you weren't holding his hand. I may never be able to make another Coney again." As he spoke, he shook his hand to let the blood recirculate.

"Don't say that, Gus. I need you there."

"Doc, you ever need *anything*, you call me. Anytime, anyplace."

"You never know, Gus," I said, cleaning up the mess I had made.

We shook hands, and I turned and made my way out of the emergency room. As I walked out the door, I saw an EMS unit bringing a patient in, a doctor at his side, squeezing air into his lungs through an Ambu bag. Watching the doctor struggle to save the man's life, and thinking about Gus's son, two things struck me. One was how I never ceased to marvel at how wonderful medicine was when it worked. The other was how much good a physician carried in his hands. *Cut it out, Dailey. You'll dislocate your shoulder patting yourself on the back.*

Still, I had to admit I felt a little euphoric after fixing Tony up, at least until I looked at my watch and realized I was running late on my main mission: self-rescue. I had just enough time to make it to the deli for my appointment.

Sister's Deli was in downtown Clarkston, where a small, quaint shopping area had recently risen from the ashes of an abandoned neighborhood. Now it was filled with trendy boutiques and art galleries. Just the kind of place a rich suburbanite like Doris Spencer would frequent.

I spotted her immediately at a table near the window. She really hadn't changed much since the days in the residency: cleavage, blond hair, and plenty of leg. Chanel, Clairol, and a private trainer could do wonders for a body past the first flush of youth.

"How are you, Doris?" I extended my hand toward her.

"Not bad, Ben. So nice to see you." I was an expert on voices—I had spent my whole professional life studying them. Hers was of the firm and self-assured variety. The kind of voice only money and security could produce.

"You're looking well after all these years," I said, sliding into the booth opposite to her.

"I try hard. You know, with all these young women around, we matrons have to keep on our toes."

"Doris, you were always beautiful." She eyed me up and down and straight through me.

"Flattery is an art form, Ben, and you do it well. And believe me, I know. I'm married to a man who needs it all the time, and gives back precious little, if you know what I mean." I now knew more than I needed or wanted to know about Doris Spencer's marital life.

"When did you learn about Larry, Doris?"

"An attorney called me yesterday. It's an awful way to hear about the death of someone you were married to for four years."

"Leave it to the legal profession to be the messenger of bad news."

"Relax, Ben. They look at it as just a job. For you it's cutting people up, for them it's cutting people out."

"It sounds as if you've had plenty of experience."

"One divorce and one prenuptial."

"I see. What does your husband do?" I asked.

"Auto business: parts and castings, corporate mergers, financial projections, market share. Anything that will keep him busy and out of the house."

"Maybe he's just involved. Believe me, medicine can do the same thing to you."

"Oh, Larry never seemed to be affected that way."

"No, medicine always seemed like a means to an end for Larry."

"The end. It sounds so final. The news reports said Larry was shot."

"You don't seem surprised."

She was about to respond, but the waitress came over and took our order. Doris had the no fat, no sugar, no taste muffin, and a skinny cap. I had a corned beef sandwich, extra mustard, and a Coke.

When the waitress left, she answered, "You asked me if I was surprised. The answer is not really. There was always a part of Larry that I never understood. A dark side that he never let me into. Even though we were married."

"How do you mean that?" I asked. I could see her hesitating before she responded.

"He would get phone calls, then leave the house. He'd always say he had to go to the hospital. Although he was probably only with that woman."

"You mean Abby MacKenzie?" Saying the name made me sink a little lower in my seat.

"I try to repress it. There are some things you don't want to think about, even after they've been over for years."

"I don't mean to pry, but did Larry ever talk to you about the events leading up to—what happened?"

"He admitted to nothing. Even afterward. Everyone had known about it but me. Talk about being a fool." She looked at me for a moment. "This isn't about the Versanti lawsuit, is it?"

"It started out that way. Somewhere along the way things went crazy. The police found some planted evidence in my office. Next thing I know, I'm a suspect for setting Larry up."

"Oh, Ben. You? Murder that poor boy to get back at Larry? Ridiculous. Of course, I knew you and Larry never got along."

"Larry told you that?"

"Only in an offhand way. You know, he would say that there was this young resident named Dailey who was trying to be a hotshot, and he was going to put him in his place. That kind of thing."

"We never got along. Let's just leave it at that."

"The mysterious Benjamin Dailey. Is that the way you want it?"

"I have no choice. After Larry got shot, the police put two and two together and got five. Now I'm a suspect in Larry's murder, too."

"Why don't you go to the police and try to explain things to them?"

"The police? Let me ask you a question. Do you know how water flows?" She gave me a blank stare. "It flows the easiest way it can. It's the same way with the police. They've got dozens of cases in front of them, so when they get something easy, they take it."

"You sound like you're talking from experience." Obviously, Mrs. Spencer hadn't heard about my previous problems. Life is insulated for some of us.

"The one thing I know is that when you have a predicament, you can't depend on other people to do your thinking for you."

"Wait a minute. Isn't that what patients depend on you for?"

"Touché. Maybe we should just look at my coming here as getting a second opinion. We doctors do that a lot. I want to know more about Larry. Who he hung out with, what his habits were. Most of all, how he always had plenty of money when the rest of us residents were struggling." By this time the waitress was delivering our food.

"Money was never a problem for Larry. No, I take that back. It was, when we were first married, but after a while we had everything we needed. Time was our problem. We never could go anywhere. No vacations. So we spent money on expensive things." I remembered Larry's Stingray during the residency.

"Where did Larry get the money?"

"He told me he had a trust fund from a rich uncle who died. I never asked."

"Did he ever talk to you about another resident named Belender?"

"I met him once or twice. But Larry never had many friends. We always stayed home or went out to the movies. That was his idea of fun." She picked off a small piece of her muffin and seemed to chew on it forever.

"Anyone you can remember that he used to talk to a lot?"

"Once in a while someone named Buzz would call. It was always a brief conversation."

Buzz. That was the name Samantha Burkinette had mentioned.

"Do you know who that was?"

"I never met him."

"Anything else that might be of interest? Contacts, people who were angry at him. Bad deals he might have made."

"Larry never said much about his professional life. In fact, he made a point of avoiding the subject. He always said that when he left the hospital is when his being a doctor ended."

"Did you believe him?"

"I didn't want to, but one day I had to believe it. I remember driving past a wreck once on the beltway near our house. It had just happened, and the police hadn't arrived. Larry slowed down for a minute, saw there was someone trapped inside, and then kept on driving."

"What did you do?"

"I screamed at him to stop and help that poor soul. He just said he was off duty."

"You still cared for him even after the divorce, didn't you?" I asked, trying to speak gently. I felt sorry for her. Another of Larry Burkinette's victims. Although at least she was still alive.

"Maybe I loved him. Sometimes it was hard to tell with Larry. But after Abby MacKenzie, I couldn't stay any longer." She sipped on her cappuccino and stared out the window for a moment. A tear rolled down her cheek. "But looking back, as bad as it was with Larry, it was better than what I've got now. I know I'm just an aging showpiece whose husband cheats on her. He takes me out for an airing every now and then before jetting off to some meeting to play around with his girlfriends."

"Things haven't changed much. Women want love and men want sex."

"That's it in a nutshell. I must be a poor judge of marital prospects. I go out as seldom now as I did with Larry."

"They paved paradise and put up a parking lot."

"Huh?" she asked blankly.

"It's an old Joni Mitchell song. Listen to the words sometime." I think Doris could sense I was getting ready to leave.

"You know, Ben, I'm glad to see you. Things seemed so much simpler back then."

"Be careful when you look backward, Doris. Sometimes you have to be sure the easy truth isn't misnamed 'simplicity.'"

"What do you mean?"

"I mean things are a lot more complicated than they seem. Larry Burkinette was never a simple man." I got up from the table. "Doris, I've got to run. It was great to see you." The more I lied, the better I got at it.

"I hope I'll see you around," she said. "Give me a call if there's anything I can do to help clear yourself."

"I'll remember that. Thanks." Three offers in one afternoon. My famous charm must be holding up.

I left her sitting there sipping her drink and staring out the window as I walked up to the cashier to pay the bill. If I hadn't turned to look at her one last time, I would have missed the evening edition of the *Times* on the newsstand, with a quarter-page photo of me under the headline: "Local Doctor Suspect in Death of 2 Detroiters."

# CHAPTER 14

Sources close to the Times have indicated that Dr. Benjamin Dailey, a noted surgeon at St. Vincent's Hospital, may be implicated in the death of two people: a young boy undergoing a tonsillectomy, who died of a strange bacterial infection, and another surgeon with whom Dr. Dailey was known to have a long-standing dispute. This is not the first time Dr. Dailey has been involved with the law. In a strange case that received national attention, Dailey uncovered a scheme to implant experimental devices in several indigent patients in the Detroit area, in the process toppling Charles Thornton, one of the most influential businessmen in the community. An informed source refers to Dailey as "a hero gone wrong."

Nice touch, that last line. Hats off to Robert Versanti. Any sympathy lingering in me for a grieving father vanished. I felt like killing the bastard.

I also felt like killing another hard-nosed son-of-a-bitch. I went over to a pay phone near the restaurant and dialed Sennett's number. He picked up himself.

"Ben, where the hell are you? You left the Holiday Inn and—"

"You told me you'd have me followed, but I just couldn't believe you'd do it, George."

"It was for your own good."

"Just like the front page of the Times? To say nothing of the other stories."

"I had nothing to do with that."

"Who the hell is 'an informed source'?"

"Robert Versanti has a lot of powerful friends in the media and at City Hall."

"What's the real story, Lieutenant?"

"The real story is that we found your fingerprints all over Burkinette's car."

"I was there that night. I already told you that. I confronted him and told him to lay off me. There was nothing else. I jerked his coat to give me long enough to get away."

"You shouldn't have gone there."

"Yeah, well, shoot from the hip, that's me."

"You mean shoot from the *lip*," he jumped on me, sounding fed up with me. "Damn it, Dailey, *think* before you open your big mouth. I've got twenty people here who'd take what you just said as a confession."

Touché. But I had one ace in the hole still. I retorted triumphantly, "If all your people are so sure I did it, where's the murder weapon?" There was a moment of silence. *Answer me that, Lieutenant*, I thought smugly.

"We found it in your boat, under a settee."

I was stunned.

"George, I've been set up. You know it and I know it."

"I believe you, Ben."

"Yeah. Sure. That's why you want to know where I am, right?"

"Ben, I swear to you —"

"Forget it, Sennett. I'll see you around."

I couldn't go back to the boat. I couldn't reach Jordan. I couldn't do anything in Detroit except get arrested.

Time to get out of town.

A CAB DROPPED ME OFF NEAR THE WATERFRONT, only a couple of blocks from the Joe Louis Arena. I quickly blended into the throng going to see the Dallas Stars play the Red Wings. The hockey game would be an unlikely place for Sennett to be looking for me, thus a good place to clear my mind.

The stadium, right on the riverfront, stood as a reminder of one of the greatest athletes to hail from Detroit. Unfortunately, it looked like a low budget concrete mausoleum, hardly a fitting tribute to the Brown Bomber.

I huffed and puffed my way up to the ticket booth and bought a standing room only ticket. Once past the entrance, I melted into the crowd and shouldered my way to section 122, center ice, right behind the Red Wings bench. The noise inside was deafening, like a gladiator ring with people waiting on the edges of their seats for confrontation.

I paid the usher ten bucks and he showed me to an empty seat. I sat down just in time to see a big defenseman from Dallas lower his shoulder into Detroit's league-leading scorer. Their gloves came off quickly and they grabbed each other's jerseys. A slow waltz around the ice between the two men ensued. The Detroit scorer ducked his head and wriggled his hand free. A tremendous scream of encouragement from the fans as his fist crashed against the Stars player's nose. It was a release of the pent-up irritation of a tough city, a fist in the air to the crowded expressways, a laugh at the bottom-line bean counters in the white-collar offices and production lines that ringed the city.

I felt the same emotion. The ebb and flow of the game had made me feel better. I had been right—the excitement had helped to calm me down and focus my thinking. I was a wanted man now, and I needed to find a means of escape.

I knew there was a telephone at a corner of the stadium near the exit. It was the only phone you could hear through in the raucous stadium, the one I always used to call in when the hospital paged me. I dialed the number and then cupped my hand over my ear. I shouted when the call connected.

"Gus, this is Ben Dailey."

"Doc, where are you? It sounds like a party from the old country."

"Almost. It's a hockey game."

"What are you doing there? Don't you know the cops are after you?"

"I didn't do it, Gus."

"Don't insult me, Doc. I wouldn't believe you did it even if you confessed."

"Gus, remember you said I could call you anytime for a favor?"

"Sure, Doc, anything. What do you need?"

"A car."

Gus had it waiting for me in the cab line on Atwater Street. A nondescript, powder blue, four-year-old Chevy. Ideal.

The keys were under the mat. I slipped in behind the wheel, put it in gear, and slid quietly out of the line. A short drive to the Chrysler Expressway and I was on my way north, in the right hand lane and driving the speed limit. I had two names—Dr. Belender and a man named Buzz. Both of them last known to be in Minneapolis.

West of Northville I pulled off into a shopping mall where I knew there was a twenty-four-hour cash machine. I quickly picked up five hundred bucks and headed back onto the expressway. On edge, I cruised northward, past Grand Blanc, past Flint, on toward Bay City. I had a moment of panic at the Zilwaukee Bridge when I saw two state police cruisers swing past me. *Okay, gumshoe. Keep your speed, stay in the right lane, and don't panic.*

At about one o'clock in the morning I pulled off at the Evergreen Cottages, a mom and pop place near the interstate in West Branch. My name was entered as G. Howe in the computer. I left with the key to find the end cottage. Cautiously, I opened the rickety screen door and took a quick look around at the knotty pine room. All clear. After securing the lock, I collapsed onto the bed, too tired to undress. I didn't have time to hear the creaking box spring or feel the lumpy mattress. I was already asleep.

The next morning, I woke up to the sun bursting through the window. The leaves were already off the trees, so I had a good view of the highway and my car. Everything was where it was supposed to be.

I showered quickly, deciding not to shave. Looking around, I found a pencil in a drawer. After stripping off the wood, I took the graphite and crushed it on a piece of paper. I put the black powder in my hands and rubbed it through my salt and pepper mane. Combing my hair again, I looked different enough to elude a passing glance from a trooper who'd have my photograph circulated by my friend Sennett.

West Branch was a small tourist town on the way up north. In the summer it was hopping. I figured in November it would be empty. In my preoccupation I'd once again forgotten the hunting season, Bambi's annual gift to the local economy. The only ones not having a good time were the deer.

At the Blind Hunter, a small diner on Main Street, I sat at a corner booth and ordered the breakfast special. The booth next to me held two men in red and black wool shirts, one with a bright orange cap. They were chewing on steak and eggs and discussing world events.

"Did you see that article about that doctor in the *Times*?" Mr. Orange Cap said.

"Yeah, can you believe that guy? The article said he might be involved in the deaths of two people, one of them a patient. Think about it, a doctor."

"I'll tell you, if I found this guy, I'd string him up like one of those bucks I'm going to shoot. Then I'd pop him right between the eyes." I watched as he raised an imaginary rifle in his arms and squeezed off a shot. My stomach jumped as his arms recoiled.

I finished quickly, paid the bill, and made my way out to my car. I had to make it across the bridge to St. Ignace before noon if I was going to make it to Duluth by nightfall.

The bridge was the Mackinac Bridge, the five-mile span of engineering genius that connected the upper and lower peninsulas of Michigan. Crossing it was tantamount to entering another country. Gone were the fancy condos on Lake Michigan and the endless sea of resorts that attracted visitors from around the world. The Upper Peninsula was desolate and destitute even during hunting season.

True to form, no sooner had I left St. Ignace than the crowd of hunters thinned out. It was as if the bridge separated the real out-of-doorsmen from the party boys interested only in a few sound shots and a weekend of carousing with their friends. Once through St. Ignace and past the Soo Locks, there was nothing but a two-lane highway. The country was poor and the Upers, as they were called, subsisted on farming, lumbering, and iron ore mining.

Thank God for the open highways and thank Gus for not being into Mercedes or BMWs. My Celebrity blended perfectly with the pickups and rusted sedans plying the highway.

I made it through Marquette and out toward Iron Mountain. The endless miles of Highway 2 through the desolate north country, strung along the south shore of Lake Superior, past Ashland, past Lake Nebagamon, into the town of Duluth.

Actually, Duluth was two cities—Duluth and Superior. At one time a twin mecca for the iron ore business, both now struggled for survival in a world economy that had realized their sole precious natural resource could be had a lot cheaper elsewhere. People talked about Appalachia, but the poverty-stricken south shore of Lake Superior had its similar misery.

I arrived around dusk into town and headed for the business district, past Darlington Observatory, down to the small strip of motels near the docks. I knew Duluth well. When I was a resident, I used to crew for Norm Larson on the sailboat he kept at the Deep Water Marina there. The town seemed to have been frozen in that time.

The Crystal Light Motel was still there, much the same as I had left it twenty-five years ago. The kind of place at which everyone in a small town leers.

I parked the car in the lot, walked into the office, and took the $29.95 overnight special. The clerk paid no attention to my T. Lindsay signature as he stroked it in on his computer keyboard.

It was seven o'clock by the time I was settled. I got washed, and then walked down the street to a diner. This time there was no talk about Detroit, or murders, or a doctor on the run. Instead it was quiet, a couple of elderly couples and a menu devoted to cholesterol.

When I finished, I looked at my watch. It was already eight o'clock. My nervous energy had been depleted. I made it back to the motel, flopped down on the bed, and switched on the TV. If I was national news, I wanted to know about it. CNN, TBN, C-SPAN, nobody mentioned my name. The omission gave me no comfort. I had worked with George Sennett before. When he wanted to find me, he would. I hoped I'd have time to clear myself by uncovering Burkinette's past before that time.

The next morning, I made an early phone call. Gus picked the phone up on the first ring.

"How's Tony doing?" I asked.

"Doc," he said excitedly, "Where are you? What are you doing?"

"The less you know the better, Gus. But there's one more thing I need, then I won't put you at risk anymore."

"Can that noise. What do you need?"

"I want you to call Jordan. She'll be back tonight. Tell her to check out the production line. Don't say anything else. The police will be tapping her line."

Gus repeated the message.

"I'll tell her. What the hell does that mean?"

"She'll know. I hope."

"Anything else?"

"No. I'm going to walk the coals if I can't get all this straightened out, Gus."

"I got a lot of confidence in you, Doc. Hell, you fixed up Tony just like that." I heard him snap his fingers.

"Thanks again for the car, Gus. Remember, if the police come by, you never heard from me."

"Even Sennett?"

"Especially Sennett." I hung up.

I was all alone again.

# CHAPTER 15

I<small>T MIGHT HAVE BEEN TWENTY-FIVE YEARS</small> since I had been at North Central University Medical School in Minneapolis, but I still had some friends at the school. From my Duluth motel room, I called the surgery department, asked for the few names I remembered, and finally found a secretary I had known, Jenny Richardson.

Jenny had been Dr. Larson's secretary before he'd retired. Now she worked in the dean's office. A quick greeting and suddenly we had restored our friendship.

"How is it working in the dean's office?"

"It's not as pleasant as working for Dr. Larson, but it pays the bills."

"How is your husband?" I knew he had suffered a stroke.

"He's amazing. He's seventy-five and still active. The stroke limited his speech, but he gets around pretty good."

"I need a favor, Jenny," I said, changing the subject.

"As long as I'm able, I'll see what I can do."

"There was a resident back in the seventies named Belender. I don't know the first name." I spelled it out for her, and she punched the information into her computer.

"Here it is. Jeff Belender. General Surgery."

"Who was the chief back then, Jenny?"

"It was and still is Jeremiah Tolbert. Do you want his number?"

"Sure," I said with trepidation. Anyone who knew Jeremiah Tolbert would have felt trepidation. Honest to a fault, demanding by nature, he was a man feared by every surgeon who trained under him. Fortunately, he'd never been my chief.

I remembered the only time I'd ever scrubbed with him. We were doing a laryngectomy, and Tolbert and his group were in charge of the reconstruction. We had just finished our part when Tolbert shouldered his way into the table. It was as if we weren't even there.

"Knife," he demanded. Tolbert never took the instruments from the scrub nurse, only from the residents. It was his theory that if they knew how to pass the instruments, they would get into the flow of the case. He held his hand out, palm up. The other resident audibly slapped the steel-handled blade into his hand. Tolbert stopped and glared at the resident, his bushy eyebrows furrowed over his half-glasses.

"Dammit, Doctor. This is not a test of wills." He took the blade handle and slapped it back into the resident's hand.

"Don't ever forget that surgery requires patience, delicacy, and discipline. If you ever hand me an instrument like that again, you'll be in the lab for a year. Understood?"

Understood.

It was strange, I would have expected Tolbert to have lost his bark. It took one sound bite on the phone to realize he hadn't.

"What is it, Doctor? I have to be in surgery in a few minutes."

"I wanted to ask you a couple of questions about a former resident of yours."

"Who is that?"

"Jeffrey Belender," I replied tentatively.

"Who the hell are you?" he demanded.

"An old colleague trying to track him down."

"Well, you won't find anything out about him from me."

"Isn't there anything you can tell me about him?"

"Nothing." Flat tone, no emotion.

"Would your secretary know anything? Maybe through the department's alumni network?"

"Alumni network? You've got to be kidding. He's no alumnus of my department. I kicked him out of our department after three years."

"For what?"

"I don't know who you are or what you're after, but I'm under a permanent gag order by the courts, so I consider this conversation over, Doctor." The phone clicked.

On a roll, I dialed the AMA in Chicago on their 800-number. It was a simple matter to call for some information. After years of paying dues, I was actually going to talk to someone in the organization.

My confidence that I was finally going to get something out of my membership was dashed when the secretary said, "I'm sorry, but we're not allowed to give out that information over the phone."

"Look, miss, I know you're right, but I'm a member of the AMA and I'm in town. I could very easily get the number from my directory at home, but that would take a couple of days."

"Oh, I didn't realize you were a member. Do you have your membership number?"

I did have my membership card with me. I always took it to get a discount on rental cars. But for my present need it did me no good. The AMA had never heard of Jeffrey Belender.

I sat there looking at the phone, wondering what to do next. Larry's friends, Belender and Buzz, were my one link to his past. And I had a hunch I'd only find Buzz through Belender.

I WASN'T SURE HOW LONG I COULD STAY around a small town like Duluth without being noticed, but I assumed I had at least one more day. I went to a sporting goods store and got a small cook stove, a tent, extra clothes, and some freeze-dried food. I stowed them in my trunk for a quick getaway.

After breakfast at a small diner, I surveyed my options. I do better when I write things down, so I reached in my front pocket to get out my pen. I pulled out a piece of paper. It was the list of doctors and cases the CDC had sent me.

There were still those three names left on the list. What did I have to lose? *Acinetobacter* had gotten me into Larry Burkinette's business and into hot water. Maybe—just maybe—it could get me out. In any case, I was facing a dead end. Anything was worth trying.

Today they were all in. The first two were on the East Coast. The cases turned out to be minor infections in two AIDS patients who had had dermatologic biopsies for Kaposi sarcoma. The last one, Francine Watkins, was in Beverly Hills.

"This is a doctor's office calling from Minneapolis. We're treating a family member of Francine Watkins, a patient who was at your hospital. We are planning to perform surgery on her, but she informed me that her sister was treated at your hospital for some unusual ailment. She wants us to check it out to see if it could affect her in any way."

"Let me look that up that name for you," she replied. There was a short wait before she came back on the phone.

"I've got the chart from about a year ago. It was in our specials file. It's pretty thick. It would take us quite a while to copy it and would probably cost us a hundred dollars to send it out. It's standard policy to charge for that service."

"I don't think I need the whole chart."

"What parts were you interested in?"

"I need the discharge summary, the operative report, and the culture reports if you have them."

"That's fairly simple. We use a computerized color-coding system for all reports. It's the latest in scanning technology."

"Great. I wonder if you could fax it to me."

"No problem. Just fax me your medical release form from a family member along with a doctor's name, address, and medical license number. Put on a return fax number and I'll get it to you." She gave me the number and hung up, leaving me to ponder how to get her the release form. At least I was doing something. My adrenalin was flowing, even though the odds were a million to one I'd find out anything useful to my case. I put my gumshoe-scamming faculties to work.

My answer came through a Kinkos shop I found in the Yellow Pages. It was America's answer to the portable office: a few computers, a copying machine, and two or three fax modems.

A young woman, curly red hair snatched back in a ponytail, freckles, and inquiring blue eyes, politely asked me what I needed.

"I need to type up something and then fax it. I wonder if you could help me."

"Sure, over by the window we have a couple of IBM compatible 486's. Let me show you." We walked over and she sat down in front of the screen.

"Just turn it on here." She pushed a button on the hard drive and the screen came up. "Now type whatever you need and when you're done hit 'file.' The print screen will come up and you hit 'print.' When you're done bring up the file menu again and hit 'exit.' That's it."

"That's great. All I need is your fax number so the people can send it back to me." Another customer came in, so she wrote it down quickly and went back to the front desk.

Pretty easy stuff for the computer literate. For me it took a few tries, but finally I had forged a medical release form that would pass muster. I had to use my own name because of my license number, but with all the requests that come through a hospital someone would really have to be looking for it to nail me.

I pulled up the file menu and hit the print button as she had showed me. In a couple of seconds, the paper came out. I used my name with the address of North Central University Medical School and the fax number of the store. Then I signed the consent: Georgette Watkins. I gambled that like most hospicrats, the records room lady was more interested in having a signed document than in its authenticity.

I touched the file menu, made a couple of wrong hits with the mouse, and finally found the exit. I was actually proud of my mendacious self as I walked back to the desk. The red-haired girl was just finishing with her customer.

"Did it work?" she asked, friendly.

"No problem."

"Computers are easy once you get used to them."

"Yeah. Now I need to use your fax machine."

"Just use that one over on the counter."

"How much do I owe you for all this?"

"When everything is done, we'll settle the bill."

I put the release form in the machine, dialed the number, and waited for the connection. Within twenty seconds the rollers had captured the paper and sent it electronically. All I had to do was wait. I took the release form, folded it, and put it back in my pocket.

Just as I was starting to feel uneasy at the delay—paranoia striking deep—I heard the beeping sound of the fax machine, then the mechanical hum of the paper coming out of the machine. I picked up the four or five sheets, glanced at them briefly to make sure they were mine, and casually put them in the pocket of my jacket.

"How much will all of this be?" I asked. She used a small pocket calculator and quickly totaled up the amount.

"Ten seventy-five." I opened my wallet on the counter and pulled out the bills.

In the car I unfolded the papers and started reading. It was the discharge summary that first caught my eye. Thirty-five-year-old female coming in for routine facial cosmetic surgery. No previous medical problems, no medications, no allergies. Physical examination showed a well-developed, well-nourished female, normal heart, lungs, abdomen, bones, and joints. So far so good. Preoperative laboratory values within the range of normal.

Next the hospital course. Surgery without incident, then a postoperative fever of unknown origin. Patient's condition progressively worsened. Blood cultures drawn showing *Acinetobacter calcocetious*. Patient started on third generation cephalosporin antibiotic, but even so went into cardiogenic shock. I could just see the scene as this young woman was dying. People scurrying around, shouting orders, administering drugs. Then the flat line. That was it.

I shook off the vivid visualization the shorthand of the report had brought to me, experienced in that kind of tragedy, and followed the text of the report to the end of the page. I bolted upright in the driver's seat. Which was exactly where I was again.

The surgeon's discharge signature was Jeffrey Belender.

# CHAPTER 16

RESIDENCY BUDDIES JEFFREY BELENDER and Larry Burkinette both had patients who died postoperatively from a highly unusual infection by the same organism. I desperately needed to talk to Belender. There had to be some connection between that and Burkinette's fate.

My mind buzzing with facts, issues, uncertainties, I barely noticed the motel until I was upon it. I was lucky I saw them in time. Two Duluth-Superior police cars were parked in the front of the place. I just kept moving.

How had they found me? The Kinkos, my open wallet? My name in the computer? My AT&T card! How could I have been so careless?

I shook my head back to reality. The panic had passed. I wasn't ready to give myself up to the police just yet. I swung my car out onto I-35 heading south. I looked in my mirror. No one was following.

At State Route 210 I turned west at the Carlton exit. Mostly farmland and lakes now. A front had come across the northern plains, offering a hint of warmth, generating a light ground fog, forcing the majority of the population to huddle in their homes. A good day for being hidden from view, but terrible for driving.

Fortunately, I knew exactly where I was going. After the town of MacGregor, I turned south again, on Highway 65. It wasn't long before the entrance to the Rice Lake Wildlife Refuge came into view. I had been here many times when I'd had a day off during my residency. At this time of the year and in this weather, I knew there would be no one at the park.

I circled in through the entrance road, past the 'Park Closed' sign and pulled off to the side to wait. I hated the feeling of running like a hunted animal. Besides, running from things wasn't in my nature.

It took a few minutes of waiting before I was sure there was no one behind me. I pulled back onto the gravel road. There'd been a secluded campsite about a quarter of a mile down the road near the lake. To my relief it was still there.

I set up my tent in short order. Compared to the old stake-it job, this dome tent was a snap. I opened up my gas stove, pulled out the grill, and put a small pot on top. A quick run to the lake for water and I was in business.

I felt a certain calm sitting in the woods, cooking my Campmor dinner, and listening to the sounds of the forest. A world in turmoil, police after me, yet here, only peace. As I waited for the water to come to a boil, I thought about Larry again. I knew that the source of my dislike for him had gone deeper than his imperious arrogance or simple envy of his wealth.

I particularly remembered one night in the emergency room back in the residency. A patient was admitted with a broken nose from an auto accident. The moment I saw him, I realized he wasn't a run-of-the-mill patient—he was clearly an affluent man, with an expensive-looking woman with him. But I was determined to treat him like everyone else: same x-rays, same call to the chief resident to let him know what was going on.

Most chief residents wouldn't give a second thought to such a minor case, especially in the middle of the night. *Patch him up and send him to the clinic* were Larry's usual words. But when I mentioned the patient's name, Larry was immediately interested. He told me he'd be down.

When he arrived, Larry was at his Mr. Staffman best. He ooh'd and ah'd solicitously as he examined the man and told him what he thought. The patient, somewhat bewildered by this flood of attention, looked over at me, as if for a cue. Larry saw the look.

"Dr. Dailey," Larry said, in front of the patient. "Have you completed the CT scans on Mr. Maxwell?"

"No," I replied. "I wasn't sure that you required one."

"'Not sure'? What do you mean, 'not sure'? I don't know how many times I have to stress to you the necessity for a complete workup. If you keep slipping up like this, we may have to discipline you." Bullshit, and Larry knew it. But try and tell the patient that.

When Mr. and Mrs. Expensive heard that, I suddenly became *persona non grata* and Larry Burkinette had become their best friend. As I walked away, boiling, I heard Larry extolling the virtues of a complete workup to Robert Maxwell, chairman and CEO of Maxwell Industries, who was offering Larry his private box at the stadium any time. I never had any doubts about Larry's motivation after that.

By the time I had finished my recollections, the Monterey chicken with rice was hot. I shoveled it down right from the pan. Eating this concoction and thinking about Larry was giving me indigestion. To say nothing about how

I was going to find Jeffrey Belender, stuck here in the woods with the police searching for me.

The answer certainly didn't appear that night, either. By the time I had finished cleaning up and settled down in the tent I was beat. I had to adjust to sleeping on a Thermarest. It took a couple of turns in the sleeping bag, until I was staring at the entrance of the tent and watching the shadowy movement of the tree branches in the light of the moon. How strange. A week ago I'd been sitting at the breakfast table, debating my future. My thoughts focused on Jordan, her long silky white legs, her arms wrapped around me, the excitement of being with someone I loved.

I rested my head on my rolled jacket and pushed myself farther down into the sleeping bag as a cold shiver of uncertainty ran through my body. What was going to come of all this? There were no answers in the woods, only the swaying branches doing their hypnotic, moonlight dance. The next thing I knew it was nine in the morning.

When I looked outside, the mist that had shrouded my view yesterday had changed to three inches of wet snow clinging to everything. Nothing like Minnesota in November to make you yearn for warm weather. *C'mon, Dailey, moaning isn't going to help.*

I dressed quickly and walked outside. By now light was starting to brighten my view. Rice Lake lay like a giant pot of steaming water.

I remembered an old cabin that the park rangers used, about a quarter of a mile from the campsite. I recalled that there was a phone there.

I boiled some water on my stove, made a quick cup of coffee and some instant oatmeal, and then prepared to find the cabin. My sense of direction was a little misaligned, but fortunately I came to the one direction sign that said 'Ranger's Cabin' with an arrow.

On a day like today, in late November, I didn't figure even the rangers would be out looking for park visitors. I wasn't wrong. The landscape was deserted, and except for the honking of the few geese who still hadn't faced the fact that Minnesota had welcomed winter, there were no sounds.

The green-planked back wall of the cabin came into view almost as I was upon it. Slowly I looked around. No tire tracks, no footprints in the snow except for mine. I walked around the side and up to the front door. Locked. I peered through a window. The telephone was there. All I needed to do was get in.

Obviously, the easiest thing to do would be to break the window, but I didn't want to leave any trace that I had been inside if I could avoid doing so. I looked at the window again. It was one of those fold-down, louvered affairs that project outward when opened. I looked at the latch and saw that it wasn't closed. All I had to do was reach with my fingers and pull it down.

I clambered over the windowsill onto the dusty wood floor of the cabin. I stood up and looked around. An old wood stove, a rickety bed, dried mouse droppings, and the telephone in the corner.

I was half-tempted to start up the wood stove to get the chill out of my system, but I pushed down the urge and walked over to the phone. It was one of those old crank-it boxes. Obviously, the modern era hadn't touched Rice Lake yet.

I looked at my watch. It was a quarter to ten in the morning. What was the chance anyone in California was up, with the time difference? But, what did I have to lose? I picked up the receiver and spun the crank, as I had seen in the movies. I kept doing it over and over. I could hear noise at the other end, but no connection clicked. In frustration I slammed the receiver back on the hook, spinning the crank viciously. The phone rang. I picked it up and heard the operator.

"May I help you?"

"Yes, operator, I'd like information in Encino, California."

It took about ten minutes of fussing through the phone system, but I finally got tapped into Valley Community Hospital in Encino, where Belender's unfortunate patient, Francine Watkins, had died. A couple more minutes and I was talking to the medical staff office. To my surprise, I found myself speaking to the assistant director, Janice Martin.

"Ms. Martin, this is Dr. Benjamin Dailey. I'm calling from Minneapolis. I'm from the alumni association of North Central University Medical School. I'm surprised I got anyone at this hour."

"It's Jan, Doctor, and I always come in early to clear my desk before I get bogged down in meetings. Now what can I do for you?"

"We're looking for some of our former residents. The chief of the department is retiring, and we want to have a get-together. I thought I'd call early today because I have a full schedule in the operating room. I'm having trouble locating a former resident, named Jeffrey Belender." There was a pause.

"He doesn't work at this hospital anymore."

"That's strange. It was the last place listed on his resume."

"He used to work here, but he left a while ago."

"I knew Jeff. I thought he had the world by the tail. Did something go wrong?"

"Wrong? I'll say. He had the whole hospital turned upside down. Almost forced us into probation with the Joint Commission on Hospital Accreditation. Why do you ask?"

"We're going to send out an invitation and have a party. I don't want to mess it up. By the way, what did he do to prompt a probation?"

"He operated on a woman for droopy eyelids. What do they call that, a bleph . . . ?"

"Blepharoplasty."

"That's it. Anyway, the patient got a weird infection after surgery and died."

"That is strange," I replied.

"Yeah, especially when they found out it was his fault. Improper sterile technique."

"What was the fallout?"

"There was a big lawsuit. The hospital kicked him off the staff to keep our accreditation. But don't worry about Dr. Belender."

"Why?"

"He must have been the richest doctor in Encino. Mercedes, big house. He'll be all right."

"Did you know Dr. Belender?"

"I'd met the man. A few of my friends knew him."

"Did your friends say anything about him when it all came down?"

"The usual stuff—rich guy, arrogant, didn't care much about his patients, high lifestyle, always fooling around. You know what I mean?"

"Yeah, I know what you mean. By the way, is there a forwarding address?"

I heard her rummaging around.

"Only thing we have is a post office box in Buena Vista, Colorado. I can give you that."

"Sure." I wrote the number down and thanked her.

Where the hell was Buena Vista? I rang the operator again. No Jeffrey Belender listed in Buena Vista information.

I called back to Valley Community Hospital. By now Jan and I were old friends.

"I'm sorry to bother you again, but I couldn't find Jeff in Buena Vista information. I wonder if he was currently married. Maybe his phone is under his wife's name."

"Good thinking. What are you, some kind of detective?" After a moment she came back on the line.

"Here it is, we always have the spouse's name. Ruth Geisling is the maiden name. Hope it works."

"Thanks again, Jan."

Another dial back to Buena Vista. Jackpot. I called. As I listened to the ringing, I wondered who would have to pay this bill.

"Hello."

"Is this Ruth Geisling?"

"Yes," she answered sleepily.

"My name is Ben Dailey. I'm a doctor from Minneapolis. I'm trying to find Jeffrey Belender and I was hoping you could help me."

"What do you want with Jeff?"

"I wanted to talk to him about an alumni meeting at North Central University Medical School."

"Forget it." An audible click.

Before I had a chance to curse, I heard a noise outside. Sound carried in the still air. I went to the window.

"Dammit, Jake, it's always some fool thing. First old man McPherson calls and tells us he saw someone coming into the park last night. Shit, he can't see ten feet in front of him. Then the operator calls with some cock-and-bull story about the phone being off the hook."

"Yeah, well, you can never tell, Walt. Just in case, unholster your gun."

I didn't need to hear more. I scrambled out the window and around the side of the house just as footsteps shook the front porch. I gently pushed the window back in place. As I tramped through the wet snow, I heard the park ranger grumble something about the mice.

Once out of range of the cabin, I circled back to my campsite. Maybe in the fog the rangers wouldn't see my footprints in the snow. I quickly put my camp stuff together and got back into the car.

The engine starting sounded like a thunderclap, so I didn't wait for it to warm up—I pulled down on the gearshift and rolled out of the park. The snow was falling more heavily now, erasing any trace of my presence.

As I left the Rice Lake Park and headed down the gravel road toward the main highway, I realized there was no perfect crime. There would always be an old man McPherson around to call the police.

By the time I was back on Highway 25, I knew exactly where I was going and what I was going to do. If Jeff Belender wouldn't come to the phone, then I would talk to him in person.

It should have been a two-hour drive to Minneapolis-St. Paul Airport. But the snowfall and my wariness turned it into four hours of stop-and-go. By the time I arrived at the airport the snow had let up, and the sun was piercing the salt slick on my windshield.

I parked in the deck and got out. One more problem to deal with here: Gus's Michigan plates, a sure giveaway. I scouted around until I found a Dodge Ram pickup with two official plates from South Dakota, backed into a spot near a corner pillar.

I casually walked down the aisle from the other side to see if anyone was coming. I bent down in front of the plate and looked again. It was perfect. One more glance to be sure that no one was coming, and I took off the plate with the appropriate attachment of my Swiss Army knife.

Once I'd made the exchange, I threw the Michigan plate into the trunk and locked up the car. When I passed the pickup, I stuck a twenty through a crack in the window and walked on.

By the time I had rationalized and acquitted myself of any wrongdoing, I was inside the terminal. I made my way to the ticket counter and waited my turn to buy a ticket. The wait seemed interminable. When I got close to the counter, I could see why. The woman in front of me was arguing with the ticket salesperson over a refund. After a couple of minutes, the agent finally called the manager over and resolved the problem. After the new ticket was issued, the agent asked for the woman's license. Shit. How could I have forgotten? As if a fugitive wanted for murder could just board a plane!

I walked out of the line and back down the corridor of the terminal, toward the street level entrance. I was near a small coffee stand when I saw the restroom. A lone man in a suit was walking in. He was about my height, build, and coloring. I waited for a minute, then followed him.

The man had hung his coat on a hook near the wash basin. Trusting soul. I went to wash my hands. As he turned to the hot-air hand dryer, I reached in for the inside pocket. The wallet was there. A first-try felony. God forgive me, but I needed his ID more than he did right now. I exited the bathroom without a backward glance, steeling my every nerve not to break into a run.

As I walked, I looked inside the billfold. My new wallet belonged to Charles Whittingdon, Dubuque, Iowa. I got back in line at the ticket counter and waited my turn. The same agent; she looked as if she was having a hard day.

"Where to?"

"First flight to Denver." It turned out I could just make one.

"When did you want to return?"

"Uh, the day after tomorrow in the afternoon." After a few minutes of checking, I had the flights arranged.

"Will this be on your credit card?" she asked. The crucial moment. I handed her Whittingdon's card and she ran it through. Luckily his credit was good. *Thanks, Chuck.*

"I'll need to see your driver's license." The last hurdle. She looked at it and then at me.

"This sure doesn't look like you," she said indifferently, as if the battles of the day had taken the steam out of her.

"It's the beard. I've been on the road for a few days and haven't been able to shave."

She shrugged, handed back the driver's license, and gave me my ticket. I boarded with three minutes to spare.

If I made it without getting arrested before I'd cleared myself, I'd mail Whittingdon's wallet back to him, intact, with enough cash to cover my expenses. In the meantime, before the airport police checked where Charles Whittingdon's credit card had just boarded a flight to, I'd concentrate on making the last leg to Buena Vista, Colorado, up in the mountains, and how to make Jeffrey Belender tell me what I needed to know.

# CHAPTER 17

THE PLANE LANDED AT DENVER INTERNATIONAL AIRPORT with no phalanx of police ready to nail me, somewhat to my surprise. Wasting no time on fruitless speculations, I passed through the baggage claim area and over to the rental car company's stand. I checked out their list of four-wheel drive vehicles. If I was going into the mountains at this time of year, I wanted something that would match up to the conditions. Signing Whittingdon's name again, I was about to skip the accident and collision waiver, but my conscience got the better of me.

Ten minutes later I was in a white Ford Explorer on I-70 heading west toward the Eisenhower Tunnel. As I drove up into the low foothills surrounding the city, I could see the smog hanging over the city in the afternoon sun. By the time I was in Evergreen the entire city had disappeared in the haze of exhaust fumes and factory smoke.

Night had fallen as my rental car made its way over Tennessee Pass and down US 24 to Buena Vista. I didn't know what I was going to find or how I was going to find it, but I did know that the answer to Larry Burkinette's death and my own freedom hinged on whatever I found. Which meant I'd damn well find something.

Buena Vista had *The Last Picture Show* look. I found a motel on the main drag for fifteen a night. Twenty minutes later, after a shower, I went back to the desk clerk.

"Hey," I opened the conversation.

"Hi," he answered. Friendly kid. "Are you passing through or staying?"

"Depends on how hard it is to find Ruth Geisling."

His eyes changed as he looked at me. It was as if I had cursed in church.

"Do you know Ruth?"

"I'm an old friend of the family. I was driving through and thought I'd look her up. She lives over on Chestnut, doesn't she?"

"Yeah, but don't look for her there. Check out the Roadkill down the street. Most people around here know Ruth." *Hmm.*

It was close to nine o'clock when I walked into the bar. There were a few men in plaid shirts, jeans, and cowboy boots sitting on tall metal stools. It was dark inside, but looking around, I could make out hubcaps, license plates, and other highway paraphernalia. If not for the cowboy boots, it would have passed for a biker bar.

I walked up to the beefy, red-faced bartender. Thinning light brown hair, a handlebar mustache, and shirt sleeves rolled up to expose his tattooed forearms— green and red eagles intertwined above the legend, *Don't Tread On Me.* Big arms, big shoulders. Big gut, too. He looked about two cans short of a six-pack.

"What do you have on tap?" I asked.

"Bud bottle," he replied flatly. I nodded resignedly and he brought me a longneck and a frozen glass.

"I bet things slow down here around this time of the year."

"Yeah, a little. Except we get a bunch of bikers every year around this time."

"Bikers? In Buena Vista?"

"Oh, nothing serious. Just a bunch of rich dudes from Denver riding Harleys and making like they're something they ain't."

"I guess a lot of people do things like that."

He nodded. "Passing through?" he asked, trying to figure out what my deal was.

"Yeah. Actually, I'm looking for someone named Ruth Geisling. The clerk over at the motel told me I'd find her here."

"Ruth? She's over in the corner." He tilted his head to the back of the place. I saw her standing in the corner. The light was dim, so I moved a little closer. She was in her late thirties, with washed out blond hair, close-fitting jeans, and a tight sleeveless crop top that exposed the nipples of her braless breasts to anyone who looked. She was drowsily watching two men play pool. Neither seemed to be paying any attention to her. When she saw me, she perked up. I walked up to her.

"Are you Ruth Geisling?"

"Sure am, cowboy," she replied with a forced pool hall swagger.

"Can I buy you a drink?"

"Yeah, that'd be great." As she walked up next to me, her breast lightly brushed my arm.

"What'll you have?" I asked as she pulled a pack of cigarettes from her purse.

"Silver bullet," she smiled, putting a Marlboro languidly between her lips.

I went up to the bar, ordered her drink and another Bud for myself, and brought them to a booth in the corner. She sat down first and I slid onto the seat across from her.

"You don't have to be a stranger. You can sit next to me," she said as I sat down. I looked closer at her eyes as she spoke. They looked glassy, the skin drawn at the corners of her lids. Her mouth showed the first signs of creasing along the upper lip.

"No, it's all right."

"You upset about something, honey? I can make it feel good." She took her hand and started rubbing my thigh under the table. I lightly pushed her hand away.

"Look, Mrs. Geisling, I'm not here for that. I need to ask you some questions about Jeff Belender." As soon as I mentioned his name her brows narrowed, and her eyes glared.

"It's Miss Geisling, and forget it. I want nothing to do with anything that concerns him. Now if you'll excuse me, I've got business to do." She looked over at Mr. Mustache behind the bar. If I didn't do something, those tattooed forearms were going to tread on me.

"Wait," I said, reaching for my wallet. "Here's twenty bucks. Just talk to me. I promise I won't bother you after I'm done."

"What do you want?" she muttered for a moment, taking the bill from my hand.

"I'm a doctor from Detroit, and I was asked to investigate a death at a hospital there. In the process I came across your husband's name. After you wouldn't talk to me on the phone, I decided to come down and see you." I was hoping she didn't read the newspapers.

She snapped her fingers. "You're the guy that called the other night, huh?" I nodded. "So what's the big deal? You came all the way to this shithole of a town just to see me?"

"Actually, I came down to see your husband, but I didn't know where to find him, so I thought I would talk to you first." She didn't say anything, just stared at her drink and took a long drag from her cigarette, blowing the smoke out of both nostrils.

"What was it you wanted from him?" she finally asked.

"Apparently, your husband had a case with similar findings to the one I'm investigating. I spoke to the lady in the medical staff office at Valley Community Hospital. They said that after the case your husband was removed from the staff and you moved out here. It was an unusual coincidence, to say the least."

She eyed me suspiciously. "You talked to Jan, huh?"

"Yeah."

She took a sip of her drink. "You came all the way out here for a malpractice case?"

"Hey, the insurance company paid the freight, what can I say?"

"So you're here. What can I tell you?"

"Tell me what you know about the case in California."

"Tell? What's there to tell? Jeff operated on the woman and she died."

"Then the lawsuit, right?"

"Yeah, the lawsuit. Before then we had quite a life. Big house, fancy cars, parties. We had everything."

"Your husband was a plastic surgeon, wasn't he?"

"Yeah, I met him in L.A. when I was working as a nurse." Her eyes lit up for a moment.

"How long were you married?"

"About ten years."

"Any children?"

"No. Jeff always said he was too busy."

"What happened with the lawsuit?"

"It was an open-and-shut case. They said Jeff used improper techniques. The attorney was a real slimeball. One of those guys with the greasy smile you find in the corner of the Yellow Pages. You know, 'we'll get you the money,' that kind."

"Yeah, I know the type."

"The hospital was like a hibernating bear that had suddenly been roused. When they realized the damages, they paid off the family and kicked Jeff off staff."

"Did the suit force you to leave town?"

"Jeff's practice was big, but after the word spread around town, he fell out of favor. It didn't help that the hospital printed a public apology."

"How did you come to Buena Vista?"

"When you get booted off the staff of a hospital, it's like being a leper. Every place you go for a job, people ask you the same question: were you ever forced to resign? The Buena Vista Clinic was the only place he could get work. He was doing general practice."

"It seems like a nice enough place."

"Are you kidding? The place is a dump. I'm just trying to make enough money to get the hell out of here."

"What about Jeff, does he like it?"

"At first he seemed all right, then he started acting funny. He got anonymous calls. I always thought they were from the suit. Hate calls, from wackos. You know."

"What do you mean 'funny'?"

"Paranoid. He'd get agitated and angry over the tiniest little thing. I told him I wanted to help, that we'd survive this, but after he beat me a few times I figured I'd had enough. That's when I filed for divorce. I thought a settlement would let me start a new life."

"And it didn't?"

"What do you think?" she asked, waving her arm expansively around the Roadkill. "He had spent everything."

"Did you try to go back to nursing?"

"I couldn't—my license had expired. I took the test, but I failed. There was nothing left and nowhere to go." Tears filled her eyes in spite of herself as she faced how far she had sunk. Because of Belender. He and Burkinette really had been two of a kind.

"In your time with Jeff, did he ever mention a man named Larry Burkinette?"

"Yeah, Jeff mentioned his name several times. He said he was an old friend."

"Did you ever meet Burkinette?"

"No. I talked to him on the phone once or twice, back in California."

"Ruth, I'd like to find your husband. Do you know where he is?"

"Sure," she said coldly. "He's over on Shady and the 306."

"Do you have directions?"

"You don't need any. You'll find it easily. It's the only cemetery around."

Looked like Belender and Burkinette had everything in common: wives, lives, and death. But dwelling on their curious similarities was not going to rescue me from the calamity of finding out that my last chance to prove my innocence was in the Buena Vista cemetery.

"When did he die?"

"About a year ago. It was a single car crash. The car fell five hundred feet into a ravine and ignited." I watched a tear run down her cheek as I took a final sip of my beer.

"I guess there's not much more to ask."

"I guess not." I got up to leave, then stopped at the edge of the booth. Why not ask? It was the gesture of a hopeless ghost, not realizing he was dead.

"Listen, Ruth, did your husband ever mention a man named Buzz?"

"Buzz? That was Jeff's nickname at North Central. He said Burkinette gave it to him when they were residents. It was like a code between them." She made the rotary motion next to her temple. "I had the feeling they were both a little crazy."

"Did your husband ever talk to Burkinette after he got here?"

"If he did, I didn't know about it." As she spoke, she glanced around the bar, catching the eye of a few pseudo-bikers in unused, shiny leathers, who obviously knew her.

"Hey, Ruth, baby, come let Daddy buy you a drink," one of them called out, a little too boisterously. She looked at me, gave me a what-do-you-expect shrug, and got up from the table.

"Here," I said, palming another twenty into her hand.

As Harry Chapin said, she just stashed the bill in her shirt and stalked toward her next prey. But in this case, I wasn't sure who was the ultimate victim.

# CHAPTER 18

I GOT UP EARLY THE NEXT MORNING to drive back to Denver. Before I left, I drove over to the cemetery to look at Belender's grave. I guess I couldn't let my last hope go without actually seeing Belender's death carved in stone.

The sun had risen as I got there. A flat, treeless plot next to the highway with a wire farm fence around it and a simple sign designating it as the Buena Vista Memorial Cemetery.

It took about thirty minutes of brushing the light snow off the gravestones to find Jeffrey Belender's resting place on Earth. It was a simple, plain marker defaced by innocuous graffiti: three red streaks like arrows with a cross through one of them, painted on the back of the gravestone. Even in the high country of Colorado, you couldn't get away from a culture of disrespect.

Something about the design began to seem familiar. After a couple of minutes, a shiver went through me, and not from the cold. I remembered now. Larry's widow, Samantha Burkinette, had described the same peculiar design.

I looked around to see if any of the other stones had been defaced. Every other stone was unmarked. I walked back to the car and got in. As much as I wanted to understand what the sign meant, how could I? I could have spent three months looking at it, and it would have still looked like three arrows, one with a cross through it. As I waited for the car to warm up, I took my pen, made a note of the name of the cemetery on a piece of paper, and set them on the seat next to me.

Then I looked down at the scrap of paper. What difference did it make? What good could any further attempt to understand what had happened to Burkinette and Belender do me, anyway? Angrily, I pulled hard on the gearshift, spun my wheels on the gravel, and jerked back onto the highway.

In my present state, my mind was a jumble of thoughts, all of them centered on Larry Burkinette.

I knew that my dislike for him ran far deeper than his chest-thumping ego, or the petty scene in the emergency room. If Larry wanted to be an egomaniac, or a sycophant to some rich executive, so be it. It's a free country. There was more to my emotions, a sensibility that I could never quite get a handle on.

I went back to the core of our ancient antagonism. Now, when I could see no way out of the trouble he'd gotten me into, I faced the real reason I'd hated Larry Burkinette.

Toward the end of my first year in the residency, I was doing a nose operation, a deviated septum. It was one of the most common operations a head and neck surgeon could do. Freeze the nose up under local anesthesia, open the inner lining, then remove the crooked and broken cartilage and bone.

I was looking forward to a rare free weekend I had planned with Abby MacKenzie. Abby was a nurse at University Hospital: long brown hair, big blue eyes, and a delicious body—the kind of woman who made you forget the bitter cold of Minneapolis and the long hours on call. We had been out a few times and had planned a weekend of camping up at Rice Lake.

Larry was in the room observing, and Abby was circulating. He had surprised me that day by actually being helpful, setting up the local tray and prepping the patient. Then matters took a different turn.

I had taken out the powdered cocaine flakes, put them on the end of an applicator stick, and smeared the interior of the nose as I had done dozens of times before. Once I was done, I finished the local by injecting Xylocaine. I waited a few minutes and then started operating. To my surprise, the patient complained of intense pain, in spite of the local anesthetic. I'd never had such an unforeseen circumstance occur. Several times during the case Abby looked at me as if I were dispensing cruel and unusual punishment. Worse, she seemed cool to me afterward, something else I wasn't used to.

That night the patient started bleeding. It was a problem that happened occasionally. I found out about it later that evening when I ran into Larry at the cafeteria. He was sitting with Abby having coffee. Their conversation seemed a little too intense for a married man and my weekend date.

"Hey, Dailey," he called out when he saw me. "I had to take care of your patient from today. It was a stinker of a bleed."

"Why didn't you call me?" I asked.

"I figured you deserved one crack at him. After that *he* deserved a *doctor*." Abby started giggling, as if she were in on a joke I didn't understand.

What was I going to say? Instead I walked away, trying to figure out what had happened, both with the patient and with Abby.

Later that night in the resident's on-call room, I was awakened by banging on the wall from the room next to mine. It was the room Larry occupied when he was taking night calls. Over the noise I heard the moaning of a woman, then a sharp cry. Then silence.

I crept to my door and opened it a crack. After about fifteen minutes I saw the door to Larry's room open and Abby MacKenzie come out. That was the end of Abby and me, and the end of any hope of friendship between Larry and me. I drew the line at his boffing my girlfriend in the on-call room next to mine.

By the time I had roused myself from my ruminations I had already passed Granite on the way to Leadville. My common sense told me to head through to Leadville and on to Denver. But my thoughts about Larry, the days of being on the run, and the intense melancholy I was feeling demanded respite. I looked out at the bright sunshine and the glittering peaks pushing through the clouds and made a sudden decision to head over Independence Pass into Aspen. What the hell, it would add a couple of hours, but I could change my flight.

At Twin Lake I turned west. There wasn't much traffic at this time of year, only a single car behind me and a few stragglers at the reservoir, which already had an ice crust and several inches of snow. I knew that in another couple of weeks, the first big snowfall would block the pass until the spring thaw came.

The higher the car climbed, the cloudier it became. Soon the first volley of light snow flurries drifted across the road. I thought about turning back, but by this time the road had narrowed, just wide enough for two cars, no room for a turn around. My pleasant ride into Aspen was going to become a hard drive. Things weren't working out as I'd wanted. How unexpected.

I switched the Explorer into four-wheel drive and dropped down into second gear. My windshield wipers were keeping up with the snow, but after twenty minutes of climbing, a thin glaze was building up on the windshield. With the way the snow was coming down now, I could see that the pass wouldn't be open much longer.

Every now and then I would try to see over to the other side of the road. All I could make out were the green tops of eighty-foot lodgepole pines pushing up against the relentless fall of snow beginning to bury them. I looked back in my rearview mirror. Through the snow I thought I could see the lights of a car behind me. It was a little reassuring to think I wasn't the only idiot making this trip.

I continued to make my way slowly up the side of the mountain pass. I couldn't see all the way, but from driving this road before I knew the heights were dizzying, the drop-off a sheer eight hundred feet. My eyes were beginning to hurt from trying to pick out the yellow signposts that marked my way. I could see the lights of the guy behind gaining on me. All I needed was the pressure of someone on my tail.

The narrow road continued to snake its way up the side of the mountain.

Each turn became scarier as visibility dropped to only a few feet ahead of the car. I wanted to stop, but I knew I would be buried if I didn't keep moving. I was concentrating so hard that I'd forgotten the car behind me. There was a sharp jolt as I was thrown forward. My car swerved giddily across the narrow pavement.

I gripped the wheel and brought it back into the right lane, alternating between terror and anger. What a jerk, driving like that in a snowstorm! I wanted to stop the car and get out, but I knew I had to keep driving. I'd settle his hash when I got to the bottom. But I got another nasty start when I looked in the rearview again; his headlights had disappeared. Maybe I *wouldn't* see him at the bottom.

That fear evaporated when I felt a second shuddering jolt against my rear fender, this one harder than the first. Fortunately, the blow struck directly on my rear bumper, so I didn't swerve this time. But I knew that the jolt had been no accident. Whoever was behind the wheel of that car was deliberately trying to get me. But why? The police wouldn't unduly endanger themselves and me. They would want me alive, to face charges and TV cameras.

I swung a little wide on the next turn. Now I could see his lights to the side of my car. As he headed to the right shoulder, I knew his next move would be to try and force me off the road and over the cliff. My drive to Aspen had suddenly become a life or death struggle on the side of a precipitous mountain in a blizzard.

As soon as I saw him make his move, I swung back to the right, my rear fender clipping his left front grill. I could see sparks fly through the snow as his car rubbed against the red rock and granite of the mountain. He managed to straighten back onto the road.

I took his momentary recovery as my only chance and slammed on my brakes. His car came barreling ahead and hit my rear fender again, this time crumpling it. I was about to jump out when I saw his arm come out of his driver's window. A sudden flash, a ricochet off the front of my car. So much for a simple arrest with due process.

I had no choice. I slammed the car into reverse and gunned the engine. I don't think he was expecting it because his hand jerked back inside as he fired his weapon three more times from within his car, two of the bullets shattering his windshield. The shots echoed eerily in the silent whiteout.

As the back of my Explorer hit his front fender, his car spun to one side. I pressed on the accelerator harder, driving the wheels into the snow, slowly turning his car sideways across the road. In a frantic attempt to recover he must have tried to accelerate. Suddenly, I disengaged and put my car in drive. The unexpected change in force left him spinning his tires forward without resistance. I looked back and saw his car moving irresistibly toward the edge of the precipice. Through the snow I could see the man's frantic braking, his gun waving through the shattered windshield, discharging one more shot. The car twisted wildly for a second, almost completely turned around, then did a lazy slide off the side of the road, its rear end hanging over the rock curb, dangling eerily above the eight-hundred-foot precipice.

I stopped my car, got out, and walked cautiously toward the edge, the heavily falling snow stinging my eyes as I squinted at the car. I wasn't about to take any more chances, so I approached the vehicle from the opposite side and looked in. There on the front seat was a burly man dressed in army fatigues, sprawled flat across the seat, his gun lying harmlessly on the floor. But it wasn't the sight of the weapon that galvanized me. Even through the glass I could hear the unmistakable wheeze of airway obstruction; to my ears it sounded as if it issued from his voice box.

I opened the door and looked at him, face swollen and lips blue, emitting a high-pitched wheeze. Panic filled his eyes as he fought to stay alive. My instinct was to run. *The hell with it, he tried to kill me!* Then I looked at him again. He was a human being, and I was still a doctor.

I forced my hand into my coat pocket and fumbled for my keyring with the Swiss Army knife. Upper airway obstruction and a dying patient. No question: a tracheotomy.

I pulled on the zipper of his coat and ripped open the neck. I saw his blood-stained dog tags and was tempted to read the name, but that would have to wait. I rolled him on his back and saw the bullet hole in the side of his neck. From the angle of the entrance wound I figured he must have shot himself as his car had gone out of control. I checked his barely perceptible pulse. He was going into shock. No EKG, no intracardiac adrenaline, no paddles, just this mysterious assassin and me on the lonely side of a mountain pass. *Airway, idiot, maintain his airway.*

I extended his neck and felt with my cold fingers for the small notch below his Adam's apple. When I found it, I opened the knife and made a stab hole through the skin. There was a sudden rush of air as the obstruction cleared. Once I did, I looked back at his face. No longer was he gasping for air. A weak smile came over his swarthy face: almost an expression of gratitude.

I looked for something to keep the hole open. Nothing. I remembered my ballpoint pen, still in the Explorer. I could unscrew the shaft and stick it in the hole. Afterward I'd worry about the wound in his neck.

Suddenly, the car rocked. There was a grinding sound against the curb and the car dropped slightly. Reflexively, I jumped back, knife in hand, out the open door, staring at the dangling car as the wet snow pelted my face. But I had to get that pen and come back. Fear or no fear.

I raced to my car, scooped the pen up with my cold fingers, and started to run frantically toward the other car. There was another sound, this time louder. I looked in horror as the car wavered on the rock and then tipped backward, vanishing like a ship sinking into a white ocean.

My legs felt trapped in slow motion as I ran to the edge and looked down. There, through the mist and snow, fifty feet below me, the car had wedged itself between two boulders.

I walked back to my Explorer, bent and beaten.

Once inside I sat for a moment, wondering what to do. I let all my unanswered questions rumble through my brain for a few more moments, then shakily put the car back into gear.

It took a few more minutes of climbing before I reached the summit. This time there was no car behind me, only the densely falling snow ahead, as I started the descent off the pass. The farther I descended, the better the weather got. When I was about halfway down, I could actually see the road.

The action of driving was strictly mechanical, as I thought about the man dead in the canyon below. The shattering image receded like a distant memory as the clouds thinned and the light got brighter.

By the time I had reached the opening of the valley into Aspen, it was almost as if it all had never happened. The state of denial enveloped me until I turned the last switchback, made the turn onto the straightaway, and ran smack into a police roadblock.

The sight of the Colorado State Police in front of me made my heart start to race again. I gripped the wheel. Reality was back with a vengeance. I might have been able to avert disaster on the mountain, but there was no getting around the police now. I pulled the Explorer up to the barricade, pulled my hat down a little more over my eyes, and watched the officer saunter up to me.

"Rough trip down?" he asked, surveying the damage to the car.

"The worst, Officer," I grinned, every ounce of my famous charm in play.

"We're blocking the road to any further traffic. You're probably the last one down for the season. Did you notice anyone else up there?" When I realized he wasn't after me, my breath started to come in regular bursts again. Common sense told me that the appearance of innocence would be best supported by sticking as close to the truth as the right to not incriminate myself allowed.

"I thought there was one person behind me, but then I lost sight of him." The officer was still looking at my car.

"We'll check it out. Say, you're going to have a lot of explaining to do to the rental car company. Especially that hole in your left front fender. It almost looks like a bullet hole." I was really sweating now.

"I did a three-sixty near the summit and must have hit something against a rock. I'm sure that's where it happened. Anyway, I'm glad I signed for the collision insurance."

"If you can't be smart, be lucky, that's what I always say. Drive safely, sir." My sentiments exactly.

I put the car back in gear and lumbered away. If they went back up there to look for my attempted murderer, I'd have a four or five hour jump on them. The police had seen me now, and they knew my car. The only thing I could do was change my identity and keep moving. So much for my Aspen respite. I was going to get a quick bite to eat and push on back to Denver.

I took Highway 82 over the Roaring Fork River into town. Before Thanksgiving, the trendy summer crowds and their fancy clothes that bulged with east coast money were gone, the skiers not yet arrived. Even so, comparing it to the days of the mid-sixties when I'd first come here, the unmistakable smell of fast money and fast living permeated the pretty little town.

I headed over to the Golden Horn, ordered the calf's liver and roasted potatoes and a bottle of Newcastle. My traumatic trip over Independence Pass had left me grimy and disheveled, but the maître d' didn't seem to mind. At that time of year, I think they were grateful for the business.

The service and food were just as good as I had remembered. I ate alone in the corner, happy to have one moment of peace where no one knew who I was, but lonely beyond any words I have to describe. More than anything I missed Jordan. Damn, if I ever found myself back in bed with Jordan, making love, I'd never answer the telephone again.

# CHAPTER 19

As I left the restaurant, I saw a pay phone in the entranceway. I knew it was reckless, but I couldn't stand it any longer, so I picked it up and dialed Jordan's number.

I heard the phone ring twice and then the answering machine came on. I recognized Jordan's voice, but the message was new.

"You have reached Jordan Dalkind's residence. I'm not in right now so please leave a message." A slight pause. "If this is Ben Dailey calling, the phone is tapped, so be careful what you say." Then the beep.

I hung up quickly, wondering if the call had been traced. Then I realized it had been too short. I called back. This time, I let the machine run through its message. When the beep came on, I spoke.

"Remember the fifty-four Red Wings." I hung up.

I was sure that would keep George Sennett occupied for a few days while he scoured the sports pages. By that time, I would probably be in jail anyway.

It was nearly dark when I got back in my Explorer and started to head north on Highway 82. Shortly outside Aspen it widened into four lanes, abruptly signaling the end of paradise. I motored past Glenwood Springs and turned east on I-70. Any remnants of quiet and tranquility immediately evaporated once I started heading east. The huge transcontinental semis and constant stream of traffic shattered all repose.

Glenwood Canyon was dark as I passed through it on one of the great highway engineering feats in this country, a double-decker expressway spanning the twenty miles between Glenwood and Gypsum. Once I was out of the canyon, the ground rose steadily over lacy white plateau country, silver as the full moon poured light across the countryside. Formerly barren country, now retirement communities and vacation housing spread everywhere as I moved through Edwards, Avon, and into Vail.

Under other circumstances I would have stopped and made a night of it at the Christiana, but instead I pulled in at the Amoco, gassed up, grabbed a cup of the machine brew, and took off again for Denver, a hundred miles away. Vail Pass was clear and in the evening moonlight I could see all the way to Copper Mountain. Looking at the peaceful scene in front of me made the maelstrom I had encountered on Independence Pass seem doubly unreal in retrospect.

Once off the pass and into Officer's Gulch, I began thinking again. Who had been after me? And why? And, leaving that fascinating question aside for the moment, what was I going to do next now that my search for Jeff Belender's and Larry Burkinette's past secrets had met a dead end?

It took me the rest of my ride back to Denver International Airport to decide what I was going to do next. By the time I had seen the white-tented roof of the airport, I had decided. Now all I had to do was get back to Minneapolis.

It was close to midnight when I arrived at the airport, my mind full of ideas. The first stop I made was to drop my car off at Hertz, but something stopped me from going in. I had been too lucky so far. Besides, there was something about the plain blue Taurus next to the office that didn't look like the standard Hertz issue. Charles Whittingdon's credit card wasn't going to take me any farther. Change of plan in the works. Minneapolis would have to wait.

So instead of going in the rental return lot, I circled into the deck and found a spot on the second floor. They'd find the car in a few days, but by that time I'd be long gone—maybe even in prison. As far as Mr. Whittingdon was concerned, I'd pay the bill when I got back home, as I'd already promised myself.

I approached the Northwest desk from the escalator. My first view was a line of people waiting to get tickets. I swung my eyes to the left.

From working with George Sennett a year ago, I had seen the type: plain suit, short-cropped hair, dispassionate stare, apparently blind to human emotion. Cops.

I got off the escalator, walked toward the newsstand, and picked up a magazine. As I pretended to read through it, I saw one of the suits surveying me. I put the magazine back down and walked directly toward the escalator again. I heard him shout. They'd recognized me.

"Okay, mister, stop where you are!"

I didn't wait for formal introductions. Instead I positioned myself between an old lady with a cane and a young family. If they were going to shoot, it wasn't going to be now.

Once beyond view, I slid down the railing to the escalator steps below, taking them two at a time. I was on the mezzanine level. Looking around, I could see my only means of escape was the small trains that moved people from one terminal to another. I started walking fast toward the exit. Looking back, I could see the two men running after me, so I picked up my speed. Again, they yelled.

"Stop! Police!" At least they could have called me by name. I hate impersonality.

I pushed forward. The train to Terminal C had just arrived. The doors slid open. I jumped aboard just as the police did the same in the car next to mine. I held my hand in the closing door. The doors closed and the train moved. The crowd of people hid me from view as I jumped back onto the platform.

Once back on the cement, I started running. I could see the two men shaking their fists at me as the robot train disappeared down the track and out of sight.

I ran back to the escalator and over to the corridor that would take me back to the front of the airport. There was a shuttle just about to leave for the Hyatt at the Denver Tech Center. I jumped on just as the black-and-whites were pulling in. The bus was packed with a group of early season skiers, so I stood near the front door. I had an agonizing minute as the driver waited. If he were to stop at the next terminal, I was finished. Then he picked up his radio, and I listened to him tell the base control that he had a full load. I watched in inexpressible relief as he swung out into the exit lane.

The police moved back and forth, in an organized car dance, placing a net around the airport. Fortunately, the shuttlebus I was on was the last bus out. As it passed the last exit, I could see roadblocks being set up on all the passenger lanes. I settled back for the twenty-minute ride.

I had stayed at the Hyatt before, nice rooms, a good restaurant, and an anonymity that I liked: a good mix for holding meetings and conferences. Getting off the shuttle, I walked directly into the lobby and was met by loud music and groups of milling people, all trying to achieve the sales incentives the placards advertised. I shouldered my way through the crowd attending the Great Western Computer Sales Incentive Seminar. The gift shop was still open. I went inside and spied what I wanted: a wide-brimmed cowboy hat, shaving cream and a razor, and some reddish hair coloring.

I walked out of the store and into the men's room just down the hall. Once inside, I stepped into one of the stalls, closing the door behind me. I looked at the water closet carefully and quickly decided that this wasn't a time for the niceties of life. I took my shirt off, lifted the top off the tank, and dunked my head in the water. What the hell, it was clean water, wasn't it? With my hair dripping over the tank, I opened the reddish dye and worked it into my hair for thirty seconds. Then I dipped my head back in. The tank turned red. I assumed my hair did too. I rung my hair out as much as possible. I took the shaving cream, lathered my face, and shaved without a mirror. Now and then I heard people come in and out of the room. No one seemed to notice me in the stall.

When I was done, I flushed the chain and the reddish mess went into the bowl and out. I waited a minute and then flushed again. This time the water ran clear. There was nothing to dry my hair off with, so I put my hat on, slipped on my shirt, and walked out of the stall. Thankfully, the room was empty as I walked up to the mirror over the sink. When I took my hat off, I was pleased at the change in my appearance, clean-shaven, reddish-blond hair. I even looked a little younger. After splashing some water on my face and wiping it off with a paper towel, I looked almost presentable for my ex-wife's country club.

My new appearance gave me more confidence as I walked back into the lobby. Great Western must have been going all-out with their party—the place was hopping. I stood by the doorway for a few minutes listening to the music, watching as the cars came and went. I waited until the car valets were all in the back lot and approached a man who drove up in a brand-new Continental.

"I'll park your car, sir," I said quickly. He looked at me for a moment.

"Do I need a ticket or something?"

"Are you with the convention?"

"Yeah."

"We're parking them all in one corner of the lot. You don't need anything else."

"Thanks a lot. I'm late already."

I got behind the wheel as he went inside, I drove off down the exit drive. I felt bad. But not bad enough to go to jail for murders I hadn't committed.

I circled back onto I-25 and then to I-70. There were cop cars every now and then, but nothing that roused my attention. I was home free. No one was looking for a new Continental. I looked at my watch: it was one-thirty in the morning. No one would be out now.

I hit the roadblock just past Denver International Airport. Up ahead traffic had slowed, and I saw flashing police car lights.

I waited anxiously as they let one car after another through the barricade. By the time it was my turn, I could see the police weren't letting anyone off easily. I carefully slowed down to a proper speed. The cop motioned me to pull up.

"Where you headed, mister?"

"Limon, I hope." He shone the light on my face and then looked at his picture.

"I need to see your driver's license, sir." I had no choice but to show him Charles Whittingdon's. He examined it and gave it back to me.

"Limon is about an hour's drive from here. Have a nice trip." Obviously, he was in need of an eye exam. I was going to leave, but my criminal curiosity got the best of me.

"What's the roadblock for?"

"Some guy we're looking for. He killed a man up on Independence Pass." A shiver went through me.

"Any idea who?"

He shook his head. "No, but rest assured, we'll find him."

"Is it safe to drive?"

"Just keep your doors locked and listen to the radio." Having a desperate killer like me out on the road was certainly enough to scare the average citizen.

I drove away slowly, picking up to the speed limit when I could no longer see the police cars lights in my rearview. Once out of sight, I set the cruise control at the speed limit and watched the eastern Colorado Plateau pass by. As I drove, I kept my eye on the rearview. Two in the morning, just the parade of transcontinental trucks plying the interstate. So far I was safe, but my anonymity wouldn't last. I knew the police. They'd find this car, and sooner or later, they'd find me.

I got off at the H Street exit and made my way into Limon, a small farming town whose existence had gained relative importance with the building of the great interstate highway system. Now truck stops, motels, and a few restaurants had sprung up on the eastern Colorado plains.

I looked around for the tallest, brightest lit sign near the interstate and found it at Al's Truck Stop. I needed to get rid of this car in a hurry. The police would spread a net out from Denver for a hundred miles.

I pulled up behind the restaurant next to two Ford half-tons. I thought for a moment, then changed my mind, parking near the dumpster. A fancy Continental would stick out like a sore thumb between two trucks. I left the car locked with the keys under the floor mat and walked into the restaurant. Three in the morning. The place was full of drivers taking their breaks.

I'd been successful with truckers before. They were, as a group, a friendly bunch relegated to the loneliness of the highway, anxious for company when they could get it.

I was exhausted, and maybe that showed when I sat down at the counter. The trucker next to me started up a conversation.

"Rough ride?" he asked. I assumed he assumed I drove a rig. Good.

"Yeah. The company sent me down with a load, then my rig broke down. They say it's a broken drive shaft. The repair guy says they'll fix it in three days."

"Three days in Limon? You got to be kidding!"

"I'm not, and my wife is in the hospital in Minneapolis."

"Who do you work for?" He had a thick accent that spoke of Lexington and Concord, Minutemen, and baked beans.

"Allied Trucking out of Minneapolis." I remembered the name from a billboard.

"Who's going to pick up your rig?"

"I called the company. They're sending a guy down to drive it. The only thing is that if I wanted to get home earlier, I'll have to find my own way back to Minneapolis." The man took an enormous bite from his chicken-fried steak. "How about I give you a lift?"

"For real?" I asked, hardly able to believe my act had worked.

"Hey, truckers' law. I'm headed to Kansas City. After that you're on your own."

"I appreciate that. Robert Orr is the name." I stuck out my hand. The trucker looked at me for a moment and then shook it.

"You're a lucky man."

"Why's that?"

"You're wearing the name of my favorite player."

"Oh, you mean the Bobby Orr thing. I get that all the time. Are you a hockey fan?"

"Does a hobby horse have a wooden head? You don't live around Boston and not follow hockey. My name is Charlie Schein, better known on the road as Slap Shot. Let's finish and we're gone."

WE TALKED HOCKEY FOR A WHILE, but soon the exhausting day and my fatigue took over. I struggled, but my mind started wandering and my eyes closed. In my half-sleep I began to think of Jordan again, wondering what she thought of my picture in the paper and the television blaring my crimes to the nation. Not the best way to cement our relationship. Now that relationship seemed more important to me than any foolish dream of independence I'd ever had.

I woke from a sound sleep to hear the trucker's CB squawking in the cab.

"Yeah, Big Daddy, this is Slap Shot, I copy." I looked over at the driver.

"Slap Shot?" I asked foggily. I'd forgotten his introduction.

"Yeah. Like I said, I'm into hockey."

"Sorry about falling asleep."

"Don't worry. I'm used to the ride, make it maybe thirty times a year. Besides, you went out like a light."

"Did I give you the number to my Swiss bank account?"

"No, but you kept mumbling 'Jordan' and a few other things."

"Like what?" I panicked.

"Relax. I know what it's like, being on the road and away from your family. They pay me the big bucks, but sometimes I wonder if it's worth it." As he spoke, I looked out at the sun over the barren plains. Ahead I could see the distant skyline of a big city.

"Where are we?"

"The end of my trip, Kansas City. I'm going to drop you off at the Fifth Wheel. It's a truck stop near town. That guy I was on the radio with, Big Daddy, he's a friend of mine. I told him he had a ride going with him to Minneapolis."

BIG DADDY WAS ACTUALLY ANDY PEARSON, and at six-eight, and two hunred and ninety pounds, he was imposing with his tight-shaved head and graying beard. vivid against his dark skin. He was waiting for us at the truck stop when we arrived. We ate, then he and Charlie went out and inspected their rigs. They were gone long enough to make me suspicious. Maybe they were on to me and were coming back with the police. But where was I going to run now?

I had another cup of coffee and waited nervously. Eventually Big Daddy came back in alone. I went along apprehensively as he hustled me out of the diner and onto his rig.

"It's too bad I didn't get a chance to thank Charlie," I said, climbing up the riser and into his shiny red Mack.

"He told me to tell you goodbye. He said to call him the next time you're doing the I-70."

"I'll remember that."

"You're headed for Minneapolis, huh?" he said as he went through the gears of his Kenworth.

"Yeah, my rig broke down."

"That's what Ol' Slap told me. He said you worked for Allied."

"Ol' Slap?"

"Charlie. Remember?"

I nodded, dumbly, cursing myself.

"Say, do you know Johnnie Martucci at Allied?" He had me. I didn't say anything. "You ain't a driver, are you?"

"How'd you know?"

"Ol' Slap told me," he said. "He felt sorry for you with your story. He said you kept talking in your sleep and mumbling about being in trouble."

"He's right," I confessed.

"Well, on the road it don't make any difference. You heard of truckers' law, haven't you?'

"Just recently."

"We kind of judge people on our own and decide our own justice. You looked all right. That's all that matters. Whatever story you're carryin' is your business."

"Do you always make the right decisions?"

"Most of the time. I grew up in a tough town in western Pennsylvania. You learned to size up people quickly. You ever play ball?"

"Yeah, a little."

"See, I could tell. The way you walk. You still have a little spring to your step."

"At my age?"

"What are you, in your forties?"

"Close enough. You're still in shape yourself. Not bad for a guy that spends his days stuck in the cab of a truck."

"I'm not stuck here. I chose this job. It gives me a chance to do a lot of thinking."

From the vantage of the truck cab, I could see why he liked it. It was quiet inside, and it gave him time to think, sitting ten feet off the ground and watching the miniature cars as they buzzed by us.

"What do you think about?" I asked.

"Lots of things, but mostly about people. I was going to study psychology when I was in college. I thought when I graduated, I would go to law school. Then I dropped out."

"What happened?"

"I played a little football, you know. Outside linebacker in the four-three. I wasn't bad either. Made all-conference for West Pennsylvania State. I even had a few pro scouts looking at me. But most of all I got used to everybody tellin' me how great I was. Then I got into the wrong crowd, made a few bad decisions."

"You look like you got yourself together now."

"It ain't bad. Nice wife and family. That's them on the dash." He pointed at a slim-waisted African American woman and two teenage boys.

"Big kids. They look like players."

"Nope. I told them they weren't going to get nothin' the easy way. They're going to college to learn so they can get somewhere someday."

Every now and then I would look around to survey the traffic. At this hour of the morning I assumed there wouldn't be much. I was wrong. Police cars whistled past us with disturbing regularity. And Big Daddy's CB was crackling with police information from the truckers moving up and down Interstate 35.

"Lots of action out there today," he said after a couple of calls.

"Yeah, what's the deal?"

"Some kook. It's all over the newspapers. A man got killed over Independence Pass near Aspen yesterday. They're looking for some guy." He reached over and handed me the paper. There was my picture again, a police sketch of me in disguise.

I felt a shiver go through my body. This wasn't a story about the police chasing Dr. Ben Dailey over Independence Pass. It was about some unknown killer, a shot-up wreck on the side of a mountain pass, and a nationwide manhunt. *That's great. Multiple crimes, police after me everywhere. Pretty soon they'll call me Dr. Dillinger.* According to the report, the investigation indicated that the car had been pushed off the road and over the edge. Then there was a rental car with what appeared to be bullet holes. "Murder on the Continental Divide," was what they called it. They didn't mention the identity of the dead person. It was just like the police to withhold details like that.

There was one thing good about the article: as far as I could see, they had no idea where I was. And if these police didn't know, then neither did Sennett. Then it hit me: Sennett must know I'd been involved with the death of the man on the pass. Hell, he had set the whole search thing in motion. Then the local police had done the rest, hadn't they? The whole mess was making my head spin.

"Anyone you know?" I said, while looking at the picture.

"No one I know and no one I care about," he determined, glancing over at me as I read the paper. "I'm not much on all this sensationalism around today. Guilty 'til proven innocent, that's the press's motto. Makes me sick."

"It's hard to doubt the newspapers, isn't it?"

"I've seen too much to believe them easily, especially when I was in trouble with the law as a kid. The police lock up a lot of innocent people every day. Take this article I read the other day about some doctor in Detroit who might be involved in the deaths of two people."

"What do you think?" I asked after a few minutes of silent riding.

"About what?"

"This doctor, do you think he's guilty?"

"No telling. I haven't heard his side of the story. A man has to wait to decide and hear all the evidence. It's the fair way. Let him show he didn't do it. We fought a revolution and a civil war so people could get freedom, didn't we?"

"It's hard to argue with history."

"You know, from what I read, this guy's been through it before. He solved a big case. I kind of like him just from reading the papers. He's the underdog, you know."

"I know what you mean."

"Some people are like that," he continued.

"Like what?"

"They attract trouble. Just like this doctor. Then they spend their lives getting out of scrapes. But that still don't make this guy guilty."

*Try and tell that to a jury, Big Daddy.*

BIG DADDY DROPPED ME OFF on Ninth Street and Hawthorne in Minneapolis at seven-thirty that night. My body ached as I stretched the stiffness out of my legs. I assumed that the police would never suspect that I would be headed back to Minneapolis. But I knew that eventually they would find me.

I also knew that the key to my freedom lay in the connection between Belender and Larry. *Acinetobacter calcocetious* hadn't just suddenly appeared in two patients whose doctors, longtime friends, were now both dead. Whoever had killed Larry had something to do with the death of Belender. And the only time the two of them had been together in the last twenty-five years was during the residency in Minneapolis.

I knew it was going to take time, something I didn't have a lot of. I needed a place to hole up in, somewhere in the city itself. But first I needed some wheels.

I caught a cab back to the airport to pick up Gus's car. It was where I had left it. Having my own wheels gave me the illusion that I was in charge of my fate again.

But illusion was all it was. My fear had intermingled with deep weariness from my long trip. While every shadow was a cop, and every car that pulled up alongside me knew my identity, in my fatigue I almost didn't care, half wishing they'd catch me and put me out of my misery. I had to force myself to keep my eyes open as I drove out of the terminal and headed back toward the city.

I opened the window slightly and let the cold air blow against my face. As I did, my alertness returned. By the time I was at the I-94 interchange, I was awake again, driving toward the center of town, viewing a cityscape that I had once spent so much time in. After twenty-five years it was hardly recognizable.

But then, I guess, so was I. As a resident, I'd been young and naive and certainly not smart enough to understand Larry Burkinette. As an adult I was wiser, more cynical, and understood him to a tee. Maybe if I had been a little more assertive when I had the chance . . . oh, hell. No point in rehashing that ancient nastiness.

Except that it was still with me.

By the time Larry Burkinette was finishing his residency he had become a constant thorn in my side. I tried as much as possible to stay out of his way, asking questions and responding to him only when necessary. In truth, whatever I did or felt never seemed to make much of a difference to him. Larry was the most important person to Larry.

Over the months since he had started his affair with Abby, I had managed to stow my anger toward him. I had lost before, and I'd probably lose again. But my opinion of him had steadily worsened. I'd watched him bullshit his way through Saturday conferences and slough off his work on the floors.

But I was the only one who noticed. To everyone else, Larry was the darling of the department, charming the secretaries, conning the attending staff. Looking back, maybe I should have said something, but even if I had, where was my proof? That he had taken my girlfriend?

So I let it ride. But no self-justification could lessen the hurt or salve the guilt that I felt even now. I should have warned Abby directly, been more forceful. My problem was that I'd never seemed able to break through the barrier she had set up around herself. She was convinced that Larry loved her, even to the end.

I remember hearing Larry and her arguing in the operating room one day at the end of the surgical schedule. It was late in the afternoon and the place was nearly empty. I had only come back to retrieve my glasses.

"Larry, we can't go on like this any longer," she had pleaded. When I heard her talking, I stopped outside the door.

"Come on, baby. You know I love you."

"Not anymore, Larry. I need a commitment. I can't keep doing this." I heard some muffled voices and whispering, and then the slamming of an instrument loudly on the floor.

"I love you, Larry. I just can't live like this," she shouted. There was another 'I know, baby' from Larry, and then the door shot open and Abby rushed out, crying. I ducked around a corner. A few minutes later Larry walked out. He didn't seem much worse for wear.

I waited, deciding what to do. Then I made up my mind. I went into the deserted surgeon's locker room to find him. Larry was in front of his locker, his Canoe already lightly splashed, his fingers buttoning his freshly starched white shirt.

When he saw me, he didn't say anything. I couldn't stand it any longer.

"You know, Larry, everyone in the hospital knows about you and Abby."

He looked indifferently at me. "Oh, really? I suppose that's supposed to make me feel guilty or something."

I could feel my face getting red. "No, you can feel any way you want to. I just know what's going to happen to Abby. You're going to discard her like a used car when you're done." By this time he had his coat on.

"'Used car.' Funny, that's how she referred to you. Kind of like the Chevy to my Porsche." He was at the door. "You know, I haven't planked a woman as good as her in a long time." He winked as he left.

The next morning, they found Abby dead from a drug overdose.

No one ever questioned Larry about her death. Clear-cut suicide, the police said. A suicide note hinted at their relationship, but nothing specific. I wanted to tell the truth, but who'd believe me, the man scorned? I said nothing. At the funeral Larry stood with his wife Doris at the graveside, contrite and sympathetic. I looked at Abby's parents and wondered how they would have felt if they knew.

I had swung off I-35 and into downtown Minneapolis. At Park Street I turned right and headed to the county hospital. Of all the places I could hole up in Minneapolis, this was the one place I was certain where no one would look for me. I pulled up to the emergency room entrance and waited for the attendant to come out.

"What can I do for you?" he asked, hunkering down in his blue coat against the cold wind that was blowing across the parking lot.

"My brother was brought into the emergency room with a broken leg," I said, hoping there was someone in there with that diagnosis.

"Oh, you mean that car wreck from the interstate. He's inside, but don't worry, I understand he's going to be all right. Just pull into that lot over there." I swung into the lot as he raised the gate.

I walked into the emergency room with the car attendant directing me through the maze of people and desks.

"Walk back to the triage area and when you get there the nurse will help you."

I mumbled my thanks and walked back down the corridor. Just before I entered the emergency area, I turned left. The decor might have changed in twenty-five years, but the layout was the same. I ducked into the stairwell and double-stepped down to the basement level.

There used to be a set of on-call rooms near the operating room. They were still there. The hospital provided the facilities, but a lot of the residents never used them. Most of the time the specialists took call from home. I located the one that said *Head and Neck Surgery* on it, walked in, and locked the door. The room looked as if it hadn't been entered in months. Some things never change.

There were some scrub suits on the chair in the corner, a white coat hanging in the closet, and, most importantly, a telephone. I sat down on the bed next to the phone and lay back on the pillow just for a moment.

THE NEXT THING I KNEW I was looking at the clock on the table: seven a.m. I jumped up from the bed, went over to the wash basin, and looked in the mirror. I was a mess. My beard needed trimming, and I needed a shower. Most of all I needed something to eat. Everything for cleaning up was there. By the time I was done and into the scrub clothes, I felt like a new man.

I went to the door, unlocked it, and opened it a crack to look down the hall. No one. I stepped into the corridor. Just down from the on-call room was a table full of masks, surgical caps, and boot covers. I put a hat on and walked toward the cafeteria, coolly impersonating a member of the surgical team at Hennepin Community Hospital.

In the cafeteria I stepped in line, loaded up on scrambled eggs, bacon, and pancakes, and went over to a white Formica table in the corner and sat down to eat. There were a number of people in the room, doctors, nurses, and an occasional administrator. I tried to look antisocial, but apparently my famous charm played me false this time.

An older doctor came up to the table and sat down. "Mind if I join you?" he asked.

"Sure," I said ambiguously.

"Jack Torgenson. I run the vascular testing here at the county. I don't think I've met you before."

"Bernie Geoffrion. I'm new here. Head and neck surgery."

"New staff, huh?"

"Yeah, just filling in from the university."

"Well, we certainly need new people," he replied, opening up his newspaper. "The medical profession just isn't what it used to be."

"How do you mean?" I asked, between gulps of my breakfast.

"Doctors aren't the same. When I went to school, integrity, honesty and dedication were everything. Now look; doctors running from the law, murders, intrigue. What are we coming to?" he asked, as he shoved the newspaper toward me.

My heart sank. There was another story about me, this time in the *AMA News*. I briefly glanced at it. No mention of me on Independence Pass, only the predicament in Detroit. Versanti was leaving no media stone unturned.

"It really is a shame." I bolted down my scrambled eggs.

"It wasn't like that when I started. Everyone cared about patients. Now it's money, money, money. From the time these kids start out that's all they think about, Mercedes, fancy trips, and time off. That's the big word now, they want time off. To say nothing about their fooling around."

"What do you mean?"

"Promiscuity. I see it all the time around here. One of the surgeons has a girl with her own house in the suburbs. Everyone here knows about it. Fidelity doesn't mean anything anymore, and their wives know it. They put up with it just to get the pot of gold. The whole thing is crazy." Torgenson was working himself into a froth.

"You're right about that. That's why it's up to us to make sure they stay on the straight and narrow." I put my silverware back on the tray and got up to leave.

"Well, it was nice to talk with you. What was it you said your name was again?" he asked, casually peering over his thick glasses.

"Geoffrion." I looked at my watch. "You'll have to excuse me, but I have to run. There's a big case today, and I've got to keep my eyes on the residents and make sure they don't get into any trouble."

I left the table and put my tray back on the cleanup rack. Some things never change—doctors still bussed their own tables at the county hospital and residents still cheated on their wives. The only difference was that the wives hadn't taken it lightly. I had to talk to Doris Spencer again.

# CHAPTER 20

I WALKED OUT OF THE CAFETERIA and toward the operating room just in case Torgenson was watching. When I got to the end of the corridor, I headed back to the residents' quarters. Fortunately, there was no one there when I returned. After changing back into my street clothes, I sat down on the bed and picked up the phone. My call must have given Doris Spencer more excitement than she'd had in years.

"Ben, what the hell is happening? I've been reading about you in the newspapers and on the television. A couple of days ago we were having a discussion in a restaurant, and now they're talking about you like a convicted felon."

"Doris, I didn't kill Paul Versanti and I didn't kill Larry, but until I find out who did, I'll never be free. You might be able to help me unlock a mystery that started twenty-five years ago."

"How?"

"You really loved Larry, didn't you?" There was a moment of hesitation.

"What difference does that make?"

"The difference has to do with Abby MacKenzie." Another pause.

"Why her?" she blurted.

"Listen carefully, Doris. Do you remember any connection between Abby MacKenzie, Jeff Belender, and Larry?"

Another wait. "The only thing was a stupid joke that Larry told on the phone. I always remembered it because it was so out of character for Larry. He was always smooth. Always a gentleman."

"So? Larry fooled a lot of people. What are you getting at?"

"The joke was about Abby's rear end. Larry told Jeff Belender that she had a tomato paste ass."

"What does that mean?"

"You know, eight great tomatoes in that little bitty can. I never got it, but then there were a lot of things I never figured out about Larry."

"Did you ever ask him about the joke?"

"Yeah, he said he was talking about some nurse at the hospital that one of the guys in the residency was dating."

"Nothing else?"

There was a long pause. "One day I came across some old envelopes with the name 'Abby' written on them."

"Anything in the envelopes?"

"No, just envelopes with her name on them. The other odd thing was that they were dusty."

"Did he ever explain?"

"I asked Larry about the envelopes, and about who Abby was. When I did, he was silent. Then he snatched them away from me and tore them up."

"Did Larry ever talk any more about them?"

"He only warned me not to go through his things again."

"Did you have any inkling that Larry was having an affair with Abby at the time?"

"No. I didn't find that out until the day before she died."

"What do you mean?"

"She called the house. She said she was Abby MacKenzie, and that she was my husband's good friend."

"What did you say?"

"I remember it as if it were yesterday. I asked her what she meant, and she said Larry was sleeping with her, they were an item, and I should be prepared for whatever happened." That would have been Abby, all right.

"What happened?"

"I confronted Larry when he got home. It was the first and only time I ever saw him lose control. He started throwing things around and yelling at me."

"What did he say?"

"That he was doing it all for me and what more did I want?"

"Having an affair with another woman was doing something for you? That's a pretty strange excuse, isn't it?"

"You didn't see the wild look in his eyes. I thought he was going to kill me, so I didn't say anything. All of sudden he got quiet, as if he suddenly understood something clearly. He didn't say another word, just walked out of the house."

"I remember seeing you at the funeral two days later. I never would have guessed anything."

"Believe it or not, I still wanted to make it work between Larry and me. I tried for a while, but inside I couldn't stand it any longer. A few months after the residency was finished, I packed up my things and left."

"Given Abby's phone call to you, do you think Larry had anything to do with Abby's death?"

"The police investigated. As far as they were concerned it was a suicide. They found the bottle of pills and a note. A policeman who came over to the house the night they found her told me she'd confessed in the note to being in love with Larry, and that if she couldn't have him, she didn't want to live."

"Tell me, Doris, did you ever speak to Jeff Belender after Larry left the residency?"

"I never saw Jeff again. And that was all right with me. I didn't like his looks. He was the same kind of person Larry turned out to be."

I tried to think of something else to say. "I guess there's not much more to ask, is there, Doris?"

"I guess not. You now know everything about me, as well as something most people don't know."

"What's that?"

"That I never stopped loving Larry. Even two weeks ago, if he had walked through my front door and said he was sorry, I might have taken him back."

"Do you think I killed him, Doris?"

"When I first read the story in the paper, I wasn't sure, but now I don't think so. That's why I'm going to keep my mouth shut. Just promise me one thing."

"What's that?"

"Find the person who killed Larry. At least then I'll have some peace."

AFTER I HAD HUNG UP, I sat on the bed staring at the cement walls of the on-call room, wondering what to do next. My eyes cast around, looking for an answer. All I saw was the room, a kind of resident's prison cell, like the one in *Boys Town* or some other orphanage movie. It brought back memories. I had spent many evenings in rooms like this one, listening to the other residents vent their anger against the indentured servitude that was the residency. It was always the same; fifteen years of college, medical school, and residency, always under someone's thumb. For some the thoughts were vented, then brushed aside. For others, it was a small step from hostility to getting even. I thought about Larry. Maybe it had been in a room like this one that he had first met Jeff Belender and begun whatever unsavory association had gotten them killed and me on the run twenty-five years later.

I pondered that question as I made the bed, put on my jacket, and picked up my used towel to put in the hamper down the hall. If I was going to continue to stay here at night, I didn't want to leave any evidence that someone might notice during the day. I went down the corridor, dropped off the dirty linen, and headed back to the room. I stopped just before turning the corner when I heard voices. Peering around, I saw Ralph Torgenson and two security guards.

"I know it's the guy in the newspaper that the police are looking for. I saw his eyes."

"Just settle down, Doc. We'll look inside."

The two guards drew their revolvers and stood on either side of the entrance. At the count of three they broke in the door.

"It doesn't look like anyone was here, Dr. Torgenson. But we're going to call the police anyway. We don't want to be responsible. In the meantime, let's look around."

Torgenson and the guards started walking toward me. I dove into the linen cart, burying myself under the towels. I could hear them going from room to room, talking. After ten minutes, my cramped legs were aching. Finally, I heard one of the guards.

"You know, Doc, you come to us with these stories about doctors doing all sorts of things all the time. We keep checking them out. One of these times we're actually going to find something." I listened as their voices receded down the corridor.

Waiting for another minute, I extricated myself and warily walked down the corridor. My free ride at the county hospital was officially over.

Within minutes I was back in the fresh air, headed toward my car. The police would find my fingerprints before too long. They'd know I was in Minneapolis.

# CHAPTER 21

I DROVE TO NORTH MINNEAPOLIS. It WAS gang country, the toughest area north of Chicago.

As I followed East Hennepin toward Broadway, I thought about Larry again. What had he meant when he told Doris he was doing it for her? Maybe there *was* a deeper truth, one that *would* make Larry Burkinette come off better than he looked right now. Wouldn't that be just like him?

I remembered one time in particular when we were residents. A couple of interns were sitting around the table talking to Larry about head and neck surgery. By this time, I had learned to keep my mouth shut and listen.

"Dr. Burkinette," one of them said, "I can't believe you could do all that to a person's nose under local anesthesia."

"All technique," he replied. "You have to know where to put the anesthetic, how much to use, and when to reinject."

Hearing him flaunt his knowledge didn't do anything to salve my feelings. Maybe, I thought, he *was* a better surgeon than I was.

I tried extra hard that afternoon on the nose I was operating on. It was a difficult operation to remove infection from the sinuses. With a lot of bleeding, the surgeon always had the chance of blinding the patient. After putting the cocaine in, I slowly injected the nose. All as it should be for the first thirty minutes. Then the patient became more restless on the table. The anesthesiologist gave him more sedation. I winced at the frown she shot at me. Such signs of disapproval were becoming common when I performed nasal surgery.

I was about to penetrate the maxillary sinus when the patient suddenly shouted in pain, moving his head violently forward. With the instrument in his nose, I helplessly saw the instrument penetrate into his eye socket.

A cold shiver of fear went down my spine. A gush of blood started, and I could see the eye swelling immediately. If I didn't act quickly the eye would swell sufficiently to put pressure on the optic nerve; the blindness that would follow would be a permanent reminder of this operation for this poor patient.

"Nurse, hand me a tenotomy scissors!" I shouted. The nurse handed them to me. In one motion I swung the scissors toward the lateral ligament of the eye and cut the restraining tension that held the globe in place. By now the eye was red from blood inside the bony socket. Almost instantly the swelling started to recede as blood escaped into the surrounding tissues.

I remember both the anesthesiologist and the nurse anesthetist looking at me with a gaze which said that tragedy wouldn't nearly have occurred if Larry Burkinette had been operating.

My thoughts were interrupted by a garish neon sign, advertising a small, flea-bag motel: The Northern Light. Perfect for what I needed, halfway between the interstate and the gang-tough section of north Minneapolis. If I wanted to stay anonymous in Minneapolis, The Northern Light was the place.

I walked inside, afraid that someone might recognize me. I relaxed a little when I saw the desk clerk, wearing a long ponytail, thick glasses, and a nose ring. He didn't look plugged into CNN. I walked resolutely up to the counter. Even a place like this had a computer, though.

"You stayin' long?" he asked laconically.

"Maybe a day or two."

"More than one night gets you the executive rate."

"What's that?" I asked cautiously.

"Second night is half-off, the third night is free."

"What if I stay the fourth, do you pay me?"

"I don't know. I ain't never seen anyone stay that long. What's the name?"

"Abel. S. Abel." I spelled it for him, and he single-fingered the information into the computer.

"One hundred and nine dollars total, first unit on the left. The ice machine is right down the hall."

"Thanks," I mumbled, giving him the twenty-four-fifty in advance. Once in the room, I made for the phone. It didn't take me long to get through to Jeremiah Tolbert. This time I introduced myself as Lieutenant George Sennett from Detroit. I figured if I was going to jail, impersonating an officer would be the least of my crimes.

"Dr. Tolbert, I need some information about a person who would have been in your residency program in the early seventies. A Dr. Jeffrey Belender."

"What's all this interest in Belender? I just had someone else call from the damned alumni society. What do you want to know about someone I haven't seen in twenty-five years, and hope I never do?"

"We're investigating a murder. Someone in Detroit's been killed, and there may be some connection to Dr. Belender."

"I see. What is it that you want? I'm very busy right now."

"Dr. Belender was in your residency for a period of time, and then he left. Is that correct?"

"Not 'left.' He was fired. By me."

"I wonder if you could tell me why?"

"I can't. I'm under court orders to remain silent on it as part of a settlement with him when I kicked him out."

"Do you know that Dr. Belender is dead?"

There was a lengthy pause. "How did he die?"

"In a single car crash in Buena Vista, Colorado. It happened about two years ago."

"Then the gag order is moot, isn't it?" he observed.

"I'd say so, Doctor," I replied judiciously, as Sennett.

"Jeff was into drugs. That's why we fired him."

"Drugs? What kind?"

"Cocaine and some other stuff. You know, in the seventies people were experimenting with everything."

"What did he say when you confronted him with the evidence?"

"Nothing. He shrugged it off as if it was no big deal. Well, let me tell you, it was a big deal and that's why he's not on my alumni roster anymore."

"Second chances don't happen in medicine, do they?"

"Using drugs and being a doctor don't mix. There's too much at stake. Still, even I might have given him a second chance if he had shown some remorse. There was none."

"Dr. Tolbert, did Belender ever mention a doctor named Larry Burkinette?"

"Not that I can remember. Why?"

"Part of the case. When is the last time you talked to anyone about Belender?"

"Aside from that call a few days ago, the last call I got was from someone in a small community hospital out on the coast asking for a reference on him."

"Did Belender ever mention someone named Abby MacKenzie?"

"Was that the scrub nurse who committed suicide?"

I was surprised he remembered. "Yeah. That's the person."

"He never mentioned her from what I recall. But Belender wasn't the kind to get involved with troubled people requiring sensitivity. He was only interested in money. He always had the fanciest things, especially for a resident. Big car, nice clothes. He was better off than I was, and I was his professor. Until the drug thing I could never put my finger on what was wrong."

"My records show that he wound up being a plastic surgeon in California."

"You see? Making money off of other people's inadequacies. He was the worst mistake in judgment I've made in thirty-some years as chief of surgery. I never forgot it."

Fast cars, fast women, and big bucks. It sounded a lot like Larry Burkinette.

# CHAPTER 22

I UNDERSTOOD NOW EXACTLY HOW SIMILAR Belender and Larry had been. But what had driven them? Had it been merely their love of material goods, or did Belender share the same malignant competitiveness that impelled Larry, a cutthroat ambition that steamrollered anyone in his way?

Shortly after my fiasco in the operating room when the patient had nearly lost an eye, the residency chief held his morbidity and mortality conference at the department's Saturday conference. It was the monthly meeting that the department held to air its dirty laundry, discuss the problem cases, and try to find ways to prevent mess-ups from happening again.

When it was time to discuss the county hospital, I stood up to talk about my case. I didn't expect any help from Larry; none offered. I explained how I had screwed up the sinus case, almost costing the patient his eyesight. I remember that I had been more nervous than I had ever been.

Dr. Larson, the chief, was in the front row by himself; judge, jury, and executioner. He hid his feelings behind a set of bushy eyebrows and droopy lids that overhung his piercing eyes. The eyes held Norm Larson's character: they spoke of fairness, and compassion, and especially discipline. I had started to explain what had happened when he stopped me.

"Dailey, this isn't an inquisition. Slow down and explain in detail what happened. We all want to understand what occurred, so we won't make the same mistake."

"I don't understand it, Dr. Larson. I gave the anesthetic as I've always done, but I couldn't get it to work. The patient kept moving."

"Did you think of general anesthesia?"

"By that time, it was too late."

Larry spoke up from the back of the group. "Dr. Larson, I think I could shed some light on this problem." All eyes turned to the back of the room.

"I was present when Dr. Dailey performed the procedure. It's my opinion that the lack of anesthesia was more a problem of poor technique than anything else." I could feel my face redden as he spoke.

"Go on, Doctor," Larson said gravely.

"I've been watching Dr. Dailey for some time. This was not the first occasion that he has had trouble. My opinion is that he has a poor understanding of the anatomy. Because of that, he didn't inject both the infraorbital and nasal palatine nerves. If he had, I don't think what happened would have happened."

"Is this true, Ben?" Larson asked.

"I don't routinely inject that area for a procedure such as this." The chief studied me for a moment, almost as if determining my fate in life.

"Well, perhaps you should reconsider your technique. Potentially blinding a patient is something quite serious. I think before you do any more of these cases I would like to have you do a couple with either myself or one of the other staff in attendance."

As humiliated as I was, I was equally in shock over my reprieve. I had thought for sure that the old man was going to can me. But I would never forget the silent stares of the entire department as I returned to my seat. At that moment I hated Larry Burkinette more than I had ever hated anyone in my life up to that point.

In retrospect Dr. Larson's decision was the best thing that ever happened to me. I left the county hospital and went back to the university where I had a chance to spend some time working one-on-one with the greatest surgeon I had ever met. Instead of rebuking me, Norm Larson guided me through a number of operations. My technique turned around almost miraculously.

Life has strange twists, sometimes too strange to understand, sometimes more purposeful than we suspect. I had always suspected that Larry had a purpose in trying to get me canned. I'd never fathomed the reason. But somewhere the answer lay buried. I just had to find where. I picked the phone back up and dialed my pathologist friend, Tim Fenninger, in Detroit. I had one more question to ask him.

"You're the last person in the world I would have expected to hear from again," he said, his voice hushed but excited when I'd identified myself. "You're on America's Ten Most Wanted list. I figured you'd be long gone to some Pacific island. Do you realize I'm committing a felony by talking to you if I don't report the fact to the police?"

"Do you think I'm guilty, Tim?"

"Everyone knew you didn't get along with Larry."

"That's not what I asked."

"I've known you for a long time. Dedicated, passionate, angry sometimes . . . But, no, Ben, I don't think you could have done it. That's why I'm still on the phone with you."

"Will you give me a personal reference when I get out of prison?"

"Gallows humor—you were always one for that, Ben."

"Guilty as charged. But that's not why I called. Do you remember a few days ago, when I talked to you about Larry? You told me the hospital was looking into things he had done, Medicaid fee fraud for one."

"Right."

"What were the other things, Tim?"

"With Larry dead I don't think it will matter anymore. The hospital was looking into the possibility of certain possible illegal usage of drugs."

My heartbeat quickened. "What kind of drug usage?"

"Prescription writing."

"Did you have any facts?"

"A couple of people were picked up with some scripts for Percodan and Dilaudid. Huge quantities. Larry's name on the scripts."

"Not much to go on, was it?"

"It was a beginning. We'd had some suspicions of him to start with. Erratic behavior, a few patient complaints."

"What was the result of the investigation?"

"After he got served with the malpractice suit on the Versanti kid, he went into a shell. His caseload dropped, there were no more prescriptions, and no one cared anymore."

"Maybe they figured that with the lawsuit, justice would be served anyway."

"Probably. All I know is that he was an embarrassment that no one wanted at the hospital anymore."

How well I knew that feeling.

"That explains the crowd at his funeral."

"Huh?"

"Nothing. I was just commenting on Larry's popularity."

"Ben, the police have already called me."

"What do you mean?"

"They told me you might call."

"Go ahead. It's all right, Tim. If they're going to get me, it's not going to be because of you. The last thing I want is to make trouble for loyal friends."

"Thanks, I appreciate that. Just take care of yourself. I have a vested interest in you."

"Why's that?"

"You've got too much of my money. Back on the links when you've got this mess straightened out, okay?"

"Okay." I clicked the phone back down. I looked out the window at the gray sky overhanging the squalid neighborhoods of north Minneapolis. I wondered what it was to die and have only two women care. But in another moment, I was dialing my retired chief, Norm Larson, again. He sounded more subdued than the last time I had spoken with him.

"It's a shame what's happened to you, Ben."

"Obviously you've been reading the papers."

"I may be eighty years old, but I know better than to believe nonsense. What really bothers me is that it's all over Larry Burkinette."

"We were always like two freight trains on a collision course."

"That's not what I meant. Larry turned out so bad, and you're taking the heat. What a waste to have you get in trouble over him."

"Maybe it wasn't a waste after all. It's possible that some truth will come out of all this."

"Such as?"

"Do you remember that day in conference when he castigated me in front of the department?"

"As if it was yesterday."

"I always wondered why you didn't send me to Siberia. I saw you can residents for less. Why?"

"Maybe I just liked you."

"That wasn't it, was it? You had a fair play rule. Everyone got treated the same. I should have paid with an extra year. Instead, you took me under your wing and taught me what I needed to know. The reason for that was something to do with Larry, doesn't it?"

Pause.

"About that time, I was getting worried about Larry. It was before I found out about his lawyer business."

"Why?"

"He had too high a lifestyle, too much too quick. I liked my residents poor, self-sufficient, and determined. There was a cockiness about him that spoke of self-indulgence. When he spoke out against you at rounds, he broke one of my most treasured rules. I never respected a man who berated a fellow resident and tried to humiliate him. That's not to say I wouldn't have listened to him in private, but not in that way."

"So that's why you took me under your wing?"

"That's it. Now you can understand the magic of being an educator. I have you as living proof of my theory."

"I'm not much now, am I? Just another fugitive from the law."

"I have faith in you, Ben. I always have and always will. I wish I could have said the same for Larry."

"I know you said he did legal work for a lawyer in Minneapolis. Was there anything else incriminating that you knew about Larry?"

"I had a vague feeling that that legal business was a smoke screen for something even worse. But I could never prove anything, nor did I really want to. By the time he finished I was just glad he was gone. Not that I didn't have some regrets sending him out as one of my graduates. But then I couldn't prove anything."

"And now Larry's dead and there's nothing else to tell." I heard my defeat in my voice even as I felt desperation twist in my gut.

"What are you going to do now, Ben? Go to the police and turn yourself in?"

"Maybe. But let me check one thing with you before I do. Do you remember any rotation that Larry and a resident named Jeff Belender worked together?"

"Not offhand. Sorry, Ben."

"Is there any way you could find out if they ever had any rotations together?"

"Sure. I'll call my old secretary and ask her. They have all the records in the hospital. Where are you going to be?"

"Nowhere you can reach me easily, Dr. Larson. How about if I call you back in half an hour?"

"Make it an hour. I'm older now and don't move that fast."

"I'll call you then."

I spent the next hour at the diner down the street, wolfing down the blue plate special and watching a couple of Chicago toughs mix it up with some Native American youths on the corner. A few packets were passed, a few dollars exchanged, a little bit of swagger exhibited on both sides.

When I called Norm Larson back on the phone, he sounded excited.

"I got what you wanted, Ben."

"You mean they did cross rotations at some point during their residencies?"

"Yep, and in an out-of-the-way place."

"Where was it?"

"Stanfield State Penitentiary."

# CHAPTER 23

STANFIELD, MINNESOTA, WAS AN UNLIKELY SPOT for a state penitentiary. If you talked to most people in town they would talk about the scenery, the drive to Taylors Falls along Highway 95, and the town's history as a logging center. But the logging days were long gone, and now, if you pressed the locals, they would grudgingly admit that along with manufacturing and tourism, the state penitentiary was the town's main employer.

In spite of this admission, Stanfield State Penitentiary remained an anomaly, because out of something bad, something good had emerged. This was nowhere clearer than in the infirmary it housed and the university residents who staffed it. To these young physicians it was a place that evoked both a primal fear of being in a prison environment and a heady sense of finally working, for one moment, on their own. For their part, the inmates conditionally accepted their fate as the recipients of inexperienced care from young residents trying their best to learn their trade. Stanfield housed some the most hardened criminals in the state, prisoners with long memories and quick justice. On the wrong inmate, a resident's honest mistake would usually bring an instant request for transfer by the resident.

As Larson had said, Stanfield was an unlikely location to find Jeff Belender and Larry Burkinette together, two materialistic and socially unconscious residents whose idea of public service was throwing their empty champagne bottles in the trash can. I could just see them leaving the prison now, smirking in disgust as they brushed its dust off their camel-hair sport coats and got into their fancy cars.

But then I had hated Stanfield too. Simple fear. Just the thought of the metal gates slamming behind me gave me a cold shudder. At present the prospect seemed far more real than my self-created fears. But right now, I had no choice. If Stanfield was where the paths of the two men had mysteriously crossed, then that was where I was going.

I drove north and east on Highway 36 from Minneapolis. The countryside hadn't changed much in twenty-five years. A few subdivisions had crept up on the farmland since I had last been there, but that was all. For that matter, the prison hadn't changed much either. Same dark brick front, same unimposing building overlooking the St. Croix River. It was my guess that the inmates hadn't changed much either.

As I drove there, I wondered how I was going to find whatever it was that I was after. Any connections I might have had with the people who worked there were probably long since defunct. What could anyone tell me about two people who hadn't been there for so long?

It wasn't until I turned off the expressway, through Oak Park Heights, and down Highway 95, that I remembered Joey Dunbar. A trustee on life sentence. He'd told me once that he kept stealing just so he could get back into the yard. It was the only place he could ever call home. I only hoped Joey was still there.

I drove past the building one time and then circled down the frontage road to make sure I wasn't being followed. The whole idea of going back in was giving me the creeps. With the entire country's police force on the lookout for me, I couldn't believe I was walking into a prison.

A feeling of *deja vu* enveloped me as I parked my car in the same lot as I had my '66 Chevelle so many years before. Now that I was back it didn't seem so long ago. I slung my cap low over my forehead and raised up the collar of my coat. The surveillance cameras that focused on me as I walked in would have had a hard time matching me up to the photo that had graced almost every daily newspaper in the country.

I walked up to the information desk, a wire-enclosed office with a uniformed woman sitting before a number of television monitors. No more Leon from 1972, no more bulging muscles. The power of electronics had far outweighed brute force.

"I'd like to see an inmate named Joey Dunbar." When I said his name, the guard blinked.

"Joey? You've got to be kidding. He never gets visitors."

"Well, he's got one today. Is he available?"

"Sure. Sign in on the registration list and I'll tell him you're here."

I signed the name "T. Sawchuk," then waited. I wondered if Joey had ever heard of the greatest goalie ever to wear a Red Wings uniform.

In a few minutes a gray-haired man, slightly stooped and moving slowly, shuffled over to the visitors' booth. When he saw me, his wizened face twisted slightly, as if he recognized me. But the remembrance seemed only momentary as he sat down behind the bulletproof screen. Reaching for the desk in front of him, I could see his hand tremor, as if rolling something between thumb and forefinger. It was the classic roll-a-pill tremor of Parkinson's disease.

"Joey," I whispered hoarsely. "It's me, Ben Dailey. Remember, the head and neck surgery resident you used to play football with?"

There was another slight grin of recognition, and the shaking of his hand seemed to increase. But nothing came out of his mouth except some garbled words I couldn't understand. The guard watching from a distance must have noticed, because she came over.

"Try and write to him," the guard said. "It's the only way he understands. If he understands, he'll nod his head or try to write back." I picked up a piece of paper in front of me.

*It's been a long time*, I wrote. He grimaced a smile. Saliva ran from the corner of his mouth.

*When did you start getting sick?*

He held up his right hand with his left and showed me five fingers.

"Five years ago?" I asked out loud. He nodded.

"Are you taking medicine?" This time, when he shook his head, he shrugged his shoulders as if to say, *What's the use?* I picked up the pencil again and began writing.

*Joey*, I wrote, *I'm trying to find out something about two doctors who worked out here, back around my time. One was named Burkinette and the other named Belender.*

At the mention of the two names his face tightened in recognition. He picked up the pencil, held his right hand at the wrist with his left, and started scribbling almost illegibly. When he was done, he slid the paper through the slot in the window. I picked it up and tried to decipher it. After a couple of minutes of straining the only word I recognized was "dust."

"Something 'dust,' Joey?" He nodded his head in frustration.

"There was something bad, wasn't there?"

He nodded and grunted again. It was apparent to me that I wasn't going to get anything else out of him. I felt as frustrated as he.

"I understand, Joey. You want to tell me something, but you can't. Don't worry, I'll find it out. There's one thing for sure, I'm happy I got a chance to see you again. Remember our last football game?" He smiled.

"Even in college I never saw anyone lay out flat for a catch like the one you made. My old coach would have loved you." I was about to get up and leave when he started grunting once more. He reached for the pencil and scribbled something again. I looked at the paper and couldn't understand the words. But I didn't want to make him feel worse than he already did.

"I understand what it says, Joey, and I'm going to follow up on it." This time, as I stood up, I could see the gleam back in his eyes as he feebly raised his hands to wave. I put the papers in my pocket and turned to leave.

"Thanks, Joey. You take care," I said. I felt sad. I knew what was going to happen to him. Maybe he did too.

As I was walking out of the interview room, the guard stopped me.

"I don't know how you know Joey, but I want to thank you for coming. I haven't seen him that animated in years. Most of the time he just sits around and stares off into the distance."

"I was just passing through the area, so I thought I'd see him. His father used to work for my dad in California back in the sixties," I lied. "I knew him for a brief time back then. Kind of a family favor to see him."

"Well, whatever brought you, I'm sure it helped Joey. He's been a trustee here for years. Most likable guy you'd ever want to meet. He just couldn't make it on the outside."

"You see many people like that?"

"Occasionally, but none as nice as Joey." I was getting uneasy over my prolonged conversation with the guard, so I turned to leave.

"Well, listen, I've got to run. Thanks very much for your help."

"You're welcome," she answered. "You know, your face is familiar. Haven't I seen you somewhere?"

"I doubt it. But I get that response from a lot of people. I just have one of those faces, I guess," I mumbled.

"Probably so," she gave me a cheery leave-taking.

I walked down the hall without looking back at the guard. Once out of the door, I turned right, around the corner, and waited. Something told me that the parking lot wasn't where I wanted to be right now.

Sure enough, in a couple of minutes the guard came out the door with a man in uniform and walked across to the cars. They looked around for about ten minutes and then began writing down license plates. I waited in the cold for about twenty minutes, until they had finished writing down the numbers and returned to the building.

When they were back inside, I made my way deviously to my car. I got back inside, started the engine, and pulled out of the lot. About a hundred yards from the prison there was an employee parking area. I drove in, found an open space, and maneuvered between two cars. As I eased out of the car I looked around. There was no one around. I took my Swiss Army knife behind the car next to me, ostensibly looking for something on the ground. I got on my knees and deftly removed the license plate. I exchanged it with the one on my car.

As I drove out, the visitor parking lot was swarming with policemen. I saw one standing at the edge of the sidewalk, checking out the license tag on my car. When he saw that it didn't match any on his list, he turned away. My heart was beating at twice its normal rate as I reached Highway 36, heading back to Minneapolis.

I needed to calm down, so I pulled into a roadside diner near Pine Springs. It was one of those family restaurants where they serve a hundred items off a laminated menu. If you order eggs, you're all right.

I ordered three, poached in a cup, and some dry toast and tea. My nervous stomach couldn't take anything else. While I was waiting, I pulled out the scraps of paper that Joey had given me. I turned them upside down and sideways, trying to decipher the message. All I could see on the first one was the word "dust." On the second I couldn't make out anything for a while. My eyes lost focus. Then, all at once the word seemed to come clear. I realized what Joey had written.

I jumped up from the table, went over to the pay phone, and dialed information. When I'd got the Stanfield Penitentiary number, I called and asked for the employment office.

After telling them I was from Social Security, looking into the records of an employee to increase her retirement benefits, they were only too happy to help me locate her. Within a few minutes I had the address and phone number of Marge Frederickson, the name on the second piece of paper, and the head nurse at the Stanfield infirmary when I was a resident.

# CHAPTER 24

THE NOOSE WAS TIGHTENING. Police cars were everywhere. But right now I had to meet with Marge Frederickson.

If she had made a connection between me and the creature of the headlines, it wasn't apparent when I talked to her on the phone. She seemed weak and preoccupied, but happy to hear from me nonetheless. I made an appointment to see her that afternoon.

Marge's house was a neat single-story brick bungalow near the Lake of the Isles. The front had a gabled entrance, like a lot of houses built in the late fifties. The low shrubs struck an even border on either side of the raised cement porch. I wasn't surprised. Marge had always been an orderly type of person.

What did surprise me was how Marge looked. She came to the door dressed in a floral housecoat and padded slippers. Her washed-out blond hair looked frowzy, there were dark circles beneath both eyes, and her skin had the sallow look of someone who had spent too much time inside. I wanted to tell her how good she looked after all these years, but I had done enough lying for one day. It didn't matter, she let me off the hook.

"I know I look terrible, Ben. I've been so sick lately."

"You were always the picture of health, Marge," I said, crossing the threshold of her house.

"'Was' is the key word. Too many cigs and not enough self-control. It's gotten worse in the last couple of months. Come on in and we'll sit in the living room." As she moved forward, she released a couple of deep, throaty coughs that seemed to issue from the bottom of her toes.

"Are you sure you're all right?"

"Just a passing thing. I'm going to be okay. The doctor says I just need a little treatment, that's all," she wheezed as she collapsed into a large easy chair in the front room of the house.

I looked around for a moment. The living room turned out to look just about like Marge: papers on the floor, furniture askew, and a breathing machine next to her chair. She must have noticed my look.

"Don't mind about the mess. I've just been a little too tired to clean up this morning." She paused a moment to catch her breath. "I don't understand how I could go downhill so fast. I know I had some emphysema, but the doctors say my vital capacity has dropped considerably over the past few months."

"Emphysema can be a tough disease."

"You're right about that. But that's not why you came here after all these years, is it?"

"I need some information, Marge. Information that might mean the difference between life and death for me." She wrinkled her nose and furrowed her brow.

"Life and death?" She coughed spasmodically for a few moments, then recovered herself.

"I'm in some trouble, and it revolves around a resident you used to know."

"Who?"

"Larry Burkinette. Do you remember him?" I studied her eyes closely as I mentioned his name. She blinked a few times.

"Larry? Of course I remember him. How strange you should mention his name. What happened?" Marge must have been too sick to have read the papers.

"You know I haven't kept up with much of anything, Ben. My doctor is this close to putting me in the hospital." She held her fingers about an inch apart as she spoke.

"Was there ever anything peculiar about Larry?"

"In what way?"

"I'm wondering if you know anything about him and a resident named Jeff Belender?" At the mention of Belender's name, I could see her frown.

"The gold dust twins."

"'Gold dust? What's that supposed to mean?"

"It means that those two rich boys led charmed lives. They were two of a kind."

"Did you ever have any problems with them at the prison?"

"They were two of the most popular doctors we ever had out there. The inmates got along well with them. Always joking, telling stories. I'll bet every inmate had seen them for one thing or another during the time I was there."

"That must have been some clinic."

"Not really. Those two boys had 'private practice' written all over them. They knew how to move patients in and out. Treat the symptom and move to the next one."

"Was there any other kind of problem while they were there? Maybe with another official?"

"Only the infectious disease audit."

"What was that?"

"Before they left the rotation, Jeff and Larry had called my attention to a series of infections they had noted while operating out there. Whenever a doctor raises a question like that, the state mandates that we do an audit."

"What happened?"

"I retired before the audit was completed so I never found out. You know the bureaucracy. It takes them forever to complete anything."

"Why's that?"

"Forms, regulations, and the ACLU. They've got everyone breathing down their necks to make sure nobody is being treated unfairly." She had another coughing fit. I waited until she regained her composure.

"Even prisoners?"

"Even prisoners, especially prisoners like Johnnie Willson."

The name struck a faint chord of remembrance in my mind. "Who was he?"

"Johnnie Willson was the Big Chief. Sioux Indian. He was the highest profile prisoner we had in Stanfield when I was there."

"What did he do?"

"He shot and killed a Bureau of Indian Affairs agent who was investigating a string of bank robberies that occurred in and around the reservation near Bemidji. They found the agent shot with a steel-tipped arrow through his heart."

"Sounds a little like cowboys and Indians."

"That wasn't the worst of it."

"What do you mean?"

"According to his file, Willson scalped the agent and hung the scalp outside his cabin like a trophy. It took the jury in Minneapolis thirty minutes to find him guilty. If they'd had the death penalty, he would have gotten it. Instead they gave him life with no parole."

"Under the circumstances I would agree, wouldn't you?"

"Sure, except it's too bad they couldn't execute him."

"Why?"

"The prison became another reservation for him to terrorize. The inmates were frightened to death of him. He was the gang leader; he ruled the place with an iron hand."

"Mr. Congeniality."

"He got his."

"What do you mean?"

"He died after surgery."

"At the hospital?" Familiarity was stirring my memory.

"Yeah. It was one of the cases we reported to the state."

"Did they ever find the cause?"

"I never found out. My mother got sick about that time. I took a leave of absence that turned permanent when I had to take care of her. After she died, I never went back. I was getting prison burnout anyway."

End of story. And I was no farther ahead than when I'd started. I could feel the jail house chill in my bones. Marge began coughing again. I took it as my cue.

"I appreciate the help, Marge," I said, getting ready to leave.

"I'm glad to see you. I get so few visitors. Since my mother died, I haven't had much company." She hesitated a moment. "What ever happened to Larry and Jeff?"

"They both died."

I could see her face pale. "How?"

"That's the sixty-four-dollar question. Belender died in a single car crash in Buena Vista, Colorado, and Larry died violently in Detroit."

"Violently?"

"Shot in his car outside his house."

"Maybe it's dangerous to have worked at the prison," she muttered, agitated.

"Why?"

"Two people already dead, and I've got one foot in the grave."

"Come on, Marge, you don't believe that, do you?"

"I wouldn't, except for some phone calls on my answering machine that I've gotten over the past few months."

"From whom?"

"That's just it. They could have been from almost anyone, except I thought I almost recognized the voice."

"What did they want?"

"The man on the phone said his company was doing a survey and wanted to know how my respiratory therapy equipment was working." She held up the card of the company on the table next to the machine.

"Sounds straightforward enough."

"It was, except for the voice. It seemed so insistent. Not at all like a person doing a boring survey."

"Did you check with the respiratory therapy equipment company?"

"That's what's even stranger. They claim they had no survey in progress."

"Maybe it was some kind of crank call," I said reassuringly.

"You know, I believed that until you came and told me those two are dead."

"What's the connection?" I asked.

"I don't know." As she spoke, she reached inside the drawer of a small table next to her chair and pulled out a microcassette tape cartridge. Her hand shook as she held it out to me.

"Ben, when you were at the prison you used to do some research on voices, didn't you?"

"Sure, but I'd have to have a sample to compare a tape against to be sure what I'm listening to."

"You're my only hope," she entreated. "This is the tape from my answering machine. It's cued up to the message. I'm going to give this to you. See what you can do with it. I can't help but believe there's something more than a co-incidence going on here." I took the tape, not knowing what I was going to do with it, and rose from the sofa opposite her. Hopelessly, I asked my last question anyway.

"Marge, what did Johnnie Willson die of?"

"You mean the septicemia?"

I nodded. "More specifically, the organism."

"It was something strange. I can't remember the name, but I remember filling it out for the state report."

"Does *Acinetobacter calcocetious* ring a bell?"

Marge snapped her fingers weakly. "That's it. How did you know?"

My head was reeling. "Just a lucky guess."

"I don't believe in luck," Marge said, her face turning even more ashen than before. She launched into another fit of coughing. The doctor in me said she was too sick to be home. I felt guilty leaving her there, so I went and got her a glass of water from the kitchen. When I got back, her jag had almost run its course. I handed her the glass.

"I've got to run, but if I find out something I'll call. In the meantime, you should call your doctor. I think you should be in the hospital."

Dead end. I'd said it before, but this time I was really here.

On the walk back to my car I experienced a feeling of suffocation from the gathering avalanche of deaths. It was time for me to come out from the cold and get help before I became one of the victims. The only question was, get help from whom? Not Jordan. I had to keep her out of this. Not Gus—he'd done too much already. Not Sid—I didn't want him singing the blues on my account. And not Lieutenant George Sennett, my erstwhile friend. No one.

It looked as if I could only depend on the kindness of strangers.

As I sat in my car I pondered my options. None of them looked good. Give myself up to the police? Not a chance. With my face plastered on newspapers all over the country, I figured I'd have as much chance of getting off as Lee Harvey Oswald.

Anyway, after I'd been spotted at Stanfield, they would be narrowing the net. It was just a matter of time until the police found me. Then what would I do? Tell them the story of how five people had died, three from *Acinetobacter* and two from other causes? No. The police had all the proof they needed: the murder weapon that killed Larry Burkinette, a motive, and my fingerprints on a dead man near Aspen.

I had to keep moving. But to where? *Think and don't panic.* It was getting harder. There must be a common thread that tied all of these crimes together, but how could I find it? I'd run out of leads. Or had I? I had to go over it one more time.

Johnnie Willson had died of *Acinetobacter*. So had Paul Versanti and Francine Watkins. That was the connection. I had to either explain it now or spend the rest of my life in prison thinking about it.

Norm Larson had always told me that the more difficult the problem, the simpler the solution.

I started writing down a timeline of what happened. Belender's patient died of infection. Belender died a few months later. Paul Versanti died of the same infection;

Burkinette died a few months later. The common thread was the bacteria. Almost a harbinger of the surgeons' deaths.

Someone trying to make sure Belender and Burkinette remembered Johnnie Willson. But why?

A link was missing. Whatever it was, it led back to Stanfield. I desperately wanted to go back and talk with Joey again, but how would I get in?

It was close to eight o'clock before I came to the realization that driving around was going to get me nowhere. More precisely, it was probably going to get me stopped by the police. So I changed license tags with yet another car. I hoped I had just bought myself another day.

I pulled into the drive-through of a nearby Burger King and bought the double Whopper with cheese, extra fries, and a chocolate shake. In my present state, death from cholesterol overload seemed more desirable than going to prison.

When I was done, I headed back to the Northern Light Motel. I headed straight for my room, locked and chained the door, then collapsed on the bed with my clothes on. Not even the gangs on the corner, the sound of motorcycles roaring down the street, or the thought of Johnnie Willson could keep me from going to sleep. Everything might be clearer in the morning. It might.

I WOKE UP ON TOP OF THE COVERS to see the sun streaming through the window. Pulling back the curtains, all I could see was the reassuringly empty parking lot, with only my car still there, ready.

It took about twenty minutes in the shower until I felt refreshed enough to get dressed again. Another twenty and I was at a restaurant, inhaling my eggs, toast and bacon, ruminating about Johnnie Willson. My night's sleep had not changed my intuition—the answer to what was happening to me was related somehow to his death twenty-five years ago.

I drove back to the main university library for a search through old newspapers. The *Minneapolis Herald* would have carried Willson's trial.

I parked my car in the metered area in front and made it up the stairs into the brick-and-glass structure unnoticed. Once inside, I found the periodical stacks, a good place to hide as I started my search again.

I punched up Willson's name on the computer and six pages of articles came up. Obviously, in Minnesota he'd been big news. I skimmed a few of the earlier ones. They described Johnnie Willson and his grisly crime; most of the facts were the same. Then came the in-depth sociological articles, describing his absent drunk father and the poverty-stricken condition in which his mother had tried to raise the family.

Finally, the editorials began. First came the hand-wringing liberals. What had we done to create a Johnnie Willson? Wasn't there a place in society for everyone? These were followed by the just-retribution activists, claiming the death penalty should be enacted. All of it sounded pretty empty when he had been dead for so long.

I looked at his photograph and tried to remember his face, back in my days at Stanfield. Nothing came to me.

I stared out the window at the leafless trees hanging over the campus commons. Johnnie Willson had been a heinous criminal. Known fact. Johnnie Willson had been killed by an *Acinetobacter* infection similar to that killing the patients treated by Belender and Burkinette. But *Acinetobacter* didn't kill the two doctors. Systemic infections with an organism like *Acinetobacter* are uncommon. Jeannette Wilkins at the Center for Disease Control had told me that. Now I had three cases indirectly involving three people who may have been in contact with each other twenty-five years before.

What was it Marge had said? There'd been an investigation by the state on Willson's death, hadn't there? Something of that magnitude ought to have made the papers somewhere.

I checked the periodical scanner again, this time under "Minnesota state prison system." It sounded logical, but finding an article was a little harder. No one but me seemed to think an infectious disease outbreak in a state penitentiary was newsworthy. I did find one reference, a small notation in the *Stanfield Sentinel*. The librarian showed me the microfiche, and I pulled it up under the screen.

It was just after I had left the residency program. A mention of an investigation and review of policy by the state on healthcare within the prison facility. It was the result of an eighteen-month study of the prison infirmary. The review indicated a breakdown in common health care practices. It also mentioned punitive action against several inmates. The source quoted was a Mr. Harold Pilkington, Assistant Director of the Minnesota State Correctional Facility.

I found the article, but finding Harold Pilkington after would be a different matter. I went into the hallway outside the library and started dialing. I assumed my best bet would be to call back to Stanfield Penitentiary. This time I introduced myself as a reporter doing a story on healthcare in the prison system. That got my call forwarded to the administrative department. It wasn't long before I was talking to Phyllis Garnett in the Office of Prison Management.

"Harold Pilkington?" she asked. "I haven't heard his name for ages."

"Oh, is he retired?"

"About ten years ago. He was one of those people who was old when he was fifty. He just waited until he had thirty years and then left. The receptionist told me you're a reporter, is that correct?"

"*Minneapolis Herald*. I do freelance work."

"What do you need from Harold?"

"I'm doing a piece on healthcare in the prison system. I know he had some problems back in the seventies, and I wanted to interview him."

"Well, knowing Harold, he would love to talk with you. He always had a sense of being unappreciated as a public health official."

"Do you know where I could find him?"

"Sonesta Key, near Clearwater, Florida. Harold sends us a card every year around mid-February just to rub it in. It's like an office joke." There was a moment's pause, "Here's his number."

I wrote it down, thanked her, and dialed the number. This time it was a while before someone answered. A tired, whiny voice.

"Mr. Pilkington?"

"That's me."

"My name is William Gadsby. I'm a reporter for the *Minneapolis Herald*. I'm doing a piece on healthcare in the Minnesota prison system, and I know you were involved in that field a while back."

"Don't tell me that after all these years the press is finally going to ask my opinion about something?"

"It was clear from my research that you were one of the prime movers of prison reform at that time," I humored him shamelessly.

"Tell that to my bosses. All that work, all that time consuming work, and no one cared. Just swept it under the rug."

"In what way?"

"We found one of the worst prison situations in America and no one wanted to report it."

"I don't understand."

"I thought you said you'd investigated the situation and knew who I was."

"Yeah," I stammered, "but there were so many things left out that I couldn't find all the answers. That's why I called you."

"Well, let me tell you, Mr. Gadsby, it was one of the best pieces of public health and criminal investigation ever seen in the Minnesota prison system, if I do say so myself. And the most beautiful thing was that it was all based on the scientific principle. Do you have any idea how much trouble there is getting information in a prison? How many things happen that are never reported?

"No," I mumbled. Was this going to be a cruel waste of time I didn't have?

"There are sexual assaults, beatings, and robberies. It's a cauldron of hate and fury just waiting to bubble over. And the people there are the sociopaths we all never want to see again."

"What happened exactly, in the case you studied?"

"It was unheard of, diabolical. It involved the use of bacteria to exact revenge on a convict named Johnnie Willson."

"I don't understand."

"The inmates ran the infirmary—"

"Wait a second. I thought the hospital was run by Marge Frederickson and the doctors."

"You see, believing that was everyone's mistake, including Marge. It was a false impression based on appearance and Marge's demeanor. She was a dominating figure, strong, forceful, tough. From what I understood she could have snapped some of those inmates in two. I think Marge actually believed that no one would cross her. In reality the inmates were conning her. They were the ones who ran the infirmary. They had access to the laboratory, the operating room, the wards. They could do anything they wanted."

"Do you know Marge?" he asked suddenly.

"I've met her recently. She seems pretty sick from emphysema."

"I'm really surprised. I didn't know her personally, only interviewed her once or twice, but from what I saw she was the middle linebacker type—healthy as a horse, could walk through brick walls, that kind of thing. She'd be the last person I would think would develop some chronic illness."

"Maybe, but she doesn't look too good now. She claimed she left the prison to take care of her mother and started smoking out of nervousness."

"From what I heard, my bet is that she picked up the habit from some of the girlfriends she hung around with. No man screwed around with Marge, if you know what I mean." He laughed. Then, he stopped abruptly. "You'd have had to know Marge to appreciate the joke." I had to agree, most men didn't stand up to her well.

"I take it that Marge knew nothing about what was done to Johnnie Willson."

"I think that to the prisoners she was only an obstacle to their plan, and they were just glad she was out of the way. For them it was prairie justice."

"Justice for what?"

Pilkington paused for a moment. "You know, Mr. Gadsby, in some ways I can understand why they did it."

"Oh?"

"Have you read about Johnnie Willson?"

"Yeah."

"Then you know he was one of the meanest bastards ever to walk the yard."

"I don't have a lot of experience with prisoners, but just looking at what he had done, it seems that there couldn't be too many people worse."

"That's an understatement. Johnnie Willson was a walking, talking nightmare. In one way or another he had harmed almost every prisoner who was ever at Stanfield. He was too tough. No one had the guts to stand up to him except those inmates in the infirmary."

"Stand up to him. How did they do that?"

"Let me ask you a question. If someone presented you with an instrument in the operating room and handed it to you, how would you know if it was sterile or not?"

The question struck me like a thunderbolt.

"I guess I couldn't if it looked clean."

"Exactly. That's what everyone said. But I proved it."

"How?"

"Koch's postulates," he said condescendingly.

"What's that?" I said, trying to sound dumb. Most of the time, it was with no great effort.

"See, that's what everyone else said. When I tried to explain it to them, they all walked away. Koch's postulate is the cornerstone of all bacteriology. It forms the basis for discovering and diagnosing all kinds of bacteriological infections."

"And you used this tool to determine how the infection was being passed around?"

"That's right. Those inmates were arrogant enough to leave packs stored in the cabinets with 'sterile' written on them. We just took them down and cultured the bacteria out."

"What did you find?"

"It was a process of elimination. There were only so many sources of infection for a patient. The instruments were one of them. No one else bothered to look."

"And that's where you found the bacteria?"

"It turned out that the inmates were using infected instruments. Instruments that they had purposely inoculated with bacteria."

"What did you do once you had determined that?"

"The warden brought the bastards to trial. Before a judge, as I understood it. Each one of the prisoners got another ten to twenty years."

"I take it they killed Johnnie Willson?"

"That's right, the Big Chief himself. They fed him some tainted food to produce symptoms like appendicitis. Then the attending residents from the university were called in. From what I heard, they were so anxious to operate and get experience that if there was a choice to perform surgery or not, they always chose the surgery. Once they made the incision, it was all over for Willson."

"Murder by proxy. What a way to die."

"It was ingenious, actually. Looking back, it was probably the only way they ever would have killed him."

"Did you ever isolate what the bacteria was?" I asked, for appearance's sake.

"*Acinetobacter calcocetious.*"

"Did you ever culture it from the inmates?"

"You're not as naive as you sound, Mr. Gadsby. They were all negative."

"Then how did you get them convicted?"

"That's the beauty of it all. The packs were enough. We could show by the scientific method how we traced exactly who handled the instruments from start to finish. It had to be only four inmates. They were the only ones with access."

"Did any of them confess?"

"Never. They all remained silent."

"This is fascinating. Did you ever publish your findings?" There was an angry silence at the other end.

"I tried, but no one would ever accept my results, because the state bureau of prisons wouldn't support me. They didn't want the public to know that inmates were running the prison infirmary. I was just one lonely guy with a master's in public health. Such meager credentials didn't cut it with the hotshot medical journals."

"Do you remember the names of the inmates, or do you have them written down?"

"How could I forget them? Ray Graywolf, Charlie Featherstone, Frank Strong—all Sioux Indians—and then Angel Martinez."

"I know it was a long time ago, but do you know where they are now?"

"A couple are probably still in prison. Maybe they're out. I don't follow the case. No one appreciated what I had done. No one wanted to hear about it. It was an election year, and the governor didn't need a scandal tainting his campaign. He'd had enough problems with his womanizing and drinking."

"So you packed your bags and left."

"That's right. Thirty years and out. It was the best thing I ever did. I play golf and collect my pension. I'm done in the arena of public service. I don't even care if someone publishes my work. I'm too old for any glory."

"Maybe if the newspaper takes this piece, you'll be famous," I lied compassionately.

"It wouldn't make any difference. The only thing you can't make up in life is time."

I knew the conversation was ending. "One last question. Did you ever know of two doctors named Belender and Burkinette? They were residents from the university who worked at the prison as part of their rotation."

"I never heard of them. We might have interviewed them, but that was all. They all said they didn't know anything. And that was the strange part, because the nurse who reported the incidents insisted that she got her information from an anonymous note that some of the doctors who worked there had left."

"Why anonymous?"

"You sound pretty smart, Mr. Gadsby. Figure it out for yourself. If you were a doctor who saw something wrong happening and it was committed by a convicted felon, would you want to leave your name as the stool pigeon?"

"I guess you're right. Did anyone else in the prison know about these note-writing doctors except Marge?"

"Somehow the inmates had heard about it. When I did my interviews in the prison, they mentioned that revenge would be taken. Standard posturing, of course. How could they ever find out the author or authors of an anonymous note?"

"Did you ever mention the revenge threat to the prison officials?"

"Sure, they acted true to form. No one listened, no one cared."

"Did the inmates say how the revenge would come?"

"No. I don't know how. One thing for sure, it wouldn't be pleasant."

"Why do you say that?"

"Because of the paintings on the wall after the sentencing. Three arrows in red pointed at the ground."

"What's that mean?"

"It's a Sioux Indian sign the prisoners used when they'd declared vengeance on someone."

"What does it mean?"

"'A slow death to my enemy.'"

# CHAPTER 25

RAY GRAYWOLF, CHARLIE FEATHERSTONE, Frank Strong, and Angel Martinez. The four horsemen of the apocalypse, and the fatal connection between Larry Burkinette and Jeff Belender. I had everything: motive, revenge, method—death by inoculation. Belender and Burkinette must have been the doctors who turned in the murderers of Johnnie Willson. And they'd never known the inmates were after them. Or had they?

I was convinced now that my theory that the *Acinetobacter* infections was a warning was correct, a cruel attempt to intimidate. The only question now was whether Burkinette and Belender had known it was the same bacteria that had killed Willson.

Their strange behavior in the months before their deaths, attested to by their wives, suggested that they'd been so informed. But that wasn't proof. I needed proof.

Proof could only come from the four inmates. Somehow, I needed to find them. But going back up to the prison was out of the question now. Instead, I'd have to find out where they had gone. I called the prison.

At first I'd planned to make four separate calls to Stanfield, each time asking for an appointment with one of the four inmates. But even I, rapidly growing proficient in deceit to support my status as a vocal expert, couldn't vary my voice enough to make that one pass. I decided to take the direct approach with the prison administration.

After making a couple of calls I found out that Helen McNamara was the administrator in charge. I used the Pilkington line about working on a story about Indian prisoners.

"What is the story about, Mr. Gadsby?" she asked.

"I'm interested in the four inmates who were sentenced to extra time for deliberately infecting another inmate in the infirmary." I gave their names. She recognized them instantly. She also grew chilly and distant. As Pilkington had said, it wasn't a story Stanfield wanted in a major newspaper.

"Did you have anyone in particular that you wanted to talk to?"

"I'd take any of the four, for starters."

"Well, you're going to have a hard time talking to Frank Strong. He died inside four years ago, a stabbing incident. The other three were released after time served."

"Any idea where they may be?" I asked hopefully.

"Once the inmates are released, we have no obligation to keep tabs on them, unless they commit another crime." My heart was sinking.

"I guess that ends the chapter. They could be anywhere," I said numbly. The administrator must have taken pity on me because she started speaking again.

"While I don't have any record of their whereabouts, I can tell you that many of the Native Americans that we've had in Stanfield have gone to the Twin Cities, especially to north Minneapolis. That's where I would look if I were you."

I called information. Nothing registered until the operator came to Charlie Featherstone. Miraculously, he was listed. I nervously wrote the number down and then prayed that he would be in. After a few rings a tired voice answered the phone.

"Mr. Featherstone?"

"Yeah, that's me. Who's this?"

"My name is Dailey, Mr. Featherstone. Ben Dailey. I used to be a doctor at Stanfield Penitentiary when you were there. It's very important that I talk with you." I waited breathlessly for a reply.

"There was a young man named Dailey who used to come by and do some crazy voice testing on us. Is that you?"

"One and the same."

"What could you possibly want with an old, broken-down Indian like Charlie Featherstone?"

"Something that could save my life."

I waited another few moments. "What do you want?" he repeated.

"I need to meet with you and ask a few questions," I pleaded.

"I don't see nobody at my house. But there's a gin mill on the corner of Thirteenth Avenue Northeast and Washington, just before the railroad sidings begin. It's called the Yard's End. You buy ol' Charlie a couple of boilermakers, and I'll meet you there." I thankfully agreed to meet him there at four that afternoon.

I left the library invigorated. I'd made more progress than I had ever dreamed of. Maybe I wasn't done for yet. All I had to do was talk with Featherstone. I was sure it would lead me to an answer.

I walked out of the library and back onto the street. I saw two or three cops huddled around my car. I had forgotten to put money in the meter. One of them looked up and pointed at me.

That was it. I was trapped. My throat felt as tight as if the noose were drawing close around my neck.

I ran back into the building, bursting through the door past two startled female students, running toward the rear exit. Looking back, I could see the police converging from everywhere. I slammed through the door and stumbled into the outside courtyard, still under construction. As I closed the door behind me, I could hear the alarm reverberating through the building.

Frantically, I looked around and found an old two-by-four from the construction on the ground. I jammed it under the handle, just in time to hear the police beating on the door.

The police had not yet cordoned off the back of the library, so I ran toward the corner, making it to the bus stop shelter at the corner just as a squad car rounded the library. I tried to remain calm, my pulse racing as I hunched down into my coat, praying no one would see me. Where was a bus when you needed one?

After what seemed an eternity, I looked down the street to see the bus coming. Would it get here before they found me? I had an almost irresistible urge to make a run for it, but fear of being seen kept me in the enclosure. Soon three other police cars showed up. By this time the foot patrolmen were fanning out across the university campus, getting closer. The bus pulled up. I loaded onto the downtown collector just as four patrolmen turned the corner.

The bus took off with my head below the window, panic gripping my body. Without wheels I was dead. And I had to meet Charlie Featherstone and talk to him.

The bus dropped me off at First Avenue and Fifth Street, and I quickly made my way to the series of overhead skywalks that connect the skyscrapers of Minneapolis. It was a maze, and I had to use it to hide.

I went to a small cafeteria near the Dayton-Hudson's store and sat in the corner. I bought a roll and coffee, and picked up a discarded paper on a table, hiding behind the newsprint while I tried to collect my thoughts. First off, I saw my picture again. This time the press speculation was that I was in the Twin Cities area. Articles and stories about the death at Independence Pass covered the front page. Reading wild lies about myself made my skin crawl.

I looked over the paper and saw several policemen at the entrance to the skywalk. In my haste to run I had only trapped myself.

There was a leather shop next to the cafeteria, one of those teenage places that sells motorcycles jackets, baggy pants, combat boots: what Generation X called "alternative." The place was staffed by young salespeople with earrings inserted into every orifice of their bodies. If anyone would be oblivious to me, it would be these mystifying teenagers.

I put my paper down and walked unnoticed into the shop. It didn't take me long: leather jacket, turtleneck, dark glasses, and a watch cap. I paid for it with my own credit card, figuring that by the time they ran it through I'd be dead, captured, or resurrected. The salesperson, a girl of twenty with punked hair, motorcycle boots, a nose ring, and black tights, gave me a strange look as she rang up the clothes. I didn't blame her—I had a hard time recognizing myself.

I started walking back down the skywalk, looking for an exit to the street. I had gone through two buildings when I saw police running from everywhere. That girl hadn't been as naive as I had thought.

I took the first escalator down into the lobby of the Radisson Hotel. Ahead of me I saw the street exit, and, maybe, freedom. Until I saw two more uniformed policemen standing at the tall revolving glass doors. I turned back slowly, looking for another way out. The police were everywhere.

One more turn and I ducked into The Norseman Bar. The lunch crowd was gathering. I tried to disappear among the people standing at the bar, but I quickly realized that I couldn't just stand there and hope to remain unnoticed. I saw the piano in the corner.

I went up to the bartender.

"I'm the afternoon player."

He looked at me, bewildered. "We haven't had a guy play the piano in weeks."

"I don't know, man. I was told to show up here and do an afternoon gig."

"Well, help yourself," he shrugged.

I went over to the piano, took off my hat, but left my glasses on. Cool, after all, is cool.

I started off with my Duke Ellington medley, looking up at the crowd, scanning the people for police. I got a pleasant applause after the first set. Then I hit into my Brubeck routine. Too bad I didn't have a sax man. Still, it wasn't too bad. The applause was a little better. By this time, I could see the police going through the bar systematically. I kept my head down and played.

By the time I had done the Basin Street, St. Louis, and Garden City Blues, the place was jumping. The drinks were flowing. I don't think I've ever been so nervous when playing. My set went on for over an hour. The little glass on the piano must have held fifty dollars by the time I was done. The cops were gone, empty-handed.

I went over to the bar for a Diet Coke, exhausted.

"You can sure play, mister," the bartender praised while pouring me the drink.

"Thanks," I replied, eyeing the crowd carefully. As I did, he extended his hand.

"Fred Ortega. I work the day shift."

I stuck my hand out in return. "Marty. Marty Pavelich," I replied. "Is there a back way out of here?"

"Sure, through the kitchen and down the stairs. Why, are you afraid someone didn't like your music?"

"No, it's just that I promised my girlfriend I'd meet her outside. She doesn't like my gigs. She thinks I should be doing something more productive at my age. I told her I'd meet her for a drink here. I just want to come in the front."

"Just go through that door and head straight back." He pointed to two swinging doors at the side of the bar.

I made my way into the kitchen, trying to walk slowly past the pots and pans, dishwashers, and steaming ovens. At the back of the kitchen was a small door. I pushed it open and immediately I was in the back alley of the hotel. There was a linen truck waiting to leave. No one was looking. I scrambled into the back and hid among some bags of laundry. Ten minutes later I heard the truck jolt forward. I was going somewhere.

That "somewhere" turned out to be a twenty-minute ride. When the truck finally stopped, I crawled out from behind the bags and peered around the back door of the truck. I was in a parking lot. A big sign announcing Twin Cities Cleaning was staring me in the face.

I jumped down from the back railing and looked around. Fortunately for me there was no one around. I walked out of the yard and onto the street. The afternoon traffic whizzed by me as I strode down the street with my head down, my cap pulled low. The crossed street signs ahead said Old Shakopee and Cedar Avenue, adjacent to a U-Haul sign. I knew exactly where I was and what I needed.

When I left U-Haul, Charles Whittingdon had rented a small pickup to move some furniture to his new apartment. I swung the vehicle out onto Cedar Avenue and down the expressway entrance ramp. I was on the road again and back in business.

I drove my truck down I-94 and then onto the I-35. I looked at my watch. I had twenty minutes to meet Charlie Featherstone.

A couple of construction zones and the beginning of the rush hour extended my trip to thirty minutes, before I crossed the threshold of the Yard's End, in an old brick building with the sign of a locomotive over the front door. It was not far from my motel, in the heart of the roughest neighborhood Minneapolis could provide, a place even the cops left alone.

I parked the truck in front, wondering if it would still be there when I got out. I should have worried more about whether I would get out of the bar. I entered through the single wooden door. My eyes tried to adjust to the darkened light. After a moment I could see half a dozen men dressed in Levi's jackets, worn jeans, and cowboy hats, with ponytails hanging across their shoulders. As I walked in, they glanced up at me. High cheekbones, aquiline noses, swarthy complexions. The Yard's End may have been a railroad man's bar, but the only customers were Native Americans. The glances they shot at me said that the welcome mat was down the street.

I walked up to the bar to speak with the bartender, but six men blocked me. Their faces were sullen and stoic. It was obvious that if I wanted anything here, I was going to have to fight my way through them. And, what with one thing after another, I didn't feel quite up to it.

I was just about to say something when a thin voice rose out of the corner. "It's all right, Buck. He's here with me." I turned around to see an old man in a booth. At his words the men turned back to the bar. Considering the alternatives, it didn't take much for me to accept the invitation.

I walked over to the scarred wooden bench and sat down across from him. There was a dim light over the table, so that I could see the white hair and weather-creased face of a man in his mid-seventies. It was the face of a man who had seen the hard side of life.

"Are you Dailey?" he asked. I nodded.

"Charlie Featherstone," he said flatly without shaking hands.

"I'm glad you could talk to me, Mr. Featherstone."

"Charlie," he said, waving for the bartender to come over.

"Okay, Charlie. You want a drink." He nodded and gave the bartender his order, Old Crow and a Bud. Club soda was fine for me. As I ordered I could feel him studying my face.

"I remember you. Nice young man. Always had your tape recorder and papers. You said you loved studying people's voices. I remember that."

"That seems like a lifetime ago. Now I'm a nice old man."

"No, *I'm* an old man. You still have your life in front of you. For me it's over," he said sadly. He waited a moment and started again. "Now what is this about saving your life?"

"After I left the prison, an inmate named Johnnie Willson died." The mention of his name made Featherstone's eyes flash. He may have been old, but the youth-giving spark of anger still lingered in his eyes.

"What about him?"

"I'm not sure. I never knew him, but it's clear to me that his death has something to do with the recent deaths of several other people."

"Like who?" he asked.

"Two patients have died from a rare bacteria. I'll spell it for you. A-C-I-N-E-T-O—"

"*Acinetobacter calcocetious*," he replied quickly, his eyes blazing with recognition.

"How did you know that?"

"I might be an old Indian, but I'm not stupid, Dr. Dailey," he said gruffly.

I apologized humbly. "I'm sorry. I should have realized you would know, considering the case and the trial."

"It's what got me another fifteen."

"Were you involved in Willson's death?"

He eyed me unblinkingly. "How could dragging up something that old help you?"

"I've been accused of something I didn't do. The police think I was somehow involved in the deaths of two people, one of them infected with the bacteria." I could see him studying me closely, as if determining whether I were worthy of his time. After a couple of moments, he shrugged his shoulders.

"What could anyone do to me that they haven't done already? Yeah, I helped, but Ray and Angel, they're the ones who did it."

"What happened?"

"What happened? I'll tell you," he replied, lifting his shot and downing it as if it was my club soda. "Johnnie Willson deserved to die, and any extra time I spent in Stanfield was worth it. What he did to Angel, Ray, and Frank ruined their lives anyway."

"How do you mean?" I was afraid I knew.

"What did you think Stanfield was, play school? We were criminals and that was our home. Forget that the government stuck us on the reservation, isolated us from the rest of society, then threw us a few dry bones. Guys like Frank, Ray, and Angel tried to break out of the mold. When they got caught, they were just three more no-good Indians."

"And Johnnie Willson was the boss."

He pushed his drink away. "Mister, nobody is my boss," he flashed. "I am a Sioux. My father's father fought at the Little Big Horn. I have pride." He pointed his bony finger defiantly at his heart. "Johnnie Willson tried to take that pride away. He could dominate physically, but he could never take our pride away."

"What did he do?"

"What do you think he did? Initiation rites, he called it. Always in the laundry room. Always the young men. He and his gang would drag them into the back, strip them naked, and use them like some common whore. First Willson. He always got the first try at the virgins. Then his buddies. He always used the same routine, so it was like a staged play.

"He'd take a knife from his pocket and hold it up to your neck. Then he'd rip open your shirt and stroke your chest with it. Back and forth. Then he'd say, 'Well, what do we have here,' in a sissy voice." Featherstone imitated a travesty of a lisp.

"Then he'd pull down your pants, throw you on the laundry bags, and fuck you in the ass. It wasn't sex. It was domination. The worst kind. He tried to make slaves of my blood brothers. And we are nobody's slaves, do you understand that?"

I nodded. After a minute of charged silence, I ventured, "How could another Indian do this to you?"

Featherstone spit on the floor in a show of disgust. "Indian. He was no Indian. He was a fucking half-breed who conned his way onto the reservation. He was a lowlife who cared nothing about our heritage. But in the end we got him." Featherstone crooked the corner of his mouth as he spoke.

"What did you do?"

"It was really Angel and Ray. They had the smarts, especially Angel. He was one clever Indian. All I did was set Willson up for them." He smiled as he said it.

"How?"

"I worked in the kitchen. I gave him food poisoning with some spices we used on the reservation and made it look like appendicitis. Indians know a lot—roots, herbs, that kind of thing. My grandmother taught me. Once we got him in the infirmary, it was all Angel and Ray's job. We knew the residents would operate at the drop of a hat. They wanted the experience. When they got him on the table, everything was in place."

"How did they inoculate Willson?"

"Through the surgical instruments. Angel had cooked up a broth of bacteria. He dipped the instruments in it, dried them, and then put them in sterile packs."

I had heard Harold Pilkington's theory, but to hear it as a fact made my skin crawl. How could a surgeon tell if a simple surgical instrument was sterile? I hesitated again before I asked my next question.

"Did you ever have any contact with a Dr. Jeffrey Belender or a Dr. Larry Burkinette?"

His dark eyes lit up like coals on fire. "What about them?"

"Both of them were killed recently. Prior to that, both of them had patients who died of *Acinetobacter calcocetious*."

He smiled and raised his fist in the air. It was a strange but stirring gesture, like that of a victorious fighter standing over his opponent.

"As I am a son of Sitting Bull, I bless the spirits who bring honor on our tribe."

"How did that bring honor to you?"

"We did what we had to be done, to get rid of Johnnie Willson. The spirits will acknowledge our justice. The prison authorities said we'd left other packs with bacteria sitting on the shelf. There were never any other packs, just the ones that we used that day."

"Are you saying that Belender and Burkinette set you up?"

"I learned one thing in prison, Dr. Dailey. Every crime has a cause. Remember that." He seemed to drift off into his own thought for a moment. "He said he was going to do it and he did," he repeated.

"Who said?" I asked casually. I think he realized he had said too much. A certain calm came over him.

"I had been waiting for a call from someone like you for five years. I never knew when it was going to come, but I knew it would. I am an old man and my health is not the best. I can now rest in peace, knowing that honor has been brought back to my blood brothers."

"What honor?" I asked again.

"The honor of the death of my enemy. Why do you think I agreed to meet with you today? I had not heard the news until now. The rest of me is silence."

"I respect that, Mr. Featherstone. But I hope you will answer one more question for me. There was some graffiti on the prison walls after you and your friends were sentenced. It showed three red arrows pointing to the ground. What is its significance?"

A smile creased the corner of his mouth. It was a cruel smile, the smile of satisfied revenge.

"I will say no more. I can rest in peace knowing what you have told me." He pulled his gaunt frame from the booth and ambled toward the bar to sit among the younger men around him. It was a signal to me, and I knew it. I had a short time to get out of there.

I went back outside and walked to the rental truck. There was a tall, muscular Native American standing by the door. He was my guard, I knew it. Without him the vehicle would have been long gone. I nodded my head, got in, and quickly drove off.

I drove past my motel, to the expressway exit. The sight of the restaurant near the entrance ramp made me remember my hunger and the fact that I always did my best thinking when I was eating. I pulled the truck around back, walked in, and sat down at the counter.

Running from the law or not, nobody seemed to notice me. Such places were used to the nameless, nondescript people who came through the doors. I was only the latest. I ordered the special: turkey with mashed potatoes and gravy, a side of canned corn, and a coffee. A regular Thanksgiving Day dinner. I'd better get mine now. Who knew where I'd be when Thanksgiving came?

Three red arrows pointing to the ground. Each arrow had to mean a person, unless it was some kind of Indian symbolism similar to the Father, the Son, and the Holy Ghost. Looking in Charlie Featherstone's eyes, I knew that the only thing that had driven him was revenge. My theory was that the first two crossed arrows were for Belender and Burkinette. But there remained that third arrow. For whom?

Pilkington had mentioned three people in the infirmary: Burkinette, Belender, and Marge Frederickson. She had been as healthy as a horse and now, to my medical eye, she was dying of emphysema. And then there was the tape . . . .

I reached into my shirt pocket and pulled out the tape, along with a piece of paper. It was the first scrap of writing Joey Dunbar had given me. I looked at the tape for a long while as I ate my dinner. Something on it might tell me whether the murderer was stalking Marge. But how would I recognize it? I sat there staring at my plate, hoping for a miracle of wisdom.

Nothing came to me. I was about to get up from the counter when I looked again at Joey Dunbar's note. Suddenly it made sense. I could have sworn it said, "angel dust."

# CHAPTER 26

THE DRIVE BACK TO THE NORTH CENTRAL UNIVERSITY MEDICAL SCHOOL seemed familiar enough to me. From a distance it looked almost as if I hadn't left my residency yet. The buildings I remembered were still there, now surrounded by a series of low-rise and high-rise structures atop a hill overlooking the Mississippi River. The whole complex, nestled amongst the university's main campus, was dominated by The Main, as University Hospital was called.

As I got closer, I could see key differences I had missed, such as the new genetics center and the building for gerontology and oncology, but the clinic and research areas were still in place. They'd better be, because without them I didn't have a prayer.

I parked my U-Haul in the visitor lot and walked over to the clinics building. It was past closing time, and most people had left. I suppose if I had been walking into the hospital wing someone would have stopped me, but the Speech and Language Pathology Department was hardly a high traffic area, no more than a sideshow in the theater of medicine.

I tried the door. It was open. One more look around, and I stepped inside. No one was there, only a lab full of equipment—perturbation machine, electroglottography, videostroboscopy—and, there in the corner, the Relco spectrography machine. It was an upgraded model, but basically the one I had used as a resident to make my early voice studies.

I sat down in front of it and turned on the switch. The oscilloscope was there, the only difference was the digital readout. After I got the machine on, I looked around for a tape recorder. On the desk was a small handheld recorder. I slipped Marge's cassette in and listened to the voices. A couple of women's voices, then a man's voice.

"Hello, Mrs. Frederickson, this is Mr. Fernandez. I don't know if you got my previous message. I'm doing a survey for Reliable Home Medical equipment. I'm calling to see if your equipment is working correctly, and whether you are feeling better. I will call back later." Innocent. Except that the equipment company denied making the survey.

I needed a steady state voice, a single diphthong word. I played the tape again and found the word "got." It would have to do.

I cued up the tape and put it back in the machine. When I isolated the word, I played the tape again and activated the spectrograph. Within a minute a graph came sliding out of the machine. I studied the tracing carefully. Everything was there; the dark horizontal lines signifying the formants or harmonic ranges of the voice, the individual frequencies of movement of the vocal cords, and the breathiness. It was a pattern specific to this voice. No one else in the human race had one exactly like it.

I flicked the machine off and was about to get up when I heard a voice outside. I froze. Where could I go? The door opened. In walked a young man in a white lab coat, probably in his mid-twenties.

"Excuse me, can I help you?"

"Just the repairman. Dr. Eddington called me in from Relco."

"Funny, I just used the machine, and it worked fine."

"I agree. I didn't find anything either."

The young man shrugged his shoulders. I picked up my spectrogram and was about to walk out when the man called me.

"Say, wait a minute." I froze.

"You forgot your tape." He held it out to me. I smiled weakly.

I walked out into the hall and turned toward the center of the hospital, to the medical library. A couple of minutes later I was in the stacks, picking up the article I'd written years ago, "Analysis of the Human Voice Using Spectrography."

I walked with the volume under my arm to the library table. As I sat down and opened the book, my hands were shaking. I almost didn't want to look as I pulled the spectrograph from my pocket and compared it to the tracings on the page, all of them of inmates at Stanfield State Penitentiary twenty-five years before.

I compared the tracings until I came to number fifteen. At first glance it appeared to have the same formants and frequencies. I held them next to each other and looked at it more closely. They were identical in every way. I went back to the table and matched the number to the name. Number fifteen: A.M., Angel Martinez.

My first reaction was to call Marge Frederickson and warn her. I left the book on the table and went to the outer lobby to call, but there was no answer.

I put the phone back on the hook, wondering what to do. I couldn't wait. I had to see her.

It took about fifteen minutes to drive to her place. By the time I got there I was really on edge, especially when I saw that there were no lights on.

I pulled up to the side of her apparently deserted house. Either Marge had left in a hurry, or something had happened.

I went to the side door. To my surprise it was open. I was momentarily frozen with indecision. Finally, I rationalized that Marge *had* left the door open, hadn't she?

It was totally dark. Any light that went on would be a beacon for a neighbor who might be watching. I took a chance and turned on the small hall light. Immediately the place lit up, almost startling me. I was in a small vestibule leading into the kitchen. I called out, but there was no answer.

My first instinct was to find Marge. I turned on a small light in the living room. Her chair was empty, her respirator next to it. There was a card from the medical equipment company with someone's name on it taped to the machine. I looked at it for a moment, then walked out to the hall.

I went up the stairs, switching on the light as I ascended cautiously. No sound, no movement. I called out once more. Again, no answer.

This time I moved into the bedrooms and checked each one out. Beds made, nothing disturbed. Nothing appeared unusual. I went back into her bedroom. There was a large double bed against the wall. On the dresser were several pictures of Marge and another woman, smiling and hugging, on some Caribbean island.

Next the basement. I went back down the stairs slowly, turning off the lights as I went. I had seen the stairs to the basement in the entrance hall, so I made my way there and turned on the lights.

I felt trapped as I walked down the narrow staircase and into the low-ceilinged room. In one corner was a washer and dryer and a workbench. There was a couch and a TV, pictures ringing the wall. More vacation photos of Marge and her friend. Luxurious getaways for someone living on a nurse's salary. I looked at the other photos of various people, mostly hospital types from the look of them.

As I stepped closer, I noticed one frame was broken. Looking down on the carpeted floor, I saw the several scraps of the torn photo. I laid them together on the table in front of the couch. Two doctors with white lab coats, with Marge. The faces of the doctors had been cut out.

The air in the basement suddenly became cold and claustrophobic. I wanted to get the hell out of there as quickly as possible, but the compulsive side of me took over; I checked out the closets and the small furnace room. Again nothing.

A feeling of relief flooded over me as I bounded up the steps and back into the back hall. I walked into the kitchen, somewhat at a loss.

Most things seemed in order, except for some plates in the sink. The kitchen table was clean. A few notes on the Formica counter next to the phone: a couple of names that meant nothing to me, and her doctor's number.

The only thing I hadn't pried into was her trashcan. I remembered George Sennett telling me once that it was the place where most of the evidence in a case could be found.

The container was under the sink. I pulled it out and looked. Nothing in there but a few empty cans of one of those protein drinks, and a few napkins. The gleam of glass at the bottom caught my eye. A small vial marked "Bronchosol." The vial was empty and clean. Bronchosol was a common expectorant used in respiratory machines. I looked at the label more closely. In small letters at the bottom was the inscription "A. C. – 11/96."

I stood in the middle of the kitchen. I had no idea where Marge was. I certainly couldn't call the police. I was about to leave and try to sort out my thoughts when I heard the outside door open.

"Hello?" a female voice called out tentatively.

"I'm in the kitchen," I managed to choke out. Whoever it was, I might as well face her. Besides, she probably had my truck blocked in the driveway.

A slim woman of about forty-five or fifty appeared in the doorway. I recognized the blond short-cropped hair and freckled face: the woman in the picture in Marge's bedroom. She stood with her left hand on her hip. In her right was a .38.

"Okay, stand against the wall, feet apart and hands behind your head. And if you don't think I'll use this, just check with my self-defense instructor." Her voice was calm and firm. I had no doubt she was telling me the truth.

I assumed the position. "Okay, now tell me who you are," she demanded.

"Reliable Home Services," I lied. "I'm here to pick up some respiratory equipment." The moment I said that, the woman relaxed.

"Oh, because Marge is in the hospital?"

"Yeah, you know how insurance companies are. Cost savings and all that."

"I suppose. Do you have some kind of proof?" She still had the gun next to her.

"Well, a company card's taped to the machine. Would I know that if I was a burglar?"

She walked into the living room backward, the gun still pointing at me. "Follow me inside until I see."

We walked in. She untapped the card from the machine and examined it.

"Okay, Mr. Sanchez, is that right?"

"No, Sanchez couldn't make it tonight, so I'm filling in for him." She handed me the card. I slipped it in my pocket without thinking.

"Okay, just checking. Sanchez is the guy who usually comes out. If you had told me that was your name you would have been dead meat." *Like I always say, honesty is the best policy.* She put her revolver back in her bag.

"You know how things are," she half-apologized. "Two women living alone. Minneapolis just isn't like it used to be."

"You shouldn't have left your door open, I guess."

"We usually leave it unlocked because the respirator people come so often. The EMS unit must have left it open. I just found out Marge is in the hospital."

"Are you a friend of hers?" I asked.

"My name is Sharon. We've lived together for almost twenty-five years." She said it almost defiantly, as if her lesbianism was a challenge to me. When I didn't bite, she went on. "Say, do you guys always drive U-Haul trucks?"

"We've had some breakdowns recently. That's why I entered the way I did. It would have meant another day's rental, another trip out here, and a lot of bitching from my boss." I said it fast, hoping she wouldn't question the sufficiency of my motive to violate company rules and the law by entering.

"Well, we had a deal with Sanchez, but I don't like just anyone coming into the house like that. I'm going to call your company in the morning and complain."

"I'm certainly sorry, ma'am. Well, I've got to pick up the equipment and make my next stop."

"I hope there's someone home at the next place. You do this with someone else, and they might shoot you for breaking and entering."

"I never thought of it that way. I'm new on the job, and I'm anxious to make a good impression." I guess she felt sorry for me, because she came over to help me collect the equipment.

"Sorry I'm being so bitchy," Sharon said. "It's just that I'm so upset about Marge. I hope they can help her."

"Did the doctors say what was wrong?"

"She had been coughing a lot. She started running a fever yesterday. That's when her doctor decided to send her over to the emergency room. Then they admitted her. They told her she had an infection of some kind in her lungs."

"Oh, yeah?" I said, unplugging the unit from the wall and rolling it down the hallway. "What hospital did they take her to?"

"Methodist."

I stopped for a moment and looked down at the cloudy fluid in the humidifier.

"I'm sure they'll fix her up," I replied absently.

"You know, your face is familiar. Haven't I seen you somewhere before?"

"Most people tell me that. I just have one of those faces, I guess." I lifted the machine and made for the side door.

"People tell me that too," Sharon shrugged. "I'll back my car out so you can leave."

I waved to her as I backed out into the street. She waved back. I felt sorry for her. Marge Frederickson was her partner, just like man and wife. I knew how I would feel if something happened to Jordan. Jordan! She'd been like an ever-present vision in my mind over the last few days and nights. I wondered if I would ever see her again as a free man.

I drove back through the Lake of the Isles. The moon on the water was tranquil in the still night. Postcard-perfect for the Chamber of Commerce. Come live in beautiful Minneapolis, home of friendly people and safe streets. Safe for all except Marge Frederickson.

A fever and progressive lung disease in an otherwise healthy female. It didn't make sense in someone like Marge. I thought about Paul Versanti, Francine Watkins, and Johnnie Willson. They'd been healthy too.

The vial, the inscription, and the fluid in the humidifier of the respiratory machine fused in my mind like a lightning bolt. A feeling of panic came over me. It couldn't be that Martinez was this close.

I sat in the cab of the U-Haul and turned on the light. I wanted to call Reliable Home Services and find out about Mr. Sanchez, who made regular and unannounced visits to see Marge. I pulled out of my pocket the card Sharon had handed me. I noticed something on the back. I turned it over. Three red arrows pointing downward, two of them crossed off.

# CHAPTER 27

ANGEL MARTINEZ WAS HERE. Somehow, he was going to kill Marge Frederickson, and I had to stop it.

I pulled up to the Northern Light Motel and parked the U-Haul truck in an empty space under the parking lot light. My mind was so focused that I didn't pay any attention to the unobtrusive vehicle near my unit. I opened my door to George Sennett, pacing, and Jordan, sitting on the bed.

Before I could react, Jordan leapt up and embraced me. She was crying against my shoulder.

"It's all right, Jordan. I'm not dead yet."

"You sure look like it," Sennett growled.

"Looks can be deceiving." I was trying to size up the situation.

Jordan backed off for moment and smiled at me as she wiped the tears from her face.

"The Production Line for the Red Wings. It took me a while to figure that one out. Gordie Howe, Ted Lindsay, and Sid Abel. You knew I would track you, didn't you?"

"For a Jeopardy junkie like you I figured it would be easy. Besides, hell hath no fury like a woman with a computer."

"A computer and a list of all the motel and hotel registrations in the country. I followed you from Duluth, to Buena Vista, Colorado, and back here to Minneapolis. When you came to S. Abel, I knew that's where you'd stay."

"I just didn't figure you'd bring the cops with you."

"I'm off-duty and out of my jurisdiction, Ben. Jordan made me promise that before I came. Anyway, you don't really think I believed all that crap in the newspapers, did you?" George Sennett grinned at me from the chair in the corner where he had dropped after Jordan's embrace.

"You could have fooled me. You and your colleagues have been chasing me over three states."

"What the hell are you talking about? I had you followed to the Holiday Inn. For your own safety. Period. No other tail. The only thing I've been doing is covering your ass with my captain, hoping you'd show."

"What about the guy following me through Grosse Pointe?"

The lieutenant spread his palms open. "You're letting your imagination run away with you, running halfway across the country. What do you think this is, some spy novel?"

"It might as well be. When you tell me you found a murder weapon on my boat, that doesn't exactly make me feel warm and fuzzy."

"Trust me, Doc, this is police work. I tried to tell you on the phone, but before I'd finished you had hung up on me. The weapon and where it's found don't always match up."

"I suppose you told that to the guy following me in Grosse Pointe after I hung up on you?" Sennett shook his head in exasperation. "Listen, Doc, believe me, it wasn't my people. If I'd wanted to, I could have gotten you any time I wanted." Just as I'd said to myself more than once.

"Yeah, well, what about the police chasing my ass through airports and major metropolitan areas like Minneapolis? I didn't imagine that." He held his palms open on his lap.

"I guess I'm going to spend the rest of the day trying to convince you. As far as the Detroit police are concerned, the Burkinette matter is an internal affair—that means it's still under investigation. All that other stuff is about the Independence Pass business. What happened there, anyway?" I could feel my conviction waning.

"What about all the stories in the media?"

"Thank Robert Versanti. He had decided you were to blame, and he was going to get justice, his style. There was nothing we could do. It's his First Amendment right. The guy's a jerk," Sennett replied. "Since then, the Colorado angle's given your story a life of its own. When this is all over, Versanti'll be eating crow. Maybe you'll even have a lawsuit."

"I think Versanti'll have had enough misery already, especially when he finds out his son was the innocent victim of a revenge killing."

"What?" Sennett asked alertly, all cop again.

"Larry Burkinette was killed by an ex-con named Angel Martinez."

"For what reason?"

"I'm not totally sure of the reason, but Burkinette and another resident named Jeff Belender set up Martinez and three other inmates to take the rap for a prison murder."

"You'd better start at the beginning, Ben."

It took about an hour as I filled Sennett in on what had happened. He looked at me with wonder as I described my travels and what I had found out. When I finished, he stared at me closely.

"Doc, you ever listen to the Doors?"

"Sure. It was my music, man."

"Remember the line, 'the future is uncertain but the end is always near.'"

"'Roadhouse Blues.'"

"That's it. The more I hang around you, the more I think that's the motto of your life. It's the perfect philosophy for being a detective."

"Lieutenant, there is the one thing I am sure of. I want to leave the gumshoe work to you."

"I'm not so sure the police could have done all that you've done."

"Let's not forget we're not done yet. Angel Martinez and probably Ray Graywolf are still on the loose, and I think they've got one more victim to go. There were three red arrows drawn on the wall of the prison, remember? Each for a person. The killer has crossed off two, but one remains."

"Who is that?"

"Marge Frederickson. She was the head nurse in the infirmary. Somehow Martinez believes she's implicated in his conviction and wants to get even."

"What's your proof?"

"This woman was relatively healthy except for a mild case of emphysema for which she took breathing treatments at home. About a month ago she grew increasingly short of breath. The doctor told her it's her emphysema and ordered more breathing treatments. When I went out to the house, I found a vial in the trash can with some lettering on it. It read A.C. – 11/96."

"What do you make of that?"

"I'm willing to bet it stands for *Acinetobacter calcocetious*, the bacteria that killed Paul Versanti and Francine Watkins."

"Do you have any other proof?"

"The humidifier that I'm sure holds the bacteria is in my truck. My guess is that if you took it to the lab it would grow out a pure solution."

"And if it doesn't?"

"Then you're wrong about my career choices."

Sennett shook his head. "I've got to find out more about Angel Martinez. If we're going after him, I need to know who I'm dealing with. Where's the phone? No, on second thought, I'll call from the motel office. Give you two a moment of privacy." He grinned and picked up a small bag from the bed.

"What's that?"

"Portable computer. No self-respecting police officer would leave town without one. Especially if he was going after a notorious fugitive from the law like Dr. Benjamin Dailey."

After Sennett left, I sat on the edge of the bed with Jordan. I had never known just how beautiful she really was.

"Are you sure you know what you're doing, consorting with a fugitive from the law?"

"We'll save the consorting for when this is all over. Right now, I want to see this matter to the end. But there is one thing I want to tell you."

My heart leaped. "What's that?"

"Lose the stubble."

I laughed. "And I thought not shaving gave me that manly look."

"See, you just demonstrated one of the best reasons to let a lawyer do your negotiating."

"And that is?"

"You should always let the other side make the first offer."

We talked for a few more minutes, until the door opened, and Sennett came back in.

"Man, this is some neighborhood you're holed up in. I go to make a simple phone call and three guys tried to stick me for my wallet."

"What did you do?"

"I can get real mean when I have to. Especially through my eyes. I told them I was undercover, and if they didn't back off, I was going to rough them up. Even showed them my badge. They were punks."

"I figure it was the eye thing, Lieutenant. Around here I'm not sure a badge means much."

"Maybe." He resumed his place in the corner chair. His gaze narrowed, as if looking down the sight of a gun barrel. "Your friend, Mr. Martinez, has an interesting history."

"You found something out already?"

"He's on the internet. All ex-cons are. I got his complete dossier. It all plugged into my computer." He opened his portable up and put it on the table.

"Martinez grew up as the fifth of eight children in Velarde, New Mexico. His father worked for the highway department and his mother did day work. A couple of minor run-ins with law around Santa Fe. Back then he had a nickname, *Ojo Loco*, Crazy Eye. Something about a lazy eye. 'Strabismus' was the word.

"Nothing much until he resurfaced in Fort Bliss, outside El Paso. Apparently, he worked for the army in the hospital as an orderly. He got mixed up with drugs and got caught. The army judge sentenced him to a two-year duty in Vietnam.

"Martinez had a reputation on the base for sexual perversion, beating up some girls at a whorehouse, and a new nickname. Now they called him *El Cochon*, the pig."

"Really," Jordan said. "That's all in the report?"

"They have to put everything in. While he was at Fort Bliss, he developed a knack for medical things. They made him a laboratory technician. He even got a letter of commendation from his superior officer.

"When he went to Vietnam he was in a MASH unit situated near the DMZ. That's where he met Ray Graywolf. I picked up his rap sheet too. Full-blooded Sioux Indian from Bemidji, Minnesota. He was serving with the 101st Airborne, stationed in Da Nang. That must have been where he met Martinez. Both of them were given conditional discharges and sent home.

"Graywolf was sent back to Minnesota for rehabilitation at the Veterans Hospital in Minneapolis. Angel Martinez was picked up for soliciting an undercover police officer and then threatening her with a weapon. That got him five-to-ten at Stanfield. After a year Ray Graywolf joined him there for armed robbery."

"Batman and Robin," I said.

"While he was at Stanfield, Martinez worked in the infirmary. The rest you know."

"Anything else?"

"We pulled up the employment records from Metropolitan Hospital where Burkinette worked. At the time of Paul Versanti's death, an employee was working in the operating room, whose photo ID matches the description we have of Angel Martinez. They're going to send a copy of the photograph to Stanfield for identification."

"We don't have to wait for that, do we?"

"No. I called the Minneapolis Police Department and talked to a friend of mine whom I knew from the police academy back in Chicago. I told him the story without mentioning your name. I told him I had to meet with him. I don't think he was too happy about coming out in the middle of the night, but he's going to see me in his office in about an hour and a half. You're going to have to go with me, Doc."

I could feel the blood drain from my face. "What happens then?"

"If you're right, we catch him. If you're wrong, there's not much I can do for you. The police will have you. It's your decision."

I looked at Jordan, searching her eyes for my decision. Her eyes told me that running was no kind of life. But I knew that anyway.

"I've got to get something to eat before I go, Lieutenant."

"Why do you think I said an hour and a half?"

"One last question, George. What about Graywolf? We'll have to deal with him too."

"That's one part we won't have to worry about."

"Why not?"

"They found him dead a couple of days ago. They haven't released his name, pending family notification. According to the report, it looked as if he'd been forced off the road at a place called Independence Pass outside Aspen, Colorado. When they found him, he had a tracheotomy incision in his throat. The report said it was an expert job by someone who knew what he was doing. The local police are calling it murder. The chief suspect is a person fitting your description very closely, traced to Minneapolis."

WE ATE AT ONE OF THOSE DARK, STEAK-AND-BEER PLACES, where the fifteen types of steak they serve all look and taste the same. It didn't matter to me. In my life I don't think I ever tasted anything better. The human companionship made everything all right.

Before I knew it we were in the acting chief's office.

"George, how the hell are you?" Marvin Sprague said, slapping Sennett on the shoulder.

"Doing all right, Marv. I want you to meet my friends here, Jordan Dalkind and Dr. Benjamin Dailey." Sprague registered no reaction at the mention of my name.

"Marv, have you got a Wanted list?"

"Sure."

"Pick it up and match it to the man standing here." Sprague looked at the poster and then at me. I could almost see his jaw drop open.

"This is the man who's been tailed from that killing in Colorado. George, what are you pulling here?"

"I'm not pulling anything, Marv. I'm just trying to help. Relax, Dr. Dailey's not going to do anything but tell you a story. It's up to you to listen."

Sprague leaned back in his leather desk chair and stared at me for a moment.

"This had better be good, George, because if you're wrong, I'm going to have every newspaper tabloid in the country roasting my butt."

Sennett turned to me. "You're up, Doc. Give the chief your best shot."

I began telling my story, from the very beginning. I tried not to leave out any details, including my run-ins with Larry as a resident. When it got to the confrontation with him at his house, I stopped for a minute.

"I didn't kill Larry Burkinette. When I left him he was fine. A little shaken, but fine just the same." If Sprague was impressed by my denial, he didn't show it.

"Go on, Doctor."

I went over my trip from Detroit and my flight across northern Michigan. I told him about trailing Jeff Belender to Colorado and finding his widow. I told him about the cemetery and the three red arrows. Then I explained about Independence Pass and the death of Ray Graywolf.

"Chief Sprague, I had no intention of harming that man on Independence Pass. He shot at me, I backed up, he spun out and went over the edge."

"According to the police, they saw bullet holes in your car."

"It was self-defense. I don't even own a gun."

"Okay, suppose I believe you. Go on."

I passed lightly over my trucker friends' help getting back to Minneapolis. I dwelled on the current danger to Marge Frederickson.

"Let me get this straight," Sprague interjected. "You think this guy Martinez is going to kill this former prison nurse?"

"Right," I replied firmly.

"And the motive?"

"Revenge. Frederickson, Belender, and Burkinette were somehow responsible for getting him another fifteen years in prison. Or at least he believes so."

"And your proof is what?"

"Three red arrows, each representing one person killed. Two of them have been crossed off. The use of a bacteria to kill two more people as a warning, identical to the bacteria that killed the inmate twenty-five years ago, for whose death Martinez was convicted. I did a voice match between a phone call from the purported killer to Marge Frederickson and a study I made on voice analysis using prison inmates—the same inmates. I found a vial in Marge Frederickson's house containing what I think is the bacteria the killer has used to poison her somehow. How much more do you need?" I yelled.

"Now you settle down, Doctor. I'm not the person being sought in fifteen states. Do I make myself clear?"

"No." I stood up defiantly. "You don't. I'm the son of a bitch being chased. Not you. I'm the guy who found out all this stuff. Not you. If you knew your ass from your elbow, I wouldn't have had to do your job for you while you were too busy chasing me!" All the anger that had been boiling in me spilled over as my temples throbbed and the words poured out of my mouth.

"He's right," Jordan said quietly. All eyes turned toward her.

"Who are you again?" Sprague demanded.

"I'm Ben Dailey's attorney and also the assistant Federal prosecutor for the Fifteenth District in the Eastern Michigan District. As the doctor's attorney I can tell him to keep quiet. You can arrest him, but I guarantee I'll get him off. There is no case against him. You know it and I know it. What you'll get in return is public scorn for Marge Frederickson's murder."

Sprague looked up to the ceiling. "Some friend you are, George. You drop this pile of crap on me and expect me to sort it out."

"It comes with the territory, Marv. But I can tell you one thing. Ben Dailey is about as solid a person as you're ever going to meet. If he tells you it's so, you'd better listen. I mean it." I had never seen Sennett so earnest. I felt ashamed for ever having doubted his honesty and friendship.

"Okay, okay. You win," Sprague groaned, holding his hands up. "But even if

I believe that this Angel Martinez is the killer, you have no direct proof. All of it is circumstantial. What do you want me to do?"

"My bet is that he's going to finish off Marge Frederickson in the hospital," I said. "It's perfect. I think he infected her through the humidifier in the respirator. Now all he has to do is inject her with the bacteria. Everyone will think she died from her lung disease."

Sprague thought for a minute. "We'd have to catch him in the act."

"Surveillance of her room," Sennett said. "Arrange for her to be transferred to another room in the hospital. Have the room wired for sound and light. When we get him on tape, we make the grab."

Sprague drummed his fingers. All at once he seemed to come to a decision.

"I've made a lifetime habit of sizing people up, Dr. Dailey. Regardless of the threats of your attorney or what the lieutenant said, I can hold my ground." By this time, he was standing, stretching his broad shoulders beneath his rumpled tweed sport coat. "And, Mr. Doctor, I don't take shit from nobody, including fugitives from the law, and the legal system and the newspapers. If you're wondering why, it's mainly because I don't give a damn. If they want my ass because they think I'm not doing my job, let them come and get me." My heart sank. Just my luck, I had to run into a hall-of-fame hardass.

"But apart from all that, my gut tells me you're telling the truth. So we're going to get this bastard Martinez, and we're going to sit on him hard. Oh, and by the way, consider yourself in my custody until further notice. Now let's get going, we've got a lot of details to work out."

# CHAPTER 28

THE DETAILS TURNED OUT TO BE EVEN MORE DIFFICULT than Sprague had foreseen. He would have to get his people in place as hospital workers, maintain strict secrecy, and be able to block any escape from the hospital. Having been around hospitals all my adult life, I could see all kinds of holes in the plan.

After Sprague had everything laid out, we left headquarters for Methodist Hospital in an unmarked squad car. When we got there, we were met by a balding, fiftyish accountant type at the rear entrance to the emergency room. Sprague introduced him as Fred Hansecker, head administrator of the hospital.

Hansecker led us into a small room at the back of the E.R. where the nurses did their charting. We pulled up some metal chairs, moved some lunches out of the way, and sat down.

"It's really no big deal for us, Marv," Hansecker said. "We move patients and equipment all over the hospital every day. The problem is getting your things in place without raising any suspicions."

"We'll do the best we can," Sprague said. "No operation is ever perfect."

Hansecker took out a notebook, and what looked like a census sheet, and began examining it.

"3712, that's it. We can move her there. It's a corner room, with good visibility from across the hall and a single exit." Sprague looked at the diagram that Hansecker had drawn.

"Let's do it."

We walked up to the medical intensive care unit on the third floor through the back stairwell.

"We just had the whole place redone," Hansecker bragged. "Computer printouts, individual units, patient monitors all controlled at the central desk."

"You mean the place is already wired?"

"Of course. We need to keep constant watch on patients even if there isn't a nurse in the room."

"Can we hook it up to a computer?"

"No problem. Everything is copy ready. We did it for the lawyers. You know, like on cop cars. Now there is never a question about what is happening at any moment."

"How many people know about the TV monitors?"

"Just about everybody. We want them to remember they are always being watched. It's a good deterrent to bad patient care."

"Big brother is watching, huh?" Sprague commented.

"We like to think in terms of better patient care and fewer lawsuits."

"Well, if everyone knows about in-house surveillance, so will our killer. We'll change the camera and use yours as a dummy. He won't know what direction the surveillance is really coming from." Sprague dialed a number and talked for a few minutes.

"Tell your people that a Mr. Everson will be here in about twenty minutes. Make sure they give him every convenience. He'll be dressed in a building maintenance uniform."

"No problem, Marv." Hamsecker led us to a windowless room.

"This is where all the monitors come in. I'll put an 'out of order' sign up and you guys can hole up here."

"You got anything to eat in this place besides hospital food?" Sprague inquired, looking around.

"What do think this is, a hotel?"

"At the rates you charge, I could be at the Ritz."

Hansecker laughed good-naturedly at the rebuff. I was chiefly struck by his apparent lack of concern at the bad publicity ramifications of bacterial murder in his hospital. He would have made a better Santa Claus than a typical hospital administrator. But at least his inexplicable jauntiness made things easier on us.

"I'll see what I can do. In the meantime, I think you guys should change into scrubs. It will make you look less conspicuous."

We took Hansecker's suggestion to heart and changed in the employee locker room. When we got back to the monitoring area there was a platter of sandwiches laid out and a couple of thermoses of coffee. The repairmen came and made the installation. Within minutes we had a complete view of the room on the TV screen. Soon we saw Marge Frederickson being wheeled into the room.Sprague fiddled with the camera, zooming in on the patient and the equipment around her to record everything. Marge looked terrible. Her robust, pink-cheeked skin had turned pale. An endotracheal tube reached into her lungs while a respirator assisted her. A couple of vials of what I recognized as succinyl choline on the table indicated a need for muscle control to keep her from fighting the machine. Also on the table was a cut-down set.

Nothing happened until the following night.

At about two in the morning, Sprague called Sennett. We bolted from the cots strewn around the room.

"I've got something, George. He's coming in now. Small guy, fiftyish. Slicked-back hair. Wearing a white lab coat. He's just taped over the hospital's camera lens." Sprague picked up the photo of Martinez from the prison and studied it.

"He's our man. Let's go."

"No, wait for him to do something so we can record it."

We waited. And watched in horror as the man took a syringe from his pocket and prepared to inject it in the unconscious Marge Frederickson's IV.

"That's enough!" Sprague shouted. "Let's go!"

We bounded from our room and across the hall. Sprague motioned two men stationed outside in the hall to follow. We burst into the room just as Martinez was about to inject the syringe into the IV.

"Angel Martinez," Sprague shouted. "You are under arrest for the murder of Jeffrey Belender and Lawrence Burkinette."

The small, wiry man with the lazy eye looked up at us. I was shocked to see him. Not because it was the man I had sought for so long, but because I remembered him vaguely. It was his eyes, cruel and narrow set, staring in different directions. I had him placed now: the operating room at Stanfield. Another picture flashed across my mind: Johnnie Willson dying of septic shock in the Stanfield infirmary. Martinez had been there. And so had I. Good God. I'd been there!

"You're crazy, mister. What you talking about, man? My name is Edgar Rodriguez."

"You can tell that to the magistrate downtown. In the meantime, spread your legs and put your hands against the bed. I'm going to cuff you and read you your rights."

I watched Martinez's eyes shift around the room. He looked at the cut-down tray in front of him and the filled syringes. Before I could get the warning out of my mouth he grabbed his syringes and the syringes of succinyl choline and a number ten knife blade.

"Knife!" I yelled.

When Sprague heard me yell, he tried to jump back, but Angel was on him, slashing with the open blade. Sprague put up his arm in defense, but Martinez slashed expertly across the tendons of Sprague's right wrist. The chief cried out in pain. Martinez pushed him against the other two men behind him and ran out of the ICU with Sennett and me in pursuit. Jordan and the other two officers attended to Sprague.

We raced to the elevators, but Martinez was fast. He got to the one working elevator just as it arrived. The doors closed a second before we got there.

"I remember this guy, George."

"Whatever you remember isn't going to do us any good unless we find him."

"He's going to try to blend in with the people in the hospital."

"Well, Sprague has all the exits sealed, so he can't get out."

"Don't be so sure," I said. "A person like Martinez is cleverer than you think. There are a hundred ways of disguising yourself. I should know, I've been doing it."

"Let's go back to where Sprague is. I'll bet he'll call his men in and sweep each floor one by one. It's the police way," said Sennett stolidly.

"That may work in an apartment building, but we're dealing with a different type of person and a different environment. Do it your way and he'll be out of here before tomorrow morning."

"It's not my call, but I'll bet Sprague will do it his way. Police procedure is police procedure. It works most of the time."

By this time we had walked back down the hall and into the ICU. When we entered the room it was crowded with nurses and doctors hovering over Sprague. There was blood on the floor and a tight bandage around his forearm. He was obviously in a lot of pain.

"Did you get him?" he asked angrily.

"No, he got away, Marv," Sennett said gruffly.

"Don't worry, I've already ordered a sweep. We'll get him." Then he looked at me. "I guess you were right, Doc." As he croaked the words out, he winced in pain.

"It doesn't matter now. We've got to find him."

"Forget the 'we,' Doc. My men will do it. You guys stay put. I don't want anyone else to get hurt." The nurse gave him a shot. In a matter of minutes he began to fade out. The nurse came over and nudged us out of the way.

"Excuse me, gentlemen, but this man is going down to the operating room."

We moved aside as the nurses lifted Sprague onto a stretcher. In a moment he was being wheeled down the hall.

We sat around the table as Fred Hansecker, the hospital administrator, came in.

"All hell has broken out now. I've got police all over the place. They're going from floor to floor. I'm sure they'll find him quickly." I felt a nudge of human satisfaction at the worry and anxious calculation for damage control on the administrator's formerly sunny face.

FORTY-FIVE MINUTES LATER, THEY STILL HADN'T found Angel Martinez. Sennett and I paced the hallway. We were by the elevators when Hansecker came out of one looking for us.

"Marv is in the operating room. The doctors figure four or five hours to repair the damage. Anything happening?"

"Nothing," I replied. Just then the overhead intercom started squawking.

"Code Blue, sixth floor, dietary room. Code Blue, sixth floor." The female voice was even and plain, as if announcing the blue light special.

"What's that about?" Sennett asked.

"Cardiac arrest or something like that. Standard announcement for a hospital."

"Maybe you were right, Ben," Sennett acknowledged. "Martinez may be getting away as we stand here."

"He's expecting the police to do the police thing. I think he'll go from being an employee, to being a patient. It's what I would do in his place."

"Where could that be done?"

"Some place where they would do a test, like the lab or the radiology department."

"Let's take a look," he said.

"Sprague told us to sit tight," I said.

"Since when did you take orders from anyone?"

I looked at the directory. Both the lab and radiology were on the first floor.

This time we took the stairs, jumping from one riser to the next. We hit the first-floor landing at almost the same time, then barged through the stairwell door and into the hallway. It took us a moment to get our bearings, but soon we found the lab.

Bursting through the door, we ran up to the clerk at the desk.

"Anyone down here at this hour waiting for tests?"

"The E.R. has been crazy, I've got three people waiting for electrolytes, two mono tests, and a stat PT and PTT. Two are waiting outside, and the rest are in the emergency room."

Sennett and I turned to the waiting room and the sullen faces of a half dozen people, sitting on the Naugahyde chairs and staring into space. No Angel Martinez.

"Let's go down to the x-ray department. More places to hide there." My voice was almost drowned out by the overhead speaker announcing the code blue again.

I had to pull Sennett by the edge of his scrub suit to move him. The sound of a cardiac arrest being announced is enough to penetrate even the toughest hide.

We moved down the hall to the x-ray department. There were twenty or so patients lined up on gurneys in the waiting room, most of them from the emergency room. We strode up to the secretary at the desk, where the lieutenant showed his badge. We both counted on the unlikelihood that anyone would challenge him as an interloper from Michigan.

"Can I see the list of patients tonight, ma'am?"

"Here." She turned the computerized list over to us.

"All these patients are scheduled, right?"

"We don't get anyone in here without a wristband and an authorization. It's the rules. There've been too many lawsuits."

"Have there been any patients added?" I asked.

"None in the last hour. We've been so busy they've been stacked out in the hallway."

"Which ones were in the hall?" I asked.

"The ones marked with an 'H.'"

I saw the names Johnson, Fields, and Petruccio. I looked around again.

"Let's check outside, Lieutenant."

Out in the hall, Fields and Johnson were still there. We looked around for Petruccio. Gone. I ran back into the waiting room.

"What time was Mr. Petruccio scheduled for his x-ray?" I asked.

"He's going to have a chest x-ray. Right now he's tenth in line."

I picked the phone up and dialed the operator.

"Operator, I need the anesthesiologist on call, stat."

"Who is this?" she asked.

"Dr. Dailey down in x-ray. I need him now."

"He's up with the code. I don't know if I can get him."

Sennett grabbed the phone.

"Miss, this is Lieutenant George Sennett. Either you get me this doctor or I'll have Fred Hansecker and the entire Minneapolis Police Department on you like flies on flypaper. Do I make myself clear?" He handed me back the phone. When I put it back to my ear I heard the paging system in action. Within thirty seconds a phone at the other end was ringing.

"This is Dr. Sneed. I hope this is important because I'm right in the middle of a code."

"This is Dr. Benjamin Dailey. I need to know something about the patient you're working on. Look at his wristband and see if his name is Petruccio."

There was a silence. Then he came back to the phone.

"His wrist band has been cut. In the rush to take care of him we neglected to look," he said defensively.

"What's his problem?"

"We think he's had some type of respiratory arrest. We found a syringe next to him with succinyl choline. He's been deliberately endangered. Right now we've tubed him and are trying to restart his heart."

Succinyl choline, silent and deadly, a muscle relaxant capable of paralyzing every muscle in the body at once. And all for a wristband.

"What?" Sennett asked impatiently.

"Martinez took a patient's wristband and then tried to kill him."

"Where do we find him?"

"Martinez is smart. He's been around hospitals long enough to know all the places to hide. The very best way is as a patient. There are dozens of places someone could be stashed, and no one would ever know."

"Where would *you* look now?" Sennett asked urgently.

"If he's a patient, then someone has to transport him somewhere. All we have to do is find the transporter who took him wherever he went."

I went back into the x-ray waiting room and accosted the clerk.

"Who's doing transporting for you tonight?" I asked.

"Billy Edwards. He's over in the emergency room."

We ran out of the room and down the hall. The E.R. wasn't hard to find. In hospital architecture E.R. basic rules apply: a ground level entrance and proximity to the radiology department.

The double doors opened automatically as we entered the crowded area. There were people in every corner, babies wailing, nurses and doctors running from place to place. I searched for the control desk and the secretary giving out information to everybody who came past her.

"Excuse me, ma'am. Do you know where Billy Edwards is?"

"Where he always is, down in the chairs by the exit."

She pointed the way. When we got to the end of the corridor, I saw a tall, muscular youth sitting on a plastic chair, legs spread, brow furrowed, a book on physical chemistry in his lap.

"Are you Billy Edwards?" Sennett asked.

"That's me. What do you need?"

"Information," Sennett said. "You always study on the job?" A look of consternation came over the boy's face. He must have thought he had done something wrong.

"Sorry, I didn't have any orders, and I have a test coming up tomorrow at the university."

"Relax, son," Sennett said. "We need some information. Did you transport a patient named Petruccio anywhere in the last hour?"

"Sure. I had his chart. He was supposed to go down to the operating room. A resident in the emergency room came over to me and told me to take him. He said they were waiting for the patient down there. So I took Petruccio down there. I gave the nurse the chart in the preop holding area and left."

"How do you get to the operating room, Billy?"

Five minutes later we were walking the corridor near the surgery suite. I had begun to feel a little stupid, trying to play detective, taking the lieutenant on some wild goose chase. Until I saw the syringe lying on the tile floor of the corridor.

# CHAPTER 29

I WOULD HAVE MISSED IT but for the fluorescent lights reflecting off the metal barrel. I picked it up and read: "succinyl choline."

"What do you have, Doc?"

"A syringe labeled with the same drug that was used on Mr. Petruccio. The same drug in the syringes Martinez stole from Marge Frederickson's room when we cornered him. What do you think the odds are?"

"I think we're on Martinez's tail. Let's go to the operating room."

We walked around the corner and saw the sign marking the preop holding area. Inside was a large, empty room with stretchers lined in small bays. We quickly glanced around the room. No one was there except a young nurse at the desk. A pretty Filipino.

"Excuse me, Ms. Lopez," I said, reading her nametag. "Did you have a patient brought down here named Petruccio?"

"I did. It was so strange. I had no knowledge of him being scheduled for anything, so I called the floor. Nobody knew anything. I tried to ask the patient, but he was moaning so much I couldn't understand him. I went down the hall to the operating room to ask the on-call nurse. When I got back he was gone. Everybody thinks I'm crazy."

I looked down the long hallway, ending in two large doors.

"What's down there?"

"Central supply and the laundry."

"Anybody in there?"

"Central supply is closed. We don't sterilize equipment at night, but the laundry works all night. That's when the pickups and deliveries take place."

I looked down the hall again. One of the doors looked ajar. Sennett must have seen the same thing.

"Let's take a look."

We walked through the doors, into a dimly lit area. To one side was the laundry. Beneath the door sign we could see a light burning. On the other side was central supply.

Quietly we peered into the laundry. Three or four men were moving hampers and bags in and out of the trucks at the loading dock. In the corner stood several apparently empty containers. I half-expected Angel Martinez to jump out as I approached nervously. Instead, all I found were some stray towels and sheets.

Sennett called one of the men over. Sweat pouring off his forehead, he seemed to welcome the break.

"Anybody come down here that you didn't recognize?"

"Nobody I've seen." He turned to his partners. "Hey, you guys seen anybody down here?" The other men shook their heads.

One of them called back, "C'mon, Randy, let's get this done."

Randy shrugged his shoulders and went back to work.

Sennett and I walked back out of the room and looked around. The only thing we saw in the darkness was the small exit sign illuminating the central supply area.

"What better place to hide than in the central supply area," I said. "Especially since the police have already searched it. No one goes there at night. In the morning he moves out with the equipment, down to the loading dock, and he's gone."

The lieutenant nodded to me and we walked forward. A chill went down my back as I saw Sennett reach inside his coat for his gun.

He turned the knob and pushed the door open with his left hand as I stayed behind him. He motioned me to move to the other side of the door, then slid his hand along the wall until he fingered a light switch. Three or four lights came on, partially lighting a large room filled with metal racks. At the end I could see the sterilizing units, two enormous Amscos. These were the work horses of sterilization in the hospital, large enough to accommodate two or three people, with an insulated window to look inside. Right now, they looked like nothing so much as two huge burial vaults.

We walked slowly down the middle of the room, Sennett's gun in his hand. It grew darker as we moved farther in, so I stayed by the metal storage rack to the side while Sennett pushed forward, looking for another light switch. The momentary distraction took our attention off the racks next to us. Suddenly, a flash came down at Sennett's head.

"Behind you!" I yelled.

But the warning seemed to be too late. As Sennett instinctively shot his arm up to deflect the blow, a metal retractor hit a glancing blow off the side of his head. He slumped to the floor, the gun clattering on the tiles.

I looked wildly around the racks. I saw a Finechetto chest spreader, lying open. Picking up half of it, I brandished its clawlike edges and stood in the middle of the room. Angel Martinez moved out from behind the storage unit. His derisive grin and lazy eye made him look ghoulish in the dim light.

The source, not only of all I had endured, but of the answers to a murderous mystery. It was both this realization, and the further realization that whatever would happen now would soon be over, that set my mind racing.

"You're one smart Anglo, you know that, Dailey? I remember you. You're the guy with the voices, ain't you?" I nodded like a foolish puppet.

"I remember something else. You were there when Willson died." As he spoke, he casually drew a syringe from his pocket while brandishing the retractor in his other hand.

"Why did you kill them, Martinez?"

"Who?" he asked, as if bored with his laurels.

"Burkinette and Belender."

"Shit. Those two pretty boys? Squeal puppies, that's what they were. They got what they deserved. They fucking set us up, man."

"With the instruments?"

"Who told you that?"

"Charlie Featherstone. He told me everything."

Martinez smiled. "I'm glad Charlie knows they died. Now he can die in peace."

"You had no proof they planted them."

His eyes narrowed. "Don't bullshit me, man. We know they planted those instruments in the cleanup area. Do you think I would have been stupid enough to leave them there? They did it. We knew it. They turned us in." As he spoke, he moved in a half-circle in front of me. I countered his moves.

"Why are you so sure they set you up?"

"Drugs, that's why. Those two fuckers, we called them the Angel Dust Twins. They had a fucking goldmine, selling stuff to the boys."

"Where'd they get it?" I asked. I had a sick feeling I knew already.

"Burkinette told me once. He had this chick in the operating room. She'd take the cocaine that was going to be used on the patient and replace it with talcum powder. He said she did it for love. That fucker was porking her for the goods. It was good shit, too. One hundred percent pure."

Those patients in agony, my near expulsion, Abby MacKenzie's anguish and death. It was hard to argue that Larry Burkinette and Jeff Belender hadn't gotten what was coming to them.

"Why did they want to get you? Weren't you his source of income?"

Martinez shrugged his shoulders. "Burkinette told me his girlfriend died and the pipeline went dry. I figured that once that happened, he didn't want anyone talking. Who the fuck would believe a con who'd just killed someone?"

"And when I walked into the middle of your scam that day at Burkinette's house, I was your scapegoat, wasn't I?"

"I can't believe how lucky I was that you were there. I was going to kill him that night anyway. Then you showed up. The perfect setup."

"You planted the gun in my boat."

"Piece of cake, man."

"I should have figured that out. And what about Marge Frederickson?"

"She was in on it too. She had to be in order to pass the stuff through the clinic. They were a team."

"You were going to kill her with *Acinetobacter* too, weren't you?"

"How did you find that out?"

"I traced the whole thing. Killing two patients to taunt Belender and Burkinette. You were just toying with them, weren't you?"

"They fucked with me, man. Before they died, I wanted them to feel what I felt sitting in that prison cell for fifteen extra years."

"All this over Johnnie Willson?" I said, almost to myself. At the mention of that name, Martinez's face became a mask of hate.

"He deserved to die worse than he did. He didn't suffer enough."

"Scratch us and we bleed, wrong us and we revenge. Right, Angel?"

"Quit with the fancy words, asshole. We can tell our own story."

"I saw it, Martinez, the three broken arrows, your symbol of revenge."

"Not just mine. It was Ray's, and Charlie's, and Frank's."

"Poor Ray," I said.

"What do you mean?"

"I mean I took care of him back in Colorado. You should have sent someone smarter. He's dead, you know."

The hatred in Martinez's eyes swelled. "You fucking *cochon*!" he yelled. "He was just an innocent."

"He tried to run me off the road on a mountain pass. He shot at me. An eye for an eye, Angel. That's a little vengeance motto *my* people keep in mind." I was trying to enrage him into an impulsive act that might disarm him, at least partially.

It worked. As I finished speaking, he flung the retractor lethally at my head. I ducked just in time. The retractor fell, irretrievable, against one of the racks.

"You've got to do better than that, Angel!" I shouted. Martinez eyed me carefully, as he silently circled from left to right. I kept talking.

"You know, Angel, I could even buy some of this stuff you're dishing out. I knew Larry Burkinette. What he did was wrong. Maybe he deserved what he got. But Paul Versanti didn't, and neither did Belender's patient in L. A. You're just a sick bastard. How could you kill those people?"

"They were in the wrong place at the wrong time. Just like you. I'm going to have to fuck you up, man." As he said it he started to move towards me. He pulled out of his pocket the same blade he had used to slash Marv Sprague.

"How did you get Bidora to sue?" I asked frantically. He stopped again.

"That was the easiest. I'd done it before with Belender. All I had to do was go through the Yellow Pages for the lawyers and look at the ads. Not the big ones, but the little guy in the corner of the page. I went to his office, told him I had some information, and told him how to get it out of the hospital. The guy was so stupid, I almost had to draw him a road map. I knew he'd be hungry, you know what I mean? Then he gives me a hundred dollars. Can you believe that? I give him a case worth millions, and he gives me a hundred fucking dollars."

"Maybe he saw you for what you are, Martinez. A cheap punk without a future. You're done, Martinez. The police know everything I know."

"Whatever happens, man, it'll be worth it."

"For what?" I shouted. "To get even? To make innocent people suffer for your sickness? Think about that little boy you killed!"

"Just a reminder to my two rich doctor friends," he laughed, loathsomely. "It was so easy to get a job in the operating room, contaminate the instruments, even screw up their gloves."

"You mean the bacteria?"

"Sure. They both carried it on their hands. I found that out messing around with their gloves at the prison. They even showed me how to do the cultures. Hell, that's how I got the idea about doing in Johnnie."

Martinez still had the blade in his left hand, but now he changed his grip on the syringe, filled with succinyl choline.

I kept backing up toward the end of the room. I knew I was in over my head. Years of exercise had kept me in shape, but street-fighting with a killer like Martinez was something I was totally unprepared for.

Each time he circled we got closer to each other. I could smell his sweat, smell the death emanating from him. Then Angel rushed me. I tried to dodge him, but this time he was too quick, striking me across the arm with the blade, tearing my flesh. I fell back, and he followed, grinning evilly, as we moved closer to the sterilizing units.

I was staggering in pain, but my arm was still working. I could feel the blood running down the inside of my shirt. Martinez suddenly dropped and rolled against my legs, knocking me down. As I hit the floor, I saw him raise the syringe.

I grasped at both his arms. Either the knife or the needle could kill me in an instant. My hand, wet from my blood, slipped. Martinez jammed his knee into my abdomen, knocking the wind out of me. I coughed and sputtered. His hand flashed downward. He stabbed the needle into my arm and injected the succinyl choline. Pain. I felt the sting of the fluid as it swelled into my bicep. I knew I was going to die.

Fury rose in me. I swung the open claw of the Finechetto at his chest, ripping his skin with the sharp, toothed ends.

Martinez cried out in pain and rolled over on his side. I could feel my muscles start to twitch as I saw him get up and struggle to his feet to escape. He must have known I was a goner as he saw the shaking of my muscles, because he turned his back.

With my muscles beginning to cramp in tetany, I made one last effort, raised myself up, and staggered against him from behind, pushing him through the open door of the sterilizing unit. Somehow I managed to close the door and turn the wheel to lock it.

I spun to the floor with my back slumped against the sterilizer, my breath starting to come in short, painful gasps. The tear in the arm of my jacket caught against the post-conditioning lever, both pulling it down and holding me up.

For a suspended moment my face was pressed against the small window. I saw Angel Martinez's wild face directly opposite mine, against the thick interior glass. The post-conditioning phase had produced a vacuum within the sterilizer to remove all the water. As the pressure in the machine decreased, so did the oxygen level. It was like being in outer space. My breath coming in short gulps, my consciousness fading, I saw the tissues in his body expanding and the muscles in his face contorting his face into a horribly disfigured mask.

Martinez was beating against the window in a frenzy. As his face became more contorted, I saw him look upward. The last vision I had of Angel before his body exploded was the wild rolling of his eyes upward, his lazy eye still staring to one side. My jacket tore from the handle. As I slid to the floor, I heard a muffled shrieking in the background. Then, the darkness of death.

# EPILOGUE

I SLOWLY STARTED TO FEEL MOVEMENT. Then a light, something in my throat, people holding my head. Words filtered into my ears.

"Relax, mister. Everything is going to be all right," the voice said.

Things started to come into focus. I struggled against the tube in my throat.

"I think we can take it out now, he's starting to breathe on his own," the voice said again. There was a tug on the plastic thing in my mouth. I coughed for a moment. A mask returned to my face.

When I looked again, I could see a head swathed in a bandage. My eyes focused on the face; it was Sennett looking down at me. The reassuring sound of his voice.

"You're going to be all right, Doc. Someone sounded the fire alarm. Everybody is here. Do you hear me?"

I blinked my eyes slowly.

THE NEWS BROKE THE NEXT DAY. Both *The Herald* and *USA Today* ran front page headlines on the death of Angel Martinez and the odyssey of Benjamin Dailey, M.D. The story was carried on the major network evening newscasts. *The New York Times* printed an article about me. Reading about my heroics the next morning in my hospital bed made me sick. I knew I was a fool to have played the police game, and a lucky fool at that.

I should have listened to Jordan and stayed away from the insurance business. Poor Jordan, having to go through so much because of my stubbornness. Well, if she'd let me, I'd spend a lot of time making it up to her.

Just like the irritating patients I had taken care of, I began begging for my release. I guess they got tired of hearing me whine, because I got my wish the following afternoon.

Before I left, I checked on my two patients. Marge Frederickson had survived. The lab test on the home respirator showed that it was contaminated with *Acinetobacter*. According to the doctors, Martinez had planned her murder perfectly. Her emphysema had lowered her resistance and set her up to be susceptible to infection by inhaling the bacteria inoculating her. Every time Martinez had changed the fluid in the respirator, he'd been pumping her full of the bacteria. A month of inhaling the bacteria was enough to hospitalize her. His intravenous injection would have been the final stroke. No one would ever have suspected.

Even in her weakened state Marge steadfastly denied any responsibility for the prison scheme. She said she'd felt something funny was going on, but she could never prove it. And she hadn't left for any reason but being tired of harassment from people like Pilkington over her sexuality. Knowing Marge as I did, I had to believe her. The police believed her too, because Sennett told me the local officials were not going to press charges.

The only living person who might not agree was Charlie Featherstone. If he had been younger, I was certain he would have gone after her. I mentioned my concern to some of Marv Sprague's people. They told me they would have a talk with him. They assured me that when they were done talking, Charlie would be satisfied to live out his life peacefully.

As for Marv, the surgeons said his slashed arm came together nicely. According to Sennett, later, Sprague came out of the affair with a blaze of favorable publicity guaranteeing him as Minneapolis' new full-time chief.

Sennett, Jordan, and I flew back to Detroit that evening. We picked up his car at airport security and drove back to his office to get Jordan's car. Her keys were in his desk, so we stopped for a few minutes. While we were there, he checked through the pile of paper that had accumulated. One letter in particular caught his eye; he opened it and read it twice.

"Catch this one," he said. "Some attorney named Jack Rembertson opened Burkinette's will. I guess his conscience got the better of him, because here's an explanation explaining his dilemma because of client confidentiality. You know lawyers." He glanced over at Jordan and smiled.

"Don't leave me hanging, Lieutenant," I said.

"Burkinette had the whole scheme laid out on paper just like you said. Belender, the drugs, and Abby MacKenzie. He was even remorseful. Remorseful enough to leave half a million each for the estate of Abby MacKenzie and Doris Spencer. He left the house, cars, and a million bucks for Samantha Burkinette."

"Where did he get that kind of money, from practicing medicine?"

"It all came from drugs and some shrewd investing. Apparently, a number of years ago he put a lot into a company called Friendship Labs."

Well, what do you know. Larry and I had had something in common after all.

"Part of the will contained a confession of his love for his second wife, Samantha, explaining that he had made her leave his house because he feared for her life. He knew if Martinez got to him, he might get her too."

I felt a pinch of conscience. Maybe there was a little good in the worst of us. I stopped for a moment at the door; Jordan had gone ahead.

"If you had wanted me, you would have nailed me, friends or no friends, wouldn't you have?"

George was quiet for a moment. "You're right. I would have. It's my job."

I nodded. "Let's get out of here, this place is making me claustrophobic."

Sennett smiled. "Me, too."

I had just turned around when I remembered the wallet in my pocket.

"I've got a wallet I need to return. It belongs to a Mr. Charles Whittingdon." I handed it to Sennett. "Write him a note and tell him you found it, ask him for a bill, and tell him the Detroit police will pay it."

"Oh, yeah? On what basis? Should we do the same for your license plate heists and the theft of the Continental?"

"I don't know what you're talking about, Lieutenant," I said blankly. Jordan had already arranged for my freedom from those charges in exchange for compensation and apologies.

Sennett stood there looking at me. I knew he was thinking of something clever to say.

"Ben, you've got to promise me one thing."

"What's that?"

"Promise me you'll give up gumshoeing, okay?"

"Okay, I promise," I said, shaking his hand. But the only people I was ever good at keeping promises to were my patients. That's why I crossed my fingers.

BY THE TIME WE MADE IT THROUGH THE FRONT DOOR of Jordan's house I was exhausted. I didn't want the spotlight, only my life back. I got that when Jordan and I walked inside the hallway.

My body hurt all over, as if I had been in a fight with Muhammad Ali. It was a common side effect of succinyl choline. But just being there, with Jordan, helped me heal fast.

The next morning we were sitting at the breakfast room table. The sun streamed in through the lace curtains, and there was an early dusting of snow on the back courtyard. It seemed I had never left. Even the conversation was the same.

"Ben, I hated seeing you the way you were. You seemed so dissatisfied."

"Not dissatisfied, just confused. There's a big difference. I needed some direction."

"Confused about what?"

"Lots of things, none of which seem to mean much anymore."

"Why?"

"When I was about to die, a crazy thought came to me."

"What?"

"Getting old isn't so bad. Leaving a good-looking corpse is overrated."

"You're saying you're not ready for the undertaker yet?"

I nodded.

"But what makes you so sure?" she asked sweetly.

I stood up from the table and leaned over her shoulder.

"Come back upstairs with me and I'll show you."

She laughed. In all my years of research on the human voice, it was the loveliest sound I had ever heard.

Gᴇɴᴇ Rᴏɴᴛᴀʟ is a head and neck surgeon. Born in Detroit, he attended the University of Michigan, where he received his medical degree. After completing a residency at the University of Minnesota, he went into private practice in the Detroit area and began teaching at the University of Michigan Medical School. He is currently a professor in the Department of Otolaryngology/Head and Neck Surgery. His writing career started twenty years ago when he published his first novel, *Sterile Justice*. Since then he has three other books in print (*A Lethal Dose*, *The Cruelest Cut*, and *The Police Surgeon*) and has participated in promoting them with book signings and radio and newspaper interviews. In addition to his mystery writing, Gene Rontal has published over fifty scientific articles, authored chapters in medical textbooks, and has been quoted in a number of lay publications, including *Time*, *Science*, *National Geographic*, and the *Wall Street Journal*. Doctor Rontal and his wife, Ellen, enjoy skiing, traveling, and spending time with their family.